DEATH GETS COZY

An Anthony Mulish Mystery

J.R. Ripley

Beachfront Entertainment

INTRO

Death Gets Cozy is an affectionate spoof/satire/sendup? of mysteries in general and cozies in particular. I wrote a novel many years ago called SKULLS OF SEDONA of which Library Journal wrote: Readers who enjoyed Sharon McCrumb's Bimbos of the Death Sun will also get a kick out of this.

The second thing happened at a recent Malice Domestic banquet whereat one of my tablemates brought up Sharon's book. This got the old gears turning. I had not yet read the Bimbos book and made it a point to do so when I returned home.

I decided to write this story, the story of the most pompous, annoying, blowhard, takes-himself-too-seriously author that I could devise. Okay, maybe I just looked in the mirror and wrote what I saw...I'll let you, the readers, decide. Remember, I am a cozy writer too. That fun I'm poking, I'm poking at myself.

A sense of humor, especially directed at oneself, I believe is essential. In fact, I also believe Amazon Essentials has them for sale at only $2.99/yard. So, if you haven't decided to bolt (there's a bad pun in here somewhere—dig around, you'll find it), read on!

DEATH GETS COZY

1

"You wrote the book."

"It was meant to be a joke." Anthony Mulish slammed his fist against his literary agent's desk. He noticed, not for the first time, that it was an antique. Louis Quatorze. His literary agent lived better than he did.

"But you signed the contract."

"It was never meant to be published."

"But you signed the contract."

How many times was that now? Ameena Chowdary had lost count. She twiddled with her silver Mont Blanc pen, her gaze drifting to the expansive backyard. Her boys were playing on the clay tennis court. Resurfacing the old asphalt court had cost a mint but it had been worth it. This was lesson time. Their coach was a former USTA doubles champ and he didn't come cheap.

Ameena had traded living in a New York City highrise for a quaint mansion in the village of Sands Point out on the north shore of Long Island. Her husband was a successful corporate attorney. She didn't need this.

"The title is stupid. I cringe whenever I see it in print: Death Gets Cozy."

"It was *your* title." Just her luck that her most difficult client had to live within an hour's commute of her home and office. Why couldn't he live in Florida or Hawaii?

How about Tasmania?

Maybe she would suggest it someday. He might like the climate. No, take that back. Anthony Mulish did not like anything.

Except his own words on paper.

"And now you want me to go to this-this—"

She helped him out. "Mystery conference. Yes, I want you to go to *Murder Under Cover*. It will be good publicity for you."

"I don't care."

"It's the organizers' very first event." The inaugural *Murder Under Cover* mystery conference was being held at a small college in the mountains of Virginia. The College of the Alleghenies, to be precise, a liberal arts institution. She had looked them up and studied the information packet they had sent her on her client's behalf. Rugged mountains, cold, mist, bogs.

Ameena shivered. Thank goodness, she wasn't attending.

Anthony Mulish snorted derisively.

Ameena responded with more words of flattery. It was pretty much the only vocabulary Anthony—don't dare call him Tony—Mulish understood. "It's really quite an honor. You will be Murder Under Cover's very first Special Guest of Honor."

She leaned back in her deep leather desk chair with a quiet sigh of satisfaction. A Swiss Simmental cow—the very same breed used to upholster the interior of her husband's prized Rolls-Royce—had given its life for her comfort. "Think of it, Anthony. For time immemorial, you will be remembered as the first special guest of honor."

She listened to the grandfather clock tick as she waited for his response. In this case, it truly had been her grandfather's clock. It was English, by way of the state of Bihar in India. She closed her eyes for a moment, picturing the giant Buddha statue at Bodh Gaya. She had made her first pilgrimage there with her grandfather when she was five years old.

The steady and gentle movement of the clock brought back childhood memories of her seated on her father's lap in his study, her ear pressed against his chest listening to the reassuring beating of his heart.

Ameena took deep breaths, trying to emulate the Buddha's calm. Her memory tingling with the scent of her father's black cherry pipe tobacco.

"To make the situation worse, you tell me I am up for some dubious award."

"TR Ipé has been nominated for a Poe." She ran the two names together quickly:

Tripe.

TR Ipé was Anthony Mulish's self-appointed pen name. Tripe was his little inside joke. Yet another gibe at the genre he considered beneath his talents. Far beneath.

"That's I-pay."

"Sure, if you say so." She turned her head and feigned a cough, rolling her eyes instead. "If your alter ego, TR I-pay, takes home this award, your sales could triple."

Go figure. The egomaniac's rambling spoof of cozy mysteries, titled Death Gets Cozy, had not only sold, it had become a bestseller in the mystery category. All by its little old self, it had quickly outstripped all Mulish's book sales for the past twenty-seven years. She'd finally earned a commission on the man. Something she never thought would or, if she was honest, should happen. The man's books were overwrought, overwritten ego-driven flights of fancy.

As big as his head was, she still wondered how it managed to contain his even larger ego.

She should have turned down representing him years ago but, like a little lost and sad puppy, she had felt sorry for him. And now that she had him, she found it hard to give him back to the pound.

Anthony Mulish twisted his jaw side to side. "Triple?"

"Triple."

Anthony Mulish shoved his big head between his hands and gave a heartfelt sigh. It was hard, so very hard being him. He had worked hard, toiled all his life to write literary novels. Important pieces of art, as important as anything produced by Victor Hugo, Fyodor Dostoevsky or Leo Tolstoy. More important than those modern day hacks like Hemingway and Fitzgerald. And now there was freaking Bob Dylan, for Pete's sake.

The long-haired guitar strummer had won the freaking Nobel Prize for Literature!

Anthony Mulish had always known that society was coming to an end. He just hadn't realized it would come about while he was still alive.

"I don't care," Anthony Mulish said finally, surprising even himself. "I don't want to win the award. I'm sick and tired of the whole thing. I wish I had never written Death Gets Cozy."

Ameena decided this was not the time to say yet again that he had written the book and signed the contract with the publisher. "Don't worry," she told him. "You won't win." She smiled. How nice to say something nasty and nice all in three little words.

"Promise?"

"I promise." The agent knew from experience that

these awards were as much a popularity contest as they were a reflection of a novel's merits.

Who in their right mind would vote for TR Ipé to win the prestigious award once they had met him?

2

Anthony Mulish sat stiff as an old corpse in the passenger seat of Ameena Chowdary's silver BMW sedan. It was a late model too. He didn't even own a car. Perhaps it was time he did. But where would he park it in the city?

Anthony Mulish stared at the passing scenery. Boring. He hated trees. He hated mountains. He hated mud. Virginia seemed to be teeming with all of the above. Virginia wasn't for lovers, it was for masochists.

As they climbed ever further into the never-ending mountains, Anthony Mulish rued his decision to attend Murder Under Cover.

Beside him in the driver's seat, Ameena tightened her grip on the steering wheel as she fought against her natural instinct to squeeze her eyes shut each time they came to a sharp turn in the road. She hated sharp turns. She hated heights. She hated her passenger.

The road seemed to get narrower by the mile, with precipitous drops and deadly plunges, followed by stomach-turning steep inclines.

There were no guardrails anywhere. Why? Didn't the Department of Transportation care if the occasional tourist took a shortcut back to ground level?

To make matters worse, she had gloomy Anthony Mulish for company. In the end, her least favorite but suddenly most successful author had put his foot down. He had insisted that he would only attend *Murder Under Cover* if she accompanied him.

Ameena's husband, Ravi, had told her that she should tell Mulish to take a hike. He'd been telling her that for years. She was on the verge of taking his suggestion one step further. If Mulish complained once more about her driving, she was going to lean over, open his door and suggest he take that hike. Even if she was going fifty miles per hour and they were four thousand feet above sea level.

They had been on the road, cooped up with only each other in the tiny car, for eight hours or more. Not even the satellite radio had helped. Mulish had stubbornly refused to listen to anything other than classical music. A soporific if ever there was one. If it hadn't been for regular caffeine stops, she'd have been asleep at the wheel long ago.

According to her GPS, the end was almost in sight.

Truth be told, it was the only thing that kept her going.

A big rig swung around a sharp blind bend, halfway in their lane. The driver tooted his air horn like it was her fault. Ameena swore. *"Veshya kee santaan!"* and swerved to the right.

The BMW's tires bounced over loose rocks and gravel along the shoulder.

She ignored her client's curses and entreaties to the god he didn't believe in to save him from a certain and painful death as they were rattled like rag dolls.

The next minute, she was smiling as the BMW found its grip on the road again and Anthony Mulish collapsed in a blessedly silent, perspiring heap. The sign posted along the edge of the road told her that the College of the Alleghenies was a mere mile away.

That mile was practically straight downhill. Ameena was forced to ride the brakes, otherwise they might have reached the campus at one hundred miles per hour. That wasn't the sort of entrance she wanted to make.

Fortunately, they arrived unscathed. Her car bounced across a narrow, storybook-perfect wooden covered bridge with a green roof and red timber sides spanning a slow-moving creek.

The small COA campus sat in a misty bowl surrounded by thick woods. Several large, dull brown brick buildings with equally unimaginative square windows were arranged in a U-shape cradling an expanse of now brown grass, with a solitary flagpole near its center.

A Civil War-era cannon aimed toward the entrance drive. Southern hospitality at its best.

Several smaller structures, including a well-kept, two-story Colonial-style house, surrounded by beds of late-blooming flowers, sat on the outskirts abutting a broad lawn with a marble fountain. A white-tailed duck scooted around in the fountain bowl while two mourning doves circled the ground below. The sign on the lawn stated that the house was the residence of the chancellor.

"*This* is our destination?" Anthony Mulish looked out the bug-spattered windshield. "Not much, is it?"

"What do you want? It's not the Ritz-Carlton. It's a small, privately-run college. And it's not costing you a dime, remember? The conference is paying for everything."

She, on the other hand, had had to pay the three hundred dollar registration fee, plus an extra seventy-five for the banquet, plus her room charges.

Ravi complained about that. She told her husband not to worry because she'd deduct the cost of the trip from Mulish's next royalty statement. Even the gas money. He'd never know.

Anthony Mulish grunted. "I was expecting something more grand. I hope the accommodations are suitable."

"Let's go find out." She took malicious pleasure in picturing Anthony Mulish being forced to spend the night in a stark cell, better yet, a monkey cage.

Leaving the car outside a broad set of steep granite steps leading to the entrance, author and agent strode into the warm lobby. Several long folding tables, each occupied by a pair of eager volunteers, were set up directly across from them. Lines of registrants stood in front of each table.

Anthony pulled a small flask from the inside pocket of his brown tweed coat. He didn't really care for tweed but he thought it fit the part he was meant to play: author. He took a small sip of tequila and returned the silver flask to its pocket. "What's going on? Class registration? I thought you told me that students were on break at this time?"

"They are," replied Ameena. "These people are registering for the conference."

"Ah, that explains it."

"Explains what?"

"Why they don't look college age. Look at them. I mean, I see a few young people but most of them are absolutely ancient."

Ameena felt a twinge in her neck like the stony hand

of a dark forest-dwelling ogre was squeezing the life essence out of her from behind her back. It was all she could do not to tell Mulish that practically everyone in sight was either younger than him or, at the very least, no older. "People of all ages read mysteries. You, of all people, should know that."

She pulled him closer and dropped her voice. "And watch what you say around these people. These are your fans."

Anthony Mulish snorted derisively.

"Mister Ipé?" A bundled up woman in a parka and white scarf beamed at him. She was pushing a cart overladen with hard- and soft-covered books. "Oh, my lordy, it is you!" She rummaged through her cloth-sided cart. "Look, I have your book, Death Gets Cozy!" She threw open the title page. "Would you sign it for me?"

Although Ameena had seen the cover a thousand times before, it never got old. Neither did her client's expression every time he had to look at it. She found the cover cute. He found it mortifying.

Death Gets Cozy was the improbable story of a female amateur sleuth who owns a rug shop/café, has a trio of black and white cats, a chubby wiener dog who thinks he's one of the cats, and a blind hermit crab with a knack for solving murders.

The novel's protagonist, Samille Cannon, was twenty-six years old, had the body of a Victoria's Secret model and the brains of a Goddard Space Center scientist—the author's words, not hers.

Samille's best friend and sidekick in amateur crime solving was Debbie Dunse. Debbie was a cartoonish blonde with too much energy and too little brain wave activity. Yet, improbable as it seemed, the blonde had her fans among readers.

According to the story, Samille Cannon had rescued the unfortunate hermit crab along a busy Florida roadside. Ameena was positive that Anthony Mulish had never so much as stepped foot in Florida. Nonetheless, in the story, the crab had been the victim of a vehicular hit-and-run as it attempted to cross from one side of busy coastal highway A1A to the other.

Blinded in the accident, Herman "Hermie" the hermit crab was able to communicate with his rescuer, Samille, via writing in beach sand. This, the creature accomplished by dragging an over-sized claw through the sand in the wooden sandbox she had provided for him in her home.

Actually, there were two sandboxes, one in her store and one in her apartment because the crab often went to work with her. In fact, he was on the payroll with the title of Official Greeter.

With all the above in mind, the publisher's graphic artist had gone to town. The cover depicted Samille seated on the edge of a giant wood-sided sandbox in the center of Little Shop of Rugs and Refreshments, surrounded by her pets. The title Death Gets Cozy was written in the sand—by Hermie, no doubt, whose giant left claw was caked with specks of golden sand.

Ameena could only imagine what the graphic artist had thought of the book's premise. She would have bet drugs had been required in the creative design process.

Anthony Mulish had confided to her that he had given his protagonist the name Samille Cannon because he was infatuated with the older actress Dyan Cannon. Samille Cannon combined her real name with her stage name.

Maybe he thought Dyan Cannon would be flattered, call him up. Blurb his next Anthony Mulish novel. Not a bad idea on the face of it. If a mere one hundred Dyan Cannon fans bought one of his tedious literary novels, it would amount to as much as he generally sold in any given year.

On a personal level, of course, he wouldn't stand a chance with the actress. Ameena wasn't sure he stood a chance with any woman.

Of course, now he was making money. That might just change things. Even an Anthony Mulish could get lucky once in a while. Who'd have thought he'd be a successful author? Not her. But a woman? Only if he kept his mouth shut and just nodded, and let any potential mates do all the talking.

Anthony Mulish squinted at the fan before him. He had forgotten to put his contact lenses in. He had a pair of reading glasses in his jacket but kept them there. He was too vain to wear the glasses in public. "Did you purchase this novel?"

"Yes, of course, Mister Ipé."

"Here?"

"Uh. Why, no. I bought it at my local bookstore." According to her badge, she was Shelly Burns, from Austin, Texas. She was a long way from home. "I brought it with me because I knew you were coming." She angled the open book closer to him. "Do you have a pen, Mister Ipé, sir?"

Anthony retreated, waving his hands like a pair of five-fingered stop signs. "I'm sorry. I do not."

His signing pen was in his other inside pocket, on the left side, where he kept it at the ready. But he wasn't telling her that. Not now. Not under these circumstances.

"I'm afraid I can only sign books that you purchase here at this event."

"Oh?" The poor woman looked mortified and crest-fallen all rolled up into one red face of dismay and embarrassment. "I am so sorry. I-I didn't know." She de-flated like a red circus balloon.

Anthony Mulish smiled. "Now you do." He took his agent's arm and walked away.

"What on earth did you tell her that for?" whispered Ameena. "That was rude. You disappointed a fan."

"It only makes them stronger," he said, nonsensically.

"It makes them post nasty comments about TR Ipé, the goose that laid the golden egg and his novel, Death Gets Cozy, on social media."

That brought Anthony Mulish to a stop. "I'll do better next time." They both knew that wasn't true and that he was merely placating her.

"It's not even correct." Ameena pulled him up to a table.

"What?"

"Fans do not have to buy their books here for the authors to sign. I mean, it's nice. But authors can sign books fans bring with them from home. There are no rules."

"No rules?"

"No rules. You can sign their books, their bookmarks, the program, their elbows, for that matter. And you should."

"That's ridiculous," he said. What was the point in coming if nobody bought his books? "Not this author."

"Right. What was I thinking?"

"Excuse me?"

Good grief. Had she said that last bit aloud? "I said

'good thinking.' More sales that way."

"Exactly."

"Let's get you signed up." Maybe then she could go take a nap up in her room.

Ignoring the long lines, Anthony Mulish approached a large woman in a *High Crimes – Denver - Bouchercon 2000* T-shirt with a bejeweled lavender tiara atop her head. She was in charge of the A through F line but that wasn't stopping him.

She looked at them expectantly. "Names, please?"

Ameena stepped in. "This is Anthony—" Anthony Mulish jabbed her roughly between the ribs. "Ouch." Ameena rubbed her side. "This is Mister TR Ipé."

"Oh, Mister Ipé!" The woman leapt to her feet. Her tiara went tumbling to the floor behind her. "I should have known. I am a huge, huge fan."

Mulish held his hand to the side of his mouth and turned to his agent to mutter, "I'll say."

Ameena scowled and stabbed him between the ribs with her elbow. "Play nice."

The author leaned forward and extended his hand. "TR Ipé. A pleasure, madam."

The woman scooped up her tiara, plopping it atilt on her head. She moved to the G through L box and flipped through the envelopes in the plastic bin there. "Here you go, Mister Ipé, sir." Waving an envelope overhead, she returned. "Everything you need is inside."

She opened the number 10 envelope to prove her point. "Here's your nametag. That goes in your badge sleeve attached to your lanyard. And here are your meal tickets, including your banquet ticket. The conference is even providing you with two free drink tickets."

She held up two red tickets. "Anything you like. Our

treat. And, as our guest of honor, you get two more free drink tickets good at tonight's reception." She held up two green tickets as if they were magic talismans.

"Thank you, Ms...?" he glanced at the plastic sleeve of her lanyard, "Wethering." Peggy Wethering had decorated her badge with cloisonné pins and Nancy Drew novel cover stickers.

What had he gotten himself into?

"I'm looking forward to your reading later."

"Reading?"

Anthony Mulish glanced first at the Wethering—or was that Wearisome—woman then his agent. "What reading?"

"At three o'clock." She snatched a small stapled booklet from the table and riffled through it. "See? Right here. SGOH reading. That's you." She raised a massive arm and pointed. "Right there in the Raymond Chandler Auditorium. Seats five hundred."

"The Raymond Chandler Auditorium? Was he an alumni?" Maybe this little college wasn't such a third-rate degree mill after all.

"Oh, no. At least, I don't believe so. It's really the George Mason Auditorium. He wrote Virginia's Declaration of Independence. The con organizers renamed all the rooms for the event."

Disappointment edging his lip downward, Mulish accepted the envelope and turned to go.

"Don't forget your bag." With a thud, Ms. Wethering dumped a large zippered black canvas tote bag on the table.

He dragged it closer. "What's all this?"

"That's your swag bag."

"I don't want it." Mulish pushed it back across the

table.

"But all your swag is in it."

He turned to his agent. "What is this woman talking about? What is swag?"

"Free books mostly, bookmarks, plus mystery magazines, maybe some postcards and pens." She turned to the extremely patient woman manning the table who no doubt wished her client had taken his business elsewhere. That made two of them. "Hello." She extended her hand. "Ameena Chowdary. I'll take mine, please."

She turned and smiled awkwardly at the growing crowd behind them, which Anthony Mulish had rudely cut in front of.

"Let me get that for you." Peggy flipped through the plastic bin at her table. "Chowdary, Chowdary." She stopped. "Here you go." She handed Ameena her registration. "And here's your swag bag," she added with some hesitation.

Ameena thanked Peggy and turned to her client. "You should take yours too."

"Why?"

"To be polite?"

The twitch of his brow suggested he didn't think that reason enough.

"Maybe you'll find a book or two in the bag that you will enjoy reading."

"From this lot?" His eyes scanned the mostly female, mostly middle-aged and upwards crowd. "I doubt it." His finger toyed with the fabric handle. "Still, it is free and it would be rude to refuse, I suppose."

"You suppose right."

Peggy Wethering held up the bag in question. "Mister Ipé? I do think you will enjoy it." Her voice trembled and her tiara slid down her forehead, scraping down her nose. She shoved it back in place with her free hand.

"Fine. I'll take mine too," sighed Anthony Mulish, as if he were doing the woman a great favor. He could always sell the books at Monty's Books & More, his neighborhood used bookstore. Even books such as these had to be worth something.

The poor volunteer looked like she needed the hospitality suite and quick.

"You didn't tell me there would be a reading," complained Anthony Mulish. "I hate readings."

"It's customary. I thought you knew. It was in the contract you signed with the organizing committee." Peggy's lips tightened.

"I must have glossed over that."

"You have a reading, two signings, half a dozen manuscript critiques to plow through—"

"Half a dozen?"

"The committee mailed them to you eight weeks ago, Mister Ipé."

"But half a dozen?" Anthony Mulish looked in desperation at his agent.

Ameena held up her hand. "Plus a meet and greet with your fans. Check your schedule. It's in that booklet in your bag. It will have all your times listed."

"What time does the bar open?" he wanted to know. He remembered now a thick packet of twenty-page partial manuscripts arriving at his door back home. He had assumed they were from wannabe authors seeking his advice. He had immediately trashed them.

"Not soon enough," Ameena said with surprise. Not surprise that she'd thought it, only surprise that she'd said it out loud.

Another volunteer told the pair that their rooms were on the fifth floor. They rode a warm, crowded elevator upward.

On the ride up, Anthony Mulish said quietly to his agent, "I'm afraid I left the manuscripts I am supposed to be critiquing back in my apartment." A small lie. But, in his opinion, life was justifiably meant to be full of them.

"Don't worry. They sent copies to me, too, in case yours got lost in the mail. I've got them in my bag. I'll drop them off."

"Wonderful," replied Anthony Mulish in a tone that left no doubt that he meant exactly the opposite.

A large woman in a green dress who had been talking to her slender companion took one look at Anthony Mulish and stopped. "One second." She patted her friend's arm. "Do you know who this is?" She turned to the author. "You are TR Ipé, aren't you?"

Anthony thrust his hands in his coat pockets. "Yes."

"I knew it! I thought Death Gets Cozy was wonderful. And to think, it's your debut novel. You have a real gift, TR."

"Yes," he agreed.

Her red-headed companion joined the conversation. This woman wore no lanyard as of yet but was loaded down with her own conference bag. "When can we expect the next book in the series?"

Mulish visibly flinched. His agent knew this was a sore spot for him. He hated his success at least as much as he loved it. Probably more. She knew the thought of a sequel, let alone a continuing series was unthinkable to him. Though both she and his publisher had begged and begged him to continue.

"I am considering my options," he said with a flick of the tongue. "First and foremost being to slit my wrists." He jutted out said pale wrists.

The ladies laughed nervously, unsure if he was joking or not.

Ameena came forward as the elevator stopped on floor two. A couple people got off. The doors closed and they resumed their ascent. "You must be Dorothy Hall. It's an honor to meet you. I've read all your books. I'm Ameena Chowdary. I represent Mister Ipé." She turned to her charge. "Ms. Hall is a mystery author, TR. A very distinguished one, I might add."

"Why, thank you, Ameena." Dorothy Hall primped her bouffant with pride.

"Dorothy is also up for a Poe award for best hardcover original in the cozy category."

"I'm surprised." Anthony Mulish stroked his chin.

"Surprised?" Dorothy Hall blinked her green eyes at him.

"I believe I have seen your work. Nothing original about it at all."

Dorothy Hall tittered nervously, again unsure if this was the celebrated cozy author's sense of humor or if she was being dissed.

Ameena blushed with embarrassment. She knew exactly what he had meant.

The elevator stopped and the doors slid open once again. The ladies stepped out first. "See you at the banquet tonight, TR," called Dorothy Hall. The two ladies disappeared into a room near the elevator shaft.

"She called me TR," Anthony Mulish said. "I hate that." He preferred the more formal Mister Ipé. The elevator continued upwards.

"I know. But you did choose your own nom de plume." How many times had she reminded him of that too? "Get used to it. These people have read your book. They feel like they know you. More than that, you're family to them." If only his fans knew how wrong they were. "And did you have to be so rude? Do you know who that was?"

"Yes, Dorothy Somebody. Writes twee cozy mysteries."

"*You* write twee cozy mysteries. Rather, you've written one cozy mystery to be exact." She hoisted her finger. "Ms. Hall has a Grand Master Award for lifetime achievement in the field from the Mystery Writers of America."

That evoked the merest of shrugs from the author.

Ameena dug rapidly through her capacious handbag for her blood pressure meds.

The elevator came to a stop on their floor. Anthony Mulish stepped out then paused outside the door to his room. "Have you submitted *The World Is Words* to publishing houses yet?"

Ameena smothered a groan.

The World Is Words was his latest masterpiece, his magnum opus. His Nobel Prize-worthy novel that spanned the last five hundred years of Western civilization. His previous novels had sold in the low thousands. This one would sell in the millions. He was certain of it.

"Not yet." Truth be told, she fell asleep each time she tried to read it. The novel was overwrought and overworked. If she ever did make it to the end of the eight hundred-plus page novel, her husband and children would probably find her dead at her desk, a victim of boredom.

Ravi had found her slumped over the manuscript on more than one occasion, asleep, drool oozing from her mouth. He'd even gone so far as taking photographs of her on his smartphone and posting the embarrassing shots demonstrating just that on social media. She secretly plotted her revenge on her husband and her client.

Anthony Mulish frowned. He thrust his key into the slot and opened the door. The steel key was the real deal, not one of those flimsy keycards. The college was either a slow adopter or felt it simpler to give their students something more solid to hold onto and less easily frangible. "You are my agent. Strike while the iron is hot."

"Yes, Anthony." Ameena caught sight of a sumptuously outfitted suite. At least they were putting him up nicely. She wouldn't have to hear him crow about the accommodations.

"Shush." He held a cautionary index finger to his lips. "That's Mister Ipé while we are here." He hated it when others compared the author Anthony Mulish with that hack TR Ipé. "You must remember to call me that."

"Of course, Mister Ipé." She had tried valiantly to get him to drop the ruse. If everybody knew that Anthony Mulish and TR Ipé were one and the same, bookstores might finally be able to move some of his older Mulish-branded titles. But still the writer insisted on maintaining the pretense.

If only she'd dropped him as a client years ago. She had been a fool to keep him. If she dropped him now, when he was finally earning her some much-deserved commission money, she'd be double the fool.

"And remember, let's strike while the iron is hot. I pay you to get results." He slammed the door in her face.

"I'd like to strike all right," she muttered, balling her hands into fists as she slumped wearily to her own smaller room at the end of the hall next to a utility closet.

3

Anthony yawned as he entered his suite. He studied himself in the mirror hung in the foyer. He still sometimes barely recognized the man he saw looking back at him. He had dyed his mousy brown hair black and shaved his beard—all in an attempt to distance himself, Anthony Mulish, serious novelist, from the man he had become, TR Ipé, cozy mystery author.

Ugh. It still hurt even to think it.

From his earliest memories, all Anthony Mulish had wanted was to succeed in life as a serious novelist. He hadn't cared about fame or even fortune. A modest living and a modest home would have been enough for him.

For years he had struggled in vain. He'd written novel after novel, a few published, many never seeing the light of day. The reviews had been mixed at best but he had not let that stop him, although it did sometimes hurt.

Then came the age of the internet and he had to deal with inconsequential and frequently mean-spirited twits who posted the most inane and spiteful reviews of his novels for all eternity.

What sort of lives did they lead that they spent their time trying to destroy other people?

People they didn't even know.

People who had given their lives to create stories.

Then, in a fit of rage and vengeance, he had written Death Gets Cozy. For his murder victim, he'd chosen a blogger/influencer. Blogger/influencer. How he loathed the very terms. Vocalizing the words called to mind the sound of someone vomiting up a rancid sardine. He considered most of their work just as unpalatable.

He had sent his satiric novel to Ameena as a joke really. A way of venting his frustration with the world.

Nothing more.

And now he was famous for it. Every time he went into a bookstore, he was forced to endure the sight of the novel's saccharine cover with his pseudonym in bold raised letters.

He had created a monster and the monster was him. Tired, watery gray eyes blinked at him. The eyes of a sixty-year-old man. He had tried Tiffany blue-tinted contacts but the effect was disconcerting so he had gone back to clear lenses.

"Anthony Mulish," he spoke to the mirror, "look what you have done. Famous for something you never wanted. Celebrated for writing the sort of novel that you delighted in mocking others for writing."

It was horrifying. Overwhelming. And, if he was honest with himself, which he occasionally was, a little bit exciting. Several bloggers had put him up there in the ranks with Dame Agatha Christie! Why, one social media influencer had even called Death Gets Cozy the "must read mystery novel of the year!"

How could he be a cozy writer? In his mind, cozy mystery authors were little old ladies with furry, fat-bellied cats in their laps, seated in slipcover chairs, knitting booties and scarves for their grandchildren. In between, they concocted absurdist tales of small town charm and murder.

Now, according to his agent, these very same writers considered him one of the family.

If there was a god, he surely did have a sense of humor.

Or a mean streak.

Anthony Mulish removed his coat. He hung it carefully over the desk chair. Reaching into the inside pocket, he pulled out his flask and took a long drink of tequila. He deserved it.

Yanking open the curtains, he looked out at the mountains and the misty forest. The sky above was a dappled gray blanket. Three white-tailed deer, a mother and two fawn, were visible through the trees, nibbling at the sparse understory.

"How dreary."

He pulled the drapery shut again. There was nothing outside worth looking at.

The suite itself was pleasant enough. Being a college, he had feared being ensconced in some spartan dormitory, dreary and smelling of stale bargain-priced beer. Surprisingly, this suite was quite posh, meant for visiting dignitaries like himself, no doubt.

He decided to explore further. Opening a white door, he discovered an elegant, marble-tiled bathroom off the foyer.

The foyer itself opened into the sitting area, featuring velvety overstuffed chairs and a sofa. A large, flatscreen TV was attached to the wall. A decent workspace occupied another wall with one of those ergonomic black leather office chairs that he had always coveted.

Could he keep it? Would the unwieldy chair fit in the

trunk of Ameena's BMW?

In the corner of the room, he noticed a kitchenette with all sorts of stainless steel appliances. He popped open the refrigerator, delighted to see they had stocked it with fruits, cheeses and two packs of Guinness Draught, his favorite beer.

A candy dish on the dining table held an assortment of imported Belgian chocolate bars with almonds—one of his guilty pleasures. The table also held a beribboned bottle of his favorite tequila, too. This tequila was contained in a macabre yellow-and-red Day of the Dead skull-shaped bottle. He'd never seen anything like it and cradled the glazed bottle in his hands to study it more closely.

That bottle was definitely going home with him.

The organizers had listened well.

Heavy white, raised-panel double doors led to what he surmised would be the bedroom. He turned the gold knob on the right and entered. To his surprise, a young blonde woman lay atop the king-sized bed. Long hair spilled over her ripe, full breasts. There was something sexy about the scoop-necked French peasant dress that hung loosely from her shoulders, stopping a little above the knees. Her eyes were green. Her parted lips were red and inviting.

A perfect specimen.

Anthony Mulish was already devising a place for her in one of his novels. He swallowed hard. "One of us seems to be in the wrong room."

"I'm Giselle Mimieux." She pointed a finger at him. "You are TR Ipé." She balanced a wine glass in her left hand. She gave it a swirl.

Anthony Mulish considered. The woman's accent

was French. Her intent was yet unclear. "How did you get in here?"

She smiled. "I stole a master key from one of the maids earlier."

"You should go."

"But I paid for a manuscript consultation with you." Giselle Mimieux patted the white down-filled comforter.

"Now? Here?"

"Tomorrow, actually, but I was hoping for some time alone." She batted her long, curly lashes at him. "And maybe you could introduce me to your agent?"

Ah, she was one of those. "I'll see you at the appointed time. Get out." He pointed towards the door.

Giselle Mimieux set her half-empty wine glass on the nightstand and reluctantly stood. "But I paid a hundred dollars for your critique."

"You want my critique? Here it is. You," he paused for dramatic effect, "are a slut."

The young woman's face darkened as she grabbed her leather purse off the plush Turkish rug the bed sat on. She slipped her feet into a pair of high heels.

Giselle Mimieux stormed to the door.

He followed her. "And if you want to write cozies," Anthony Mulish said loudly, "I suggest you spend more time writing and less time spreading your legs."

She slammed the door behind herself.

Reentering the bedroom, Anthony Mulish noticed a large manilla envelope on the opposite nightstand. He peered inside. The envelope was stuffed with pages of printer paper. He removed them and looked at the typed title on the front: Sweet Murder by Giselle Mimieux.

"Good grief. Another load of yesterday's cow dung,"

Anthony Mulish said, after forcing himself to read the opening two pages.

With a sigh, he pulled open the bedroom curtains, lifted the sash and hurled the manuscript out the window. Pages fluttered bird-like and flew in the cold wind like the trash that they were.

An incessant banging at the door of his room drove him to open it. He slammed the window down and stomped to the door. "Yes?"

It was Giselle Mimieux. Her arms were rigidly locked over her chest. Her face was the color of a ripe radish. "I want my manuscript back!"

"You are too late. It is decorating the lawn."

"What does that mean?" Her eyes burned with hatred.

"I threw it out the window." He slowly closed the door, nearly clipping off her pert little nose.

"You pig!" she shouted at the closed door and stamped her feet.

Ameena headed toward the elevator. Her own quarters were tiny and austere, more dorm than domicile. And she was paying a pretty penny for the space.

With her was Jenny Garrett, Anthony Mulish's editor at Ackerman Publishing. AP had been responsible for publishing Death Gets Cozy. Sometimes, Ameena didn't know whether to thank them or firebomb their offices.

The pair noticed the sexy young woman banging on Anthony Mulish's door.

"Isn't that Ipé's suite?" Jenny Garrett had been forewarned about speaking Anthony Mulish's real name anywhere in public.

"Yep." Ameena kept walking.

Bang! Bang! "Open up, jerk face!" shouted Giselle

Mimieux fiercely.

"Who's the young lady?" asked Jenny.

"Another of his fans, I suppose." Ameena pushed the button for the elevator. She ignored the constant pounding on her author's door.

She breathed a sigh of relief when she and Jenny Garrett were safely inside the elevator and falling rapidly.

4

Anthony kicked off his shoes and stretched out on the soft, memory foam-topped, king-sized mattress. Thank goodness the insane woman's pounding had finally stopped.

He needed a rest. It had been an overlong day, stuck in the cramped car with his agent. Worse yet, the evening promised to be a bore. He hated people and hated worse socializing with them. Their senseless chatter was a verbal assault, pummeling his ears and squeezing his brain like the foulest device of torture ever devised by Torquemada.

If the sadistic Spaniard had really wanted to make a person suffer, he should have sent them to one of these mindless conferences.

He sniffed. The comforter smelled of patchouli, as had Giselle Mimieux. If he hadn't been so tired, he might have been tempted to let her stay. Having sex with her could have been fun. But having to read her amateurish manuscript?

No, he would rather remain celibate than be forced to read more of that twee drivel.

Read.

Drat.

He pushed himself up against the headboard. What had that volunteer woman said? He had a reading at three o'clock?

It was nearly three now. He rose, riffled through his suitcase and brought out a copy of Death Gets Cozy. There was no time to consider which passage to choose. He would simply start at the beginning and read a page or two. There was no point giving away too much of the story. He needed buyers, not free listeners. People who preferred to have the book told to them should purchase the audiobook. His royalty margin on those was quite good.

He stopped at the door to his suite, paused and pushed a smile onto his face. It was show time.

The hallway stood empty. So too the elevator. He wiped the smile off his face. No sense wasting all that energy for nothing.

Downstairs, he noticed Ameena sitting front and center in the auditorium along with several hundred attendees. There was no sign of Giselle Mimieux. Hopefully, the woman had returned to Paris, France or Paris, Texas, wherever she was from.

Reba Lonnegan gave a sigh of relief as their SGOH entered the room. Frantically, she motioned him to the side of the stage and whispered. "I'm Reba Lonnegan, one of the organizers, Mister Ipé. Your publisher, Frank Ackerman, is supposed to introduce you. He hasn't shown up yet."

Her eyes bounced nervously over the faces in the crowd. She wanted everything to go perfectly but with real-life people involved, rather than people on pages, things rarely did. That was why she preferred books. The people in books may not have always done what she wanted but they did what the author wanted. "I could introduce you, if you like."

"Not necessary, Ms. Lonnegan. These people know who I am." He planted his right foot on the first step. "I'll handle this myself."

He composed himself, adjusting the lapels of his jacket as he climbed the steps. The crowd watched eagerly as TR Ipé proceeded to center stage. He studied his audience as the faces in the audience in turn watched and waited anxiously for him to speak.

This was the sort of thing that Anthony Mulish had waited all his life for. The great author standing before his adoring fans. Reading from his critically acclaimed novel.

Sadly, these were mystery fans. Largely, cozy mystery fans. A world and a genre he knew little about. Perhaps he should have brought along his latest unsold masterpiece, The World Is Words, and read from it. That would have given them something to think about.

With a sigh only he could hear, he opened to the beginning of chapter one of Death Gets Cozy.

A hand shot up in the fourth row before one word could escape from his lips. "Excuse me, Mister Ipé," bubbled a middle-aged woman with a Southern drawl and an affection for all things magenta, including her sweater, her lip gloss and the absurd streak in her hair. "Before y'all begin, could you tell us where you got your inspiration for Death Gets Cozy? As an aspiring novelist, I'd love to know. I'm sure we all would."

Voices in the crowd murmured agreement.

Sensing imminent disaster, like a ground zero bomb detonation, Ameena jumped to her feet. "I'm sure Mister Ipé will be happy to answer all your questions after the reading."

Reba Lonnegan, who stood to the side of the stage

holding cards to indicate the passing of time, chimed in. "Ms. Chowdary is right. Why don't we hold all questions until later? Mister Ipé will be happy to speak with each of you after his reading."

The author smiled uneasily. The nettlesome women were making promises for him which he had no intention of keeping.

Ameena sank gratefully to her chair. Mission accomplished. Disaster averted.

Asking him about his inspiration!

What if he had told the truth? What if Anthony Mulish blurted out to this crowd that the whole novel had been nothing more than a joke?

TR Ipé's career and sales would come to a grinding halt. This crowd might even stone him. Not literally, of course, but they might hurl their Louise Penny or Margaret Maron novels at him. Hardcover editions, too.

Those were thick. And heavy.

The agent waved her hand at Anthony Mulish. He cleared his throat, smiled grimly and began to read.

"Samille Cannon was not expecting to discover a body the very first morning of the very first day that she opened her cozy little store, Little Shop of Rugs and Refreshments. But there it was, a dead body. At least what appeared to be one. Two polished black loafers sticking out from the center of an antique lavender-and-yellow Persian rug, with a hint of black wool trousers and matching socks leading inward."

Anthony Mulish cleared his throat and continued. "What else could it be? Samille wondered. She moved inexorably closer with two of her three cats and Fudgie the wiener dog following in her wake."

The author paused, puzzled, as he looked out into the

audience. What the devil was his agent doing? She was distracting him with her ridiculous gestures. Pushing her palms upward. What did she mean by that?

Was she trying to tell him something? Couldn't it wait?

Finally, taking advantage of Anthony Mulish's pause, Ameena pointed toward the microphone and mouthed "Move closer to the mic."

Anthony Mulish nodded and grabbed the microphone. A jolt of electricity shot through him. He heard something snap. He hoped it wasn't any of his bones.

The microphone fell from the podium, hitting the stage with a dull thud. A hundred voices rose at once.

Eyes bouncing, heart fluttering, Anthony Mulish looked up to see Reba Lonnegan looking down. At him. "Are you all right, Mister Ipé?" How, oh how, could things keep going wrong? "Matt!"

A young man appeared as if summoned out of nothing. "Sorry, Ms. Lonnegan. Must be a loose connection. Some of this PA stuff is, like, really old." He drew the word out for emphasis. "I told the head of the AV department we needed new stuff."

"See that it's fixed before somebody gets hurt." She prayed Mister Ipé was not a litigious sort. The con could not afford a lawsuit. And the college would be livid because they'd be party to any subsequent legal proceedings and hefty judgments.

"Yes, ma'am." The young man in torn jeans and a gray college sweatshirt retrieved the microphone and shook his head.

Before somebody gets hurt? thought Anthony Mulish.

Hands helped him to his feet.

"Would you like to cancel, TR?" asked Ameena.

Reba Lonnegan's mouth formed an O of horror at the thought.

"No, no. The show must go on." TR Ipé smiled, gave himself a shake and returned to the podium to continue reading, albeit without benefit of electronically-enhanced vocals. His hands tingled a bit as if he'd been goosed in the funny bone. His fingers, where they had touched the metal microphone, were lightly burned at the tips.

In the corner of the room, the college student slash con volunteer slash brunt of Ms. Lonnegan's ire, sat cross-legged on the floor, the broken microphone in his lap. He prodded the device with a screwdriver.

The great TR Ipé did his best to ignore the fellow. He'd show this crowd that nothing, not even an electrical shock, could get this author down.

Plus, there was the sympathy angle. That could sell a few more books. The brave author valiantly continuing on in spite of dire setbacks and the near loss of life itself.

Perhaps Ameena could arrange for a feature on him in the local newspaper. The New York Times was probably too much to hope for.

Yes, the author as martyr. There was some profound truth to that.

Recognizing this, Anthony Mulish thought it might be best to pretend he was in a bit of lingering pain for the remainder of the conference. Maybe affect a limp.

It wouldn't really be a stretch since being at Murder Under Cover was a bit of a pain in and of itself.

5

"Great job, TR," said Ameena as she and Anthony Mulish stood outside the auditorium afterward. Mercifully, the reading was over and nothing else untoward had happened.

The author beamed and loosened his tie. "Did you notice? After my reading, I signed fourteen brand new hardcover copies of my book."

"That's wonderful, TR." Ameena sounded less than impressed. He'd asked each autograph seeker for a receipt showing proof of purchase before signing. He had even refused to sign one fan's conference program guide unless they first purchased his book.

This weekend was growing longer by the minute. She wondered if there were any physicists remaining on campus who might be willing to explain the immutable laws of quantum mechanics and the time-space continuum as related to the sphere of Anthony Mulish around which she was now stuck in a soul-sucking orbit. No, this was a liberal arts college. She was out of luck on that score. There wouldn't be a physicist in sight.

Then again, maybe she'd find a psychology major or two, possibly willing to give her a free session?

"Let's get out of here before any more of your fans bother you." Or vice versa. Ameena held a roomy woven basket in the crook of her arm. A white cloth was draped over top.

"Good idea." He glanced at his agent's bundle. "Planning a picnic?"

"This?" She raised the basket. "These are the items you are donating for the auction."

"Auction?"

"Yes. I'll show you." Easier to show him than to try and explain the concept. "Follow me. They're combining a silent auction with a live auction. People can place bids ahead of time here on the items they're interested in buying."

"What could possibly be of interest here?"

Ignoring Anthony's remark, Ameena continued, "Then there's the live auction Saturday night where everything is up for grabs."

Anthony tagged along as she led him down one hall then another. They stepped into a good-sized converted classroom. Stacks of molded plastic chairs filled the corners. Long tables laid out along the edges of the walls held an assortment of knickknackery and books. Several tables joined together forming a square in the center of the room.

Two ladies and a lone male sat chatting in the center of the square. A third woman was jotting something down in a lined ledger.

"What is all this bric-a-brac?" Anthony Mulish puzzled at the odd assortment.

There were books, of course, but there were also straw hats, beaded necklaces, beach towels, quilted blankets, a triptych featuring cross-stitched kittens, mermaids and cheeses, plates emblazoned with tacky photo images of cozy mysteries, pots and pans, shopping bags, coffee, tea, chocolate and other items of the eat and drink variety, kitchen utensils, assorted gift cards, a free ski vacation, and bits of knitted apparel—most of which seemed cat- and dog-sized.

Some donations sat modestly with the name of the author who had donated the item listed on a folded tent card. Other more ambitious offerings were arranged as vignettes on the tables.

One particular vignette featured a dollhouse atop a plinth. The dollhouse appeared to have been made from nothing but matchsticks and glue. The interior was filled with matchstick furnishings and matchstick people. The author donating this auction item—which was sure to go up in flames the minute somebody bought it because the crafter had failed to remove the match heads—was named Cherie Maraschino.

Lined sheets of paper beside each item listed a suggested opening bid price. The opening bid for the soon-to-be-up-in-flames dollhouse was the improbable price of one hundred dollars.

"Shh. Keep your voice down. This is not bric-a-brac. These are highly sought after collectibles."

"A mug with a photo of a kitty's face on it?" Anthony Mulish dubiously rotated the gray mug seeking a clue as to why someone would pay good money, even bad money, for the cheap ceramic piece. And was that a real stray cat whisker bouncing around at the bottom of the mug?

He shivered as he set the mug down next to its mate.

Incredibly, someone had already offered fifteen dollars for the pair.

"You should have mentioned this to me prior to coming. I would have brought some of my real novels."

"My bad," deadpanned Ameena with an accompanying eye roll. Nobody here wanted any of Anthony Mulish's dense as clay, dry as bones novels. "Besides, you don't want people to know that TR Ipé and Anthony Mulish are one and the same, remember?"

"Right." The corners of the author's mouth turned downward. "Still," he sighed, "it's a shame. They could have seen what I am really capable of."

"Oh, I think they are seeing that," Ameena said for reasons of her own.

"You think so?" Anthony Mulish puffed out his chest.

"Absolutely." The agent turned to one of the volunteers. "This is TR's contribution. Where shall I set it?" The volunteer showed her where to place the item. Ameena uncovered the basket.

Inside she'd placed a hardcover copy of Death Gets Cozy, a gift card for dinner for two at a popular restaurant chain, several bars of Belgian chocolate, a bottle of expensive champagne (that she hoped Ravi wouldn't notice missing from his precious wine cellar) and a certificate good for a free manuscript consultation from both her and the author.

Anthony Mulish grabbed one of the chocolate bars, the one with hazelnuts. He wasn't happy. Chocolate, if not the cure to his discontent, was a step in the right direction. "Why do I have to do this consultation for free? I'm a successful mystery author. Shouldn't I be paid for my time? It's not like the conference isn't charging attendees a pretty penny itself."

"All the money is going to a children's hospital, TR." Ameena carefully adjusted everything in the basket. The opening bid was set at one hundred and fifty dollars. Surely, it would go for much higher. The champagne alone was worth much more than that.

It would have been nice to have offered naming a character after the winning bidder in TR Ipé's next cozy mystery. That was always a popular draw at these auctions. But since he refused to write another, that wasn't an option.

"I do not have any children." Anthony Mulish picked at the end of the chocolate wrapper.

"Thank goodness for that," muttered Ameena, snatching the chocolate bar and planting it upright in the woven basket.

"Excuse me?" Anthony Mulish cupped his hand to his ear.

"Nothing. I didn't say anything. You must be tired." Ameena encouraged her author to get some rest and he concurred. That left her free to her own devices and free of him for a couple of hours.

She spent it at the bar. This being a college and not a hotel, the bar had been set up in a hospitality suite on the second floor. The drinks were not free but the offerings were plentiful. So was the crowd.

A temporary white poster board sign hung over the double doors, affixed with cellophane tape. The organizers had dubbed this room *The First and Last Chance Saloon*, in honor of the portside bar in Oakland, California where a young Jack London frequently studied and drank. The crude drawing of a martini glass on the poster board left no doubt that this was the place to be.

If only the organizers had posted a *No Authors Allowed* sign on the door, too, it would have been perfect, thought Ameena, sipping her scotch, as she was forced to listen to a pair of over-the-legal-limit authors bemoan both their incompetent agents and their unappreciative editors.

6

Sometime later, glancing at his bedside clock, Anthony Mulish noted wearily that it was nearly time for the conference's evening welcome and opening ceremonies. He wriggled his fingers tentatively. Happily, he suffered no lingering effects of his mishap with the faulty microphone.

Fetching his tuxedo from the closet where he had carefully hung it on unpacking, he shrugged it on.

It was important to look one's best even among mystery fans. Adjusting his bowtie, he studied his reflection in the foyer once again. The only thing out of place was the hideous plastic badge in the middle of his chest. He tightened the lanyard around his neck so the badge hung a few inches below his bowtie. The badge bore the name TR Ipé and, in gold letters, let the world know that he was the con's special guest of honor.

That was something.

He practiced a smile in the mirror. It looked as phony as ever to him. But his fans would never know.

Riding down in the elevator with him were a trio of women in orange-sequined gowns with peacock blue feathers sprouting from their shoulders like some sort of bird-human hybrids, and matching masks. Were they here for a costume party?

In the lobby, Ameena met Anthony and introduced

him to two of the conference's organizers. "TR, these are our hosts. I believe you met Reba Lonnegan at your reading." She indicated a rail-thin woman in a tan shirt-waist dress. Her hair was cut short and curved around and under her delicate chin.

"Yes, of course." Anthony Mulish winced at the memory.

Ameena teetered on a pair of three-inch stilettos. Even with them on her feet, she was the shortest in the bunch. "This is Stan Dooley."

The gentleman, Stan Dooley, also hovering near the half-century mark, was Anthony Mulish's height. His dark hair was streaked with gray. He wore rumpled jeans and a black sport jacket. The shirt on his back was one of the black and red T-shirts being offered up for sale by the conference.

Anthony Mulish had seen a line of them strung up over the registration tables. He had been pleased to see that below the title of the conference, his name was highlighted as SGOH. The names of several lesser authors were listed below his in smaller lettering.

As the pair babbled on about how honored they were to have him for their inaugural event, Anthony Mulish surveyed the crowd. While he had opted for formal attire, the tuxedo which he had purchased secondhand some years ago, he was pleased to see that a number of attendees had chosen suits and formal dresses. Unfortunately, many others wore jeans and T-shirts and shabby jackets.

Still others wore wacky outfits and quirky regalia, like the women he'd ridden down in the elevator with. They hadn't been going to a costume party at all. They had been coming here!

He saw puffy pink feather boas, preposterously large cowboy hats and perilously pointy cowboy boots, flamboyant Victorian dresses featuring generous amounts of décolletage and everything in between. One fellow had clumsily made himself up to look like Sherlock Holmes. His companion made a dubious Watson.

It has to be the wife, figured Mulish. Who else would open themselves to such public ridicule?

A large, stout man interrupted Anthony Mulish's thoughts.

"Anthon—I mean, Mister Ipé, so glad you made it okay." This was TR Ipé's publisher, Frank Ackerman. He looked the author up and down. "Looking snazzy, TR."

"Thank you." Anthony Mulish tugged at his coat sleeves. He did look rather good. He had hesitated to purchase the tuxedo secondhand, but the clerk had insisted that it had once been worn by the noted playwright Arthur Miller. That had sealed the deal.

"Hello, Frank," said Ameena, planting faux kisses on both the publisher's cheeks. She introduced the publisher to the organizers.

"We met earlier." Frank Ackerman nonetheless thrust out his meaty palm and shook with Reba and Stan. "Good to see you again. Great event. Great event." Frank's black suit looked twenty years out-of-date and meant for a man forty pounds lighter.

Ameena noticed beads of sweat along the edges of Frank's bushy beard.

"Can I get a word with you, TR?" Frank inquired.

A passing server offered Anthony Mulish a flute filled with champagne. He took a sip. "This is not a good time. How about later?"

"Ticket, sir?" interrupted the server, palm up.

"Go away," Anthony Mulish told him.

"Here, take one of mine." Frank dug into his pocket for a ticket and threw it down on the serving tray. The waiter withdrew.

What Anthony Mulish needed now most was alcohol and plenty of it. It promised to be a long evening. Glancing at the schedule, he had seen that he was expected to make a speech at the end of the opening ceremonies.

Following this, the organizers had scheduled a classic murder mystery movie: *Strangers on a Train*. Although the movie veered far from Patricia Highsmith's excellent novel, it remained one of his favorite film adaptations.

"I'd really like to talk to you now, TR." Frank Ackerman appeared nervous. "It's about your book." He pressed his fingers against the author's forearm and gave a gentle squeeze.

Anthony Mulish handed Ameena his glass. "Refill this for me, would you?" Turning to Stan and Reba, he said, "You'll excuse me a moment. It seems I am in demand."

"I'd better come too." Ameena balanced her glass as well as Anthony Mulish's. Looking at Stan and Reba, she added, "TR is a brilliant writer but he doesn't understand a thing about business or contracts."

"That's what he pays you for, right?" Stan hoisted his own glass and drank. This being an organizer wasn't what it was cracked up to be. Too long hours, too many hassles, and it seemed all he got paid in was insults and complaints.

"Right." Personally, she felt that at least half her commission was her due just for putting up with him.

"No, no." The author held up his hand. "That won't

be necessary." He left her standing there and followed his publisher to a quiet corner of the ballroom. "What's bothering you, Frank?"

"Huh? Nothing." Frank wiped a line of sweat from under his bulbous nose. Talking to Mulish, merely being in his presence, seemed to open every pore in his flesh. "I read your new book." He'd bought it two months ago and only gotten around to reading it three days' prior after his copy editor had gotten through with it. "It's a doozy."

"Thank you."

"I am a little nervous keeping Ameena out of the loop on this one." Frank glanced back nervously over his shoulder at the agent.

Anthony Mulish loomed over his publisher and said harshly, "It's none of her business." He wasn't sure what had possessed him at the time, the attraction of more money, the lure of fame, however dubious, or the chance to poke fun at cozy mystery readers, but in the wee hours of morning, he had written a sequel to Death Gets Cozy. He had titled it A Cozy Ending.

Ackerman Publishing had offered him a six-figure advance and he had personally handled the contract. Why pay his agent for something he had created? She might have helped sell the first book but what did he need her for now?

"Ameena has earned plenty off Death Gets Cozy. Every time she sends me a royalty statement, I'm forced to see her collecting fifteen percent for all my blood, sweat and tears." His attitude was that, if he was going to write the stuff, he ought to be paid and paid hand-somely for doing so.

"Look at her over there." The author studied his

agent. She was dressed to the nines, swilling champagne, hobnobbing with the mystery royalty. Dorothy Hall had her ear. Was Ameena thinking of adding her to her client list?

That wouldn't do. He should be her biggest, most important client. If not her only client. His thinking was irrational considering he was planning to dump her —but that had never stopped him from such illogical thoughts before.

"I still don't feel right about it." Frank Ackerman used the cuff of his suit jacket to wipe his upper lip once more. "What if she sues us?"

"Us?" Anthony Mulish frowned. He had not considered that possibility. "Do you think she would?"

"I have no idea. Isn't her husband some bigshot attorney?" Frank Ackerman feared lawsuits. As a small publisher, he knew there was a fine line between solvency and ruin.

Death Gets Cozy had been his company's first big hit in nearly five years. Frank was only now catching up on paying off the mountain of debts he'd accumulated. His house was double-mortgaged and he had been forced to sell his beloved boat. The last thing he needed was a team of New York lawyers swooping down on him and picking over his carcass.

"Yes." Anthony Mulish mulled over the publisher's words. "She and I never had an actual written contract for Death Gets Cozy." Theirs had been an informal arrangement over the years.

Frank grabbed a plate of wheat crackers and cubed white-and-yellow cheeses off an ornate silver platter on the black-clothed table. "Still," he said between bites, "wouldn't it be simpler *and cheaper* to pay her her cut?"

"Cheaper for you, maybe. Do you want to pay her the commission out of your share of the profits?"

"No," Frank Ackerman said hastily.

"Then let me handle Ameena."

A crowd had gathered near the raised platform at the front of the room. Reba Lonnegan spoke into a microphone.

"The opening remarks are about to begin." Anthony Mulish adjusted his bowtie. "I need to get to the stage."

"Wait. There's one more thing you should know, Anthony."

"Don't call me Anthony," the author hissed.

"Sorry."

"What else did you want to tell me?"

"Jenny Garrett is here."

"Why? Why did you bring Ms. Garrett?" Jenny Garrett had been his editor on Death Gets Cozy. Anthony Mulish had not been overfond of her comments on his writing. Upon his success and the subsequent submittal of A Cozy Ending, he had put his foot down, insisting that she be replaced or he'd take his book elsewhere.

Ackerman had, albeit reluctantly, acceded to his biggest client's wishes. Jenny Garrett had been demoted from senior editor to copy editor. She had further been banned from working on TR Ipé's novels. A far fall indeed in the publishing world.

Seeing her would be awkward, thought Anthony Mulish. This whole event was awkward enough.

"Send her home," demanded Anthony Mulish.

"I can't do that. Jenny came on her own dime. She took unpaid leave from work despite my protests. She insisted. She paid her own fees and transportation, housing, the works."

"You should have put your foot down."

"What could I do?" blurted Frank. He could barely control his staff in the office. He had no control over them outside work.

"Autograph, Mister Ipé?" A shy man with pale blue eyes and a shock of unruly blond hair stood before the author. He was dressed in pleated gray pants and a blue blazer. A spot of dark ink stained his pink shirt. In one hand he extended Death Gets Cozy, in the other a fancy black ink pen.

"Later," said Anthony Mulish, brushing the young man aside. They were calling for him on stage.

7

Anthony Mulish climbed the narrow stage steps to the satisfying sound of robust applause. To his consternation, Giselle Mimieux occupied a seat in the front row. She wasn't clapping. In fact, she looked rather put out.

Anthony Mulish took the vacant seat reserved for him at the long table facing the crowd. To his right, sat Dorothy Hall. To his left, sat another woman with whom he was unfamiliar.

Dorothy Hall nodded stiffly by way of greeting. The purple pantsuit she had chosen for the occasion looked like it had been cut from the same bolt of fabric as was used to create Barney the Dinosaur's costume. Two strings of heavy pearls weighted her down.

He waved his hand several times in front of his nose. The woman smelled like she had brushed up against a magnolia tree in full bloom. He hated the scent of magnolia trees.

Anthony Mulish noted that the woman on his left made a sour face as he took his chair. Tented name cards sat in front of each person at the table. He leaned forward but was unable to read the woman's name because the cards were aimed at the audience.

Eager fans of all sorts filled the room to capacity. Everything from avid readers, published and hoping to be published writers, to agents and other book industry types.

Stan Dooley made some generic opening remarks. His lame jokes earned him a few polite titters.

Anthony Mulish took a drink from the glass of water provided for him. It tasted off, but then, why shouldn't it? Everything about this conference was a little off.

Giselle Mimieux's face bore the intense smile of a hungry predator immediately prior to striking its prey. She did have great legs, he noted, and wasn't afraid to show them. Her white dress was slit practically to her waist. Blood red stiletto heels hugged her feet, reminding him of Dracula's postprandial fangs.

The woman to his left leaned closer, rubbing her shoulder against his. "You're TR Ipé."

Anthony Mulish turned to face the woman. "That's right."

"You've got a lot of nerve showing up."

"I am the guest of honor. Have we met?"

"Not until now," whispered the woman, a hard edge to her voice despite the smile she projected to the crowd. "I'm Sharon Crumbie. You gave my last novel, *Muffins Taste Like Murder*, a lousy one-star rating online."

Anthony Mulish smelled alcohol on the woman's breath. Her green eyes were swimming in the stuff. Her red hair seemed unsure what direction it wanted to go. A glass of merlot sat next to her own glass of water.

Sharon Crumbie picked up the wine glass with a sudden move and tossed its contents down her throat. "You stink, you know that?"

Anthony Mulish glanced nervously at Stan Dooley. He handed the podium over to Reba Lonnegan. "I remember," he said through gritted teeth. "*Muffins Taste*

Like Murder. Even the title is stupid. How can muffins taste like murder?" His voice had risen a notch.

Reba Lonnegan shot him a questioning glance. Anthony Mulish lowered his voice again. "What does murder taste like?"

Sharon Crumbie gaped at him.

"It makes no sense. I'd have given the book zero stars but it wasn't an option. Pity. My review was meant with the best of intentions. Read my critique again. There's some good advice there."

Anthony stroked his chin. "Heed it. It will make your writing stronger. I should know. All you have to do is read the thousands of words of praise *and five-star reviews* that Death Gets Cozy has received to see that I am right."

Sharon Crumbie's fingers tightened around her empty wine glass. She scanned the crowd for a server. "My book is a cozy. The title is cute," she said through her teeth.

Anthony Mulish smiled indulgently, making her all the madder. "It's stupid. Besides," he continued, suddenly warming to his subject, "if I remember correctly, and I do, you write a series of historical mysteries featuring the Hunchback of Notre Dame who, along with a gargoyle named Garçon who has come back to life, solves murders in the environs of seventeenth century Paris. That," he concluded, "is inane."

"I'm a USA Today best-selling author."

"Which only proves how low humanity has sunk." He sipped from his glass.

"Listen, you—"

"And did they even have muffins in seventeenth century France? If so, what did they taste like? Sawdust, maybe. And raw sewage. Certainly not murder. And why would a hunchback and a stone statue waste their time exposing murderers? Why would they care? One's an outcast. The other," he said pointedly, "is a rock."

Anthony Mulish snorted. The microphone picked up the sound. He cleared his throat and adjusted his bowtie as with one ear he listened to Ms. Lonnegan going over the remainder of the weekend's schedule.

Why?

All the information was in the pocket guide and the big conference program book they'd been given when they registered.

Did she think no one at a conference for book readers and authors could read?

Anthony Mulish would have tuned the woman out but he didn't want to miss his cue when it was his turn to speak. He hadn't prepared any remarks. But he wasn't worried. He could say just about anything and get applause from this audience.

They adored him.

"Face it," Anthony Mulish said softly, "a hunchback for a protagonist—that's almost as absurd as Ms. Hall's work." He indicated the author to his right.

Dorothy Hall grabbed his shoulder roughly and jerked him around. "What's wrong with my work?"

Anthony Mulish looked down his nose at the mystery writer. "Your sleuth's companion is a tiny yellow-and-green alien who is trapped on Earth and helps a doltish female private detective solve cases with plots so obvious that any simpleton could see through them."

"That's Kikiyu." Dorothy Hall snarled, pushing out her not insignificant chest. "My fans adore him."

"He's a rip-off of that little green alien on The Flintstones." Anthony Mulish tapped his fingers against the table. "The Great Gazoo, I think his name was. Always helping Fred and Barney solve their problems. Watch a lot of Flintstones growing up, did you, Ms. Hall?"

Dorothy Hall pushed herself up from her chair. Her face was mottled red and purple. "I am going to rip your freaking face off!"

"Ladies and gentlemen," announced Reba, "you can see how eager she is, so let's waste no more time bringing her up. Here she is, our toast mistress for the weekend, the delightful Dorothy Hall!"

The room erupted in applause. Dorothy Hall gazed out at the audience.

Jaw slack. Stunned. Stymied.

A smile slowly worked its way onto her face. She stumbled to the microphone. It was show time.

She'd deal with TR Ipé later.

8

Ameena observed the proceedings from a front row seat near the inside aisle. Her client was surrounded on either side by Dorothy Hall and Sharon Crumbie. Two titans in the mystery field.

Once again she was amazed at the way things had changed for her client and herself over the past year. She always dreamed of having a star client. She finally did—and it had to be Anthony Mulish. The gods could be rather perverse at times.

She didn't read lips but she could read expressions. Whatever Mulish had been saying to the two women wasn't flattery. The two ladies looked about ready to tag-team him.

Should she rescue him? If so, how? There were hundreds of people in attendance. It wouldn't do to make a scene. It was a quandary because maintaining TR Ipé's image was critical to his continued success in the cozy world of mysteries.

On the other hand, watching the two titans in the mystery field take him down could be fun—the most fun she'd had in years with Anthony Mulish as her client.

Frank Ackerman tapped her on the shoulder. She smiled and lifted her purse from the chair beside hers. She had been holding a seat for him. He'd said he had some other business to attend to.

The man never seemed to stop.

"Everything okay?" Ameena whispered as he squeezed in beside her.

Frank Ackerman wiped a folded paper towel he'd pulled from the men's room dispenser and wiped his forehead. "Yeah, fine."

"What did Anthony want?"

"Huh?"

"Before. He wanted to talk to you in private about his book."

"Oh, that was nothing," the publisher said with a reassuring smile. "He wanted to know how sales were going. Hey." With a tilt of his large head, he gestured across the aisle, deftly changing the subject. "See that girl over there?"

"Which one?"

"The blonde near this end. Third seat in."

Ameena noted the pretty young blonde who seemed to be raptly absorbing Dorothy Hall's words of encouragement to aspiring writers. Wasn't that the same woman who had been banging on Anthony Mulish's door? "What about her? An author of yours?"

"No. Can you believe it? She told my wife I slept with her."

"Why would she do that?"

A voice behind them shushed her.

"Spite, I guess."

Ameena studied the publisher's face. "And did you? Sleep with her, I mean."

"Well, yeah, sure." He chuckled awkwardly. "But it wasn't my fault. The girl came on to me. Followed me to my room at a conference in Reno last year carrying a bottle of red wine. She wouldn't take no for an answer."

"How hard did you try?"

"That's not the point." The woman behind him poked him in the back and warned him to keep quiet. Frank whispered close to Ameena's ear. "Beulah found out and divorced me."

"So I heard. About the divorce, that is." She had not heard about Frank's extramarital activities. Served him right. If Ravi ever cheated on her, she'd empty their joint bank account after stripping his flesh from his bones and feeding it to the vultures.

The publishing world was a small one. Frank's divorce had made the rounds. Not that there hadn't been whispers at the bar over the years concerning Beulah Ackerman's own extramarital exploits.

The publisher's ex had set up a boutique literary agency of her own. One of Ameena's clients had left her for Beulah's agency. Worse still, Beulah had gone on to sell her former client's manuscript—which Ameena had been championing and struggling to find a home for, for over a year—to Garfield & Green for a nice advance.

"She's here, you know."

"Beulah?"

"Yeah." Frank Ackerman swiveled around searching for Beulah. "Looking for talent."

"Tell her to stay away from Mulish," warned Ameena. Now that the author was making good money, she was going to watch out for her own interests. The sharks were circling, lured by the scent of an easy commission.

Frank dabbed his wet forehead once more. "Don't worry," he said with a chuckle. "I tell *everybody* to stay clear of Anthony Mulish." The man was a royal pain in the ass.

Speak of the devil in wool, Anthony Mulish took a sip of water and set down his glass. He climbed to his feet as Dorothy Hall concluded her remarks and introduced him to the audience, despite her strong personal misgivings.

As he passed, Sharon Crumbie stuck out her foot, quite by accident, tripping him. He tottered into the podium and bumped his chin on the microphone jutting out at him.

"Sorry." She chuckled evilly then winked at Dorothy Hall as she reclaimed her seat.

"Good evening and welcome," began Anthony Mulish. His fingers toyed with his bowtie. The room was as stifling as the inside of a brick oven. He should have asked someone to lower the thermostat a few degrees.

Anthony Mulish cleared his throat. He adjusted the microphone upward. Ms. Hall was not a tall woman. Satisfied, he opened his mouth. He was relieved that touching the microphone had not send another jolt of electricity through his body. He wasn't sure his system could bear a second shock so soon after the first.

Then he promptly fell over the podium. His arms dangling like two very dead trout.

There were screams.

And there were laughs.

Ameena leapt to her feet. Lifting her billowing skirt above her ankles, she hurried towards the dais. Frank surged forward too and swept past her. He lumbered up the steps towards his author.

Anthony Mulish still hadn't moved.

Was this a sick joke?

Stan Dooley and Reba Lonnegan wrestled Anthony Mulish off the podium and gently eased him to the stage floor.

"Is he okay?" Frank's eyes bulged as he looked down at his most valuable asset.

Anthony Mulish groaned. His head rocked side to side. "I don't feel so good." He felt queasy and his intestines seemed to be doing the rumba. Hands helped him to an upright position. He braced his palms against the hard floor.

"Do you need a doctor, Mister Ipé?" asked Stan nervously. He and Reba shared a worried look. What would it mean to the future of Murder Under Cover if its very first Special GOH fell ill or dropped dead?

They had invested heavily in the event.

Anthony Mulish shook his head. "I'll be fine. Maybe an antacid."

Frank Ackerman patted his pockets. He always kept a roll of antacids on his person. Publishing was a tough business. Ulcers were part of the game. "Here you go, TR." He peeled back the wrapper and handed three tablets to Anthony Mulish.

The author took them and chewed slowly.

Dorothy Hall and Sharon Crumbie pushed past Frank Ackerman for a closer look at the fallen author.

"Is he dead, Snookums?" Sharon Crumbie planted a hand on Dorothy Hall's arm. Snookums was Dorothy Hall's nickname.

"It appears not," Dorothy Hall told her. TR Ipé didn't look so high and mighty now, sitting rumpled and dazed on the platform. "But cheer up," she said under her breath. "The night is young."

9

"Would you like to go back to your suite, TR?" Ameena nestled beside Frank. She took hold of her author's clammy hand.

"No. Help me up."

Together Ameena and Frank Ackerman aided the fallen author to his feet.

"Okay now?" asked a worried Frank Ackerman.

"I could use a drink." Anthony Mulish looked around hopefully.

"Do you have a drink ticket?" asked Peggy, shooting up from the audience. For the opening ceremony, she had dressed up as Ngaio Marsh, one of the original queens of crime fiction, in a carefully selected scarlet wool dress and matching hat. Disappointingly, no one had thus far recognized her as the inimitable Dame Commander of the Order of the British Empire.

Like her heroine, Peggy Wethering had never married and had no children. The mystery scene and its inhabitants were her family. Her only family.

"I don't think a drink ticket will be necessary," Stan said with a snap of the tongue.

"Mister Ipé, you may have all the drinks you like," confirmed Reba shooting Peggy down with a withering glare.

"Thank you, my dear." Anthony Mulish clasped

Reba's hand in his.

Ameena heard the woman titter. The co-chair of the organizing committee wasn't wearing a wedding ring. Anthony Mulish could be in trouble.

Stan Dooley excused himself. Clasping the podium, he addressed the milling crowd. "Everything's all right, folks. Mister Ipé is tired. But he assures us he is well. I suggest we enjoy the beverages and snacks so generously sponsored tonight for us by both Ackerman Publishing and Brinker and Beebo Press.

"And don't forget," he said, twisting his hand to see his watch face, "our special movie presentation begins at nine sharp in the theater. That's just down the hall to the left as you leave. Thank you."

A glass of red wine was brought to the SGOH. Anthony Mulish sipped cautiously. Satisfied, he downed the remains of the glass. The server hurried off to fetch a refill.

"Are you sure you are okay, TR?" Ameena did not want to appear responsible for the death of one of her authors. It could decimate her reputation.

"Yes. It must have been something I ate or drank."

"Drank?" The agent glanced at the table. In the commotion, Anthony Mulish's water glass seemed to have disappeared. "That's odd."

"What is?"

"Nothing," she said with a shake of the head. That was the trouble with being at a mystery conference, one saw mysteries and conspiracies everywhere.

"I'll just freshen up." Anthony Mulish dusted himself off.

"The rest rooms are on the right side of the lobby," Frank Ackerman said. "Want some help?"

The author twisted his lips. "If I ever need help going to the men's room, you have my permission to shoot me." With those words, he roughly moved the publisher aside and strode unsteadily from the room.

"You heard him, Ameena," Frank Ackerman said, his hands tightly fisted, "he gave me permission to shoot him."

"I heard." Ameena grabbed the fresh wine bottle and glass from the returning server and sent him on his way.

Anthony Mulish entered the long, narrow restroom. A younger man stood washing his hands in the basin.

The man looked at the author's image in the mirror as he shuffled past. "Are you okay, Mister Ipé?"

Anthony Mulish stopped dead in his tracks.

The young man turned around. The handwritten badge dangling from his lanyard spelled out the name Ulaf Ulafsson and announced to the world that he was from Moab, Utah. A cascade of blond hair fell across his left eye. "I mean, I saw you collapse at the podium. I'm sorry you didn't get a chance to speak. I was really looking forward to hearing what you had to say."

"I'm fine," replied Anthony Mulish, ignoring the dripping fingers of the fan's outstretched hand. He was anxious to get on with the business he had entered for. "A mere case of fatigue. A long car drive, lots of insipid speeches. A little peace and quiet and I will be good as new." He cocked a brow.

"Sorry." Ulaf Ulafsson caught his meaning and blushed. He reached quickly for a handful of paper towels. He used these to dry his dripping fingers.

Anthony Mulish waited until the young man departed then splashed his face carefully with cold water.

He wiped himself dry. The man in the mirror told him to stay strong. Only two more days of this ridiculous conference and he could go home to New York. Where he belonged.

Anthony Mulish returned to the party where he was forced to endure the ministrations and well-wishes of his agent, his publisher, and his fans.

It was a relief to hear that it was time for *Strangers on a Train*. As SGOH, Anthony Mulish had his choice of seats. He picked a spot in the last row, preferring not to have anyone seated behind him.

Ameena sat to his right. Stan Dooley walked down the aisle to the front of the theater room and stood framed by the screen. Folding his hands behind his back, he spoke a few words by way of background into the classic Hitchcock film. This was the so-called British version of the film. Approximately two minutes longer than the original US release, it included some alternate scenes and excluded the final scene from the American version.

"I wish he would shut up and get on with it," Anthony Mulish whispered a little too loudly. A film could not be made that could begin to compare to the brilliant Highsmith novel. "I don't care which version they show. Just get the reels rolling."

Reba Lonnegan, who sat on his opposite side, made a throaty little noise, rose and disappeared in the direction of the projectionist's booth.

The room went to black.

"I've been thinking," whispered Ameena.

"Yes?"

"Maybe you should play a character."

"What do you mean?"

"I mean pretend that you really are TR Ipé, a kind and generous, grateful author." The writer all these people were expecting to see. She was worried that, in the space of one afternoon and evening, Mulish was sabotaging cozy writer TR Ipé's future career. Not to mention his earning potential.

"I'm not sure I understand."

The agent thought how best to explain. "I mean that instead of simply adopting the pen name TR Ipé, adopt the persona. *Be* TR Ipé, not you-know-who."

"I am doing my best," Anthony Mulish replied testily.

Ameena sighed and sank into her seat. Sadly, that was probably true. The film title blazed across the screen. She settled in for a long night and an even longer weekend.

Finally, the movie ended and the credits rolled across the screen to a smattering of applause. Ameena glanced at her companion. His arms hung loose in his lap. His eyes were closed.

She poked him in the chest. Anthony Mulish did not budge. What was going on? Had he had a second attack of whatever had hit him earlier?

The author suddenly snorted and shook himself. He slowly unpeeled his eyelids.

"I thought you were dead," quipped Ameena.

He stifled a yawn. "It has been a long day." The house lights came up. He pried himself from his tight seat with a wince. He'd grown stiff sitting through the movie.

"Shall we get a night cap?"

"I'll pass." Anthony waved off an autograph seeker and marched to the elevator. His agent hurried after him. What he needed was a babysitter. Sadly, she was it.

She'd see him to his room then get a drink or three.

Ameena had promised her husband she would take it easy on the alcohol but playing TR Ipé's keeper was exhausting. She not only had to shepherd him everywhere he went, she had to shield him from his fans and his fans from him. Neither of which were easy tasks.

She caught up to her charge outside the lobby elevator.

"The elevator is stuck." Anthony Mulish announced as if it was his agent's fault. She had learned that most things that went wrong were, in his opinion. He repeatedly jabbed the smudged chrome button. "Now what?"

Ameena was about to joke that he ought to ask some of his fans to carry him up the fire stairs to his suite. Her better judgment—and semi-sober state—held her back.

If she were to suggest it, he'd probably do just that. She could see the photographs on social media now, several fans, in an effort to ingratiate themselves with TR Ipé, lugging him by the arms and legs ever upwards. Suffering back sprains, twisted ankles and heart attacks.

Not the best image for a best-selling cozy mystery author.

"Here it comes." Ameena stepped back from the sliding doors expecting a flood of riders exiting.

"Frank!" cried Anthony Mulish.

"Very funny, Frank." Ameena hoisted the hem of her skirt and stepped over the publisher. He had pulled a similar stunt— what was it? Two or three years ago? At BookExplosion. He had pretended to hang himself in one of the ladies rooms of the Javits Center.

Ameena wasn't falling for it this time. She and two

hotshot editors from Excalibur House had lost their lunches seeing Frank seemingly suspended from a ladies room stall with a lacy pink bra with cutouts for the nipples. It was a Frederick's of Hollywood undergarment that had belonged to his wife, Beulah, no less. She'd been peeved.

Ameena pressed floor five. "Honestly, Frank, I've seen better looking bloody chest gags at my kids' middle school Halloween parties."

"I don't know, Ameena..." Anthony Mulish held the door open with his shoe. Did he really want to get in the elevator with Frank lying there like that?

The publisher was leaning against the side of the elevator. His legs were stretched out in front, his feet sticking upward. The publisher's arms hung limp at his sides. His suit jacket gaped open.

Frank Ackerman's heavy chin sat on his unmoving chest. His half-open eyelids were looking down at the big dark red blotch that spoiled his shirt.

What if he had really been stabbed to death or shot?

Or was this the sort of prank mystery conferences went in for? Ameena should have forewarned him. Then a terrible thought hit Anthony Mulish.

If Frank was dead, would it delay the release of his next book?

"Seriously, Frank. Enough's enough." Ameena prodded the publisher with her pointed toe. "Get up. You're embarrassing yourself."

Ameena much preferred to remain behind the scenes and out of the spotlight. It was bad enough that her author was continually humiliating her whenever they were in public together, now his publisher was embarrassing her too.

The post-movie crowd had gathered outside the elevator now, taking in Frank's post-movie theatrics.

Everyone was gawking at them. Some took photos with their smartphones to share on their social media of choice.

"Frank?" The agent leaned forward and thumped him in the chest. Ameena looked at her knuckles. She blanched. She had seen blood before. This was blood. Real blood. Not the fake stuff that came in a tube at the party store.

She screamed.

Anthony Mulish drew his foot back. The elevator door slid quickly shut.

"What the hell are you doing?" screamed Ameena, pressing herself against the wall of the elevator. "Lord Shiva, save us."

They were alone in an elevator with a dead man!

A freshly dead man.

"Sorry." Anthony Mulish punched button after button to no avail.

The elevator raced inexorably upward. Ameena's heart seized up. She squeezed her eyes shut and prayed, not stopping until the ungodly box of death finally came to a stop on the fifth floor.

The doors slid open revealing a bald-headed man in a red shirt and baggy blue jeans seated in a wheelchair, waiting for the elevator's arrival.

His eyes grew big as melons when he saw the dead body on the floor and the elevator's two agitated and frantic passengers. They looked like two scared rats in a sinking ship. He spun around faster than a man in a wheelchair ought to be able to and fled to his room.

Anthony Mulish stepped off the elevator. "Good night. I'll let you handle this."

Ameena grabbed her client violently by the scruff of the neck, forcing him back inside the elevator. "You are not going anywhere."

"But the police can handle this."

"The police *will* handle this." Ameena punched the button for the lobby. She suddenly felt queasy. Was it the quickly descending elevator or seeing Frank Ackerman, who had been healthy and hale earlier this evening, now the victim of murder? "And they are going to want to talk to us."

"Why us?" Like his agent, Anthony Mulish was carefully avoiding looking down or anywhere near the vicinity of Frank Ackerman's mortal remains.

"Because we found him."

"You are my agent," Anthony Mulish pleaded. "Handle it, Ameena. It is what I pay you for."

"I am your *literary* agent, TR. And your nursemaid and your bodyguard and your accountant and your conscience." The agent's voice rose higher and higher. "What I am not is your lawyer in a murder investigation!"

Anthony Mulish clutched his hands and asked solicitously, "I've never seen you appear so agitated. Are you all right? Is everything okay at home?"

"Forget home. Frank Ackerman is dead, Anthony. It doesn't get any less all right than that." The confining space seemed to be spinning, and was somebody sucking out all the oxygen? Feeling about to explode, she willed herself to take several deep breaths in a row.

The elevator came to a stop in the nick of time. The doors rumbled open. The crowd downstairs had grown exponentially. Stan Dooley and Reba Lonnegan stood in the forefront.

Reba threw her hands to her mouth and bawled incomprehensibly.

Stan thrust her aside. "Is he really dead?"

"As a proverbial doornail," said Ameena. Chills danced all over her body. She turned her back to the elevator doors. She was not riding up in an elevator with a dead guy a second time. Not on her watch.

Stan squatted and checked Frank's wrist for a pulse. "Yeah." He looked up at Ameena and Anthony Mulish. "I wonder where security is."

He exited the elevator. "We heard what was going on and didn't know what to make of it. I wasn't sure if this was a joke or not."

Stan sighed and pushed a hand across his scalp. "I'll phone the sheriff now." He took two steps then turned around. "Did you two see who did this?"

Ameena silently shook her head.

Anthony Mulish looked at Frank Ackerman a moment. "No suspects yet," he said cagily. "But I have a few theories."

Ameena gaped at the author as if he were crazy.

Which, of course, he was.

10

Reba shooed the gawkers away from the elevator. "Please, everyone. Give him some room!"

Give him some room? thought Anthony Mulish. Frank had stopped living. What he needed was a miracle worker, not breathing space.

"Are you crazy?" Ameena pulled Anthony Mulish aside as Dorothy Hall, Sharon Crumbie and a roly-poly male in an orange leisure suit tumbled out from the stairwell.

"What's going on?" demanded the male. He peered inside the open elevator. "Is that Ackerman?"

"Oh, dear." Dorothy Hall and Sharon Crumbie clutched one another, giving each other questioning looks.

"Yes, Jay. I'm afraid so," replied Reba.

Jay Copperfield was one of a small number of male cozy authors. In his fifties, he was bearded, plump, and favored slip-on loafers and baggy T-shirts emblazoned with pictures of cats. His long-running series of novels featured Alex P. Ghostley and his ghost cat, Cuddles.

Frank Ackerman was not his publisher, although he'd once been. That didn't make it any less a shock seeing him lying there dead in the elevator.

"What happened to him?" Jay pushed to the front of the crowd.

"We don't know." Reba looked out the front windows and across the dark, empty campus. "There must be a maniac loose." Where was the security woman that the college had promised would remain on duty? "It was Mister Ipé himself who discovered the body."

"Is that right?" Jay Copperfield reversed his way through the crowd. He spotted TR Ipé and his agent standing near a potted palm and made his approach. "TR, I'm Jay Copperfield. A pleasure."

"Hello," said Anthony Mulish, forced to shake hands. "This is Ameena Chowdary, my literary agent."

"I know. I hear you found Ackerman's body. That must have been quite a shock."

Anthony Mulish nodded. "A drunken conference participant stumbling out of the elevator I could expect, if not understand. But to see poor Frank like that...apparently stabbed through the heart."

Ameena cringed. "Must you paint so vivid a picture?"

"Yes," came the voice of Sharon Crumbie who had sidled up alongside Jay Copperfield. "Quite a shock. Quite the sight, indeed."

Dorothy Hall stood on Jay Copperfield's left. "Now if Frank had been stabbed in the back, I'd think we'd have our killer."

"What do you mean?" asked Ameena.

"Come on," Dorothy said with an ugly sneer on her face. "Your client here strikes me as the sort of man who'd stab anybody in the back."

Sharon chuckled softly. "And here come the police now." The cozy author nodded in the direction of the main entrance.

Several sheriff deputies in brown uniforms spattered with melting snowflakes were making their way inside, followed by a sheepish-looking security guard dressed in blue.

A rust-colored, campaign-style hat adorned the sheriff's head. A pair of frameless eyeglasses perched on his nose. He quietly spoke a few words with Stan and Reba, glancing occasionally in the direction of Anthony Mulish and Ameena as he did so.

And it was making Ameena very nervous.

Deputies cordoned off the perimeter around the elevator with crime scene tape and urged everyone back as far as possible. The college's security guard, a slender young woman with short-cropped brown hair, was left safeguarding the body. Not that it was going anywhere.

A deputy came over to them. "Mister Ipé and Ms. Chowdary?"

They admitted that they were and the deputy asked Anthony Mulish and Ameena Chowdary to follow him. He walked them over to the sheriff.

"I'd say good evening but it's anything but," drawled the man in charge. "I'm Sheriff Winslow. I am told you two found Mister Ackerman. Is that correct?"

"Yes, that's right," said Anthony Mulish. "We opened the elevator and there he was. Sprawled out on the floor."

"And nobody got out?" asked the sheriff.

"Not unless it was, perhaps, the Canterville Ghost or the Invisible Man," Anthony Mulish replied drily.

"Excuse me?" The sheriff furrowed his brow. Colleges and insane asylums seemed to have a lot in common, in his experience.

There was a county mental health facility not far from the College of the Alleghenies. There were times, and this had the beginnings of one of them, when

Sheriff Winslow was certain that the staff and residents of each were one and the same.

"Oscar Wilde? HG Wells?"

"Anthony—" Ameena tugged helplessly at his sleeve.

"Ghosts, zombies and skeletons are quite common around here," noted the author.

"Are you trying to be funny?" Sheriff Winslow pushed his hat up his forehead to get a better look at Mulish. "A man's been murdered. Stabbed to death by the looks of it."

"Take a look at some of the book jackets in the dealers' room," persisted Anthony Mulish. "You'd think half the murders were committed by supernatural beings, and a fair number of them solved by them as well. Or their cuddly pets."

Ameena rolled her eyes.

This from the creator of Hermie the hermit crab who, in one of Death Gets Cozy's many absurd subplots, finds a nude woman's body washed up along the shores of the Atlantic Ocean. Hermie then literally sifts through the sands for clues to the killer's identity.

Compounding the absurdity, with the help of Samille Cannon and Debbie Dunse, Hermie risks his life going undercover as the lunch special at the seaside seafood restaurant owned by the main suspect.

Ameena put a hand on her author's sleeve. "Sorry," she apologized for the two of them. "We're both in shock, Sheriff." She shot Anthony Mulish a warning look.

Sheriff Winslow decided to move on. "Do you have any idea how he got there?"

"What do you mean?" Ameena asked nervously.

"I mean was he killed in the elevator or somewhere

else?"

"We have no idea."

"Isn't that your job to find out?" added Anthony Mulish, not that the sheriff appeared up to the challenge.

"We will get to the bottom of this," the sheriff assured them.

"You think Frank might have been murdered elsewhere, and then his body placed in the elevator?" Anthony Mulish asked.

"Why would the killer do that?" Ameena wanted to know.

"Maybe they were trying to move the body," suggested Sheriff Winslow. "To keep the murder from being discovered."

"That would be taking an awful chance, don't you think?" Anthony almost laughed out loud. "There are hundreds of people here at this conference. Using the elevator is the last thing I'd choose if I was trying to remove Frank's body from the building."

"Oh?" Sheriff Winslow's brow rose. "What would you choose instead?"

Ameena grabbed Anthony Mulish's arm. "Mister Mulish wouldn't choose anything. He's not a killer." If she didn't shut him up quick, he might just talk himself onto the sheriff's suspect list.

"Mister Mulish?" Sheriff Winslow lifted his wide-brimmed felt hat, scratched the top of his head then plopped the hat down again in a well-practiced move. He focused on the author. "I thought your name was Ipé?" He took a puzzled glance at his notepad.

Sheriff Winslow had mispronounced his name, rhyming it with *ripe*. "That's EE-pay. And please, keep your voice down, Sheriff," begged Anthony Mulish. "TR

Ipé is my alias."

"Alias?" Suspicion popped into the sheriff's dark gray eyes.

"He means pen name," Ameena quickly explained. "Mister Ipé is the guest of honor here at the conference, Sheriff."

Anthony Mulish raised his finger. "*Special* guest of honor."

"Right." Ameena bathed him with a dirty look. "And I'm sure we'll both do everything we can to cooperate with you in your investigation, Sheriff. Unfortunately, we didn't really see anything. When the film ended, we came to the elevator. And when the door opened—"

"There he was," finished Anthony Mulish as Ameena stopped. She swayed unsteadily on her feet. "Dead."

"Sheriff?" called a deputy. Giselle Mimieux hovered near him. She looked rattled.

Sexy, but rattled.

Sheriff Winslow turned. "Yeah?" It was late and all he wanted was sleep. His in-laws were visiting, a snowstorm was predicted to hit any time now, and he had to have a murder dumped in his lap.

And what was with all the goofy outfits? Some folks looked normal enough, others were dressed like they were attending a costume party.

Sherlock Holmes and Watson stood whispering near the registration table. Maybe he should turn the whole shebang over to them so he could get some sleep. Let them solve the damn murder.

It was bad enough the in-laws were in town. He'd been kicked out of his own bedroom. His wife had insisted that her parents get the master suite and they were stuck sleeping on a crummy blow-up mattress in the den.

"You might want to hear this." The deputy looked about a decade older than the sheriff and had a few pounds on him as well.

"Excuse me," the sheriff told them. "I've got to go but I may want to talk to you both again."

"Of course." Anthony Mulish bowed ever so slightly.

"We'll be here all weekend," promised Ameena.

If the organizers didn't cancel Murder Under Cover, which, she realized, was a very real possibility now that they had a very real murder to contend with.

11

Ameena and Anthony Mulish joined a small, nervous group seated on and around the registration tables. Some kind soul had brought down from their room a bottle of straight bourbon whiskey crafted by a western Virginia distillery and was passing out healthy quantities in red plastic cups.

"Drink tickets be damned," Ameena muttered, taking one and handing another to her author.

Dorothy Hall and Sharon Crumbie sat side-by-side behind the A-F table. Both appeared to have been drinking heavily. "Frank Ackerman was a good man," Sharon Crumbie said with a slur and a slight shake of her head.

"Yep," chimed Dorothy. "A real friend—hic—to his authors."

Sharon gave Anthony Mulish a long, ugly look. "I don't know who would want to murder such a kind, sweet soul."

"Now, suicide. That I could almost understand," Dorothy added, casting her eyes meaningfully at Anthony Mulish. "I mean, just look what he had to put up with." She bumped her shoulder against Sharon Crumbie's and the two giggled like drunken college girls.

Ameena would have stuck up for her client but she was having thoughts of her own as she sipped her bourbon. Why had Frank Ackerman been murdered? Could it have been a mistake?

Why would anyone murder such a sweetheart of a man when there was a so much more deserving victim standing right beside her?

"You had a series with Frank, didn't you, Jay?" Sharon Crumbie reached for the bourbon, spilling the bottle on the tabletop. She grabbed a conference T-shirt off the line behind her and sopped up the alcohol.

"That's right." Jay watched as the EMTs took Frank Ackerman's body away. He slumped against the table.

"The Seeds of Murder series, wasn't it?" pressed Dorothy.

"Yes. But it was a long time ago." Jay Copperfield had gotten nine books out of the series before it had ended abruptly, much to his dismay.

"Ackerman Publishing dropped you, didn't they?" Sharon hiccoughed and her cheeks glowed red. Her nose wasn't far behind.

"Something like that. We had a good run," Jay Copperfield said, defensively.

"So you are unpublished now, Mister Coppershield?" Anthony Mulish asked.

The others gasped. Ameena winced. "Jay *Copperfield* writes the very successful Alex P. Ghostley series, TR. I'm sure you've heard of it."

"No, I can't say I have." Anthony gave up on the cheap bourbon and refilled his plastic cup with tequila from his private supply. He did not offer to share with his comrades.

"Jay's protagonist, Alex P., has the most adorable ghost cat," said Dorothy, practically purring with jealousy herself.

"She's a beautiful creature," added Sharon Crumbie.

"If she's a ghost, how do you know she's adorable? Or beautiful?" Anthony Mulish asked. "You can't see her."

"Use your imagination, Ipé," snarled Sharon. "That's what we do."

Anthony Mulish snorted a reply. "From what I've read of your books, your imaginations are the last things any of you use." He swirled his drink then took a sip.

"Let it go, TR." Ameena pinched her author's forearm. She sensed a second murder. Soon. And she'd be witnessing it.

"Ouch." Anthony Mulish rubbed his arm.

"Sorry, TR."

Anthony Mulish turned to Jay Copperfield. "So, Mister Copperfield, how would this ghost cat of yours solve this particular murder?"

"You mean the murder of Frank Ackerman?" Jay turned toward the elevator, which still hung open. Most of the crowd had dissipated. Those that the police wanted to question had been sent to one of the smaller rooms for interrogation.

"Yes."

Copperfield stroked his beard. How he'd love to show up this dumb ass. "In the first place, Alex and Cuddles would examine the crime scene. Sometimes Cuddles finds clues that the police or even Alex might have missed."

"What?" Anthony Mulish chuckled. "Like a hairball?"

Copperfield grabbed Mulish by the throat. "Listen, Ipé, I don't know what your problem is but I've had about enough of you!"

Ameena dropped her glass and, with the help of Stan, pulled the two men apart.

Anthony Mulish smirked.

Copperfield readjusted his leisure suit jacket. "You'll excuse me," he said. "I'm going to bed."

"What was that all about?" inquired Stan, watching as Jay Copperfield stomped angrily to the elevator. The author was refused entrance and forced to climb the stairs.

"A little difference of opinion on the use of first person versus third person POV," Ameena lied.

Stan pinched his brows together. "If you say so. I came to tell you that Sheriff Winslow would like a word with you."

"Me?" squeaked Ameena, pointing a shaky finger at her chest. "Again?" Nothing good ever came from talking to the police.

"That's what he said. Come on, I'll walk you over. He's down the hall." Stan led her to a small office. According to the sign on the door, it belonged to a Dr. G. Early, professor of social anthropology.

The sheriff was seated behind a desk cluttered with cultural artifacts and dusty old ethnographs. Ameena recognized the young student in the visitor's chair as Matt. He was helping with the con's PA system, videotaping and recording needs.

The poor kid looked shocked and dismayed. But he didn't look guilty of anything, except maybe almost electrocuting her most profitable author through clumsiness and neglect. But certainly not by intent.

Why would Sheriff Winslow want to talk to Matt? What could he have to do with Frank Ackerman's death?

"You can go, son." Sheriff Winslow half-rose from his seat.

Matt nodded. He glanced nervously at Ameena as he

slid past her, escaping down the narrow entryway to the office.

"Have a seat." The sheriff fell back into his chair with a sigh and indicated for her to do the same. "What a night." He ran his hands through his hair. His big hat sat atop the coatrack just inside the door to the left.

Without his hat, the sheriff appeared far less formidable and far more human. Ameena relaxed a little. There was no reason to be nervous. She hadn't done anything wrong. Her head swam. If she was a little drunk, so what? She wasn't driving.

Ameena crossed her ankles and ran her tongue uneasily over her lips as Sheriff Winslow scrolled through his smartphone messages. She could smell the alcohol on her breath. Could he smell it from where he sat?

What did he want with her? Did he think she had something to do with Frank's murder?

She felt chilly in the claustrophobic office and had half a mind to go borrow one of the many handmade throws being offered up in the auction room.

Her nerves were getting to her again. Feeling ill at ease, she decided to break the silence.

"I have no idea who would want to kill Frank Ackerman, Sheriff. Now, if you had asked who might have wanted to kill my author," she said rather loudly and far too loosely—she blamed it on the alcohol—"I could have offered you up a boatload of potential murderers. An entire conference worth, at the very least."

She left out one other potential suspect: herself.

How many times had she wished Anthony Mulish would simply up and drop dead?

Sheriff Winslow managed a smile as he gently set his smartphone down atop the desk. "I didn't ask you here to hear your theories on who killed Ackerman."

"You didn't?"

"Nope."

"That's a relief." Ameena settled back in her chair. "Why did you want to speak with me then?"

"Just clearing up some loose ends. I'm told you were one of Frank Ackerman's friends. I like to know my victims as best I can."

"I see." Ameena thought over the sheriff's words. "Frank and I weren't really close. We were more business associates." Putting a little distance between herself and the dead man, as much as she had been fond of him, seemed the best approach.

"So I hear. Ms. Garrett told me that Frank always spoke highly of you. And there aren't a lot of other folks around who knew him personally."

"Jenny Garrett? That's sweet." Ameena liked Jenny. She thought it had been mean-spirited and callous of Anthony Mulish to have complained about her editing of Death Gets Cozy. The novel was a bestseller. In her opinion, Jenny Garrett's careful editing had been a key part of making it a success.

"If you don't mind my asking, Sheriff, do you have any leads? Any suspects?"

The thought of being at this lonely, practically deserted college in the middle of nowhere left her uneasy. Ameena liked reading murder mysteries, not participating in them.

She should never have let Anthony Mulish talk her into coming along.

"Better than that, we've got the murderer."

"That's great." Ameena blew out a breath. "Who was it? Was it his ex-wife? It's always the ex, isn't it?" She chuckled nervously and bit her fingernail to force herself to stop.

"Ex-wife?" Sheriff Winslow planted his palms on the desk and leaned closer.

"Yes, Beulah. I always knew that woman was a ticking time bomb."

"Interesting."

Ameena cleared her throat. "Isn't it Beulah?" she asked, doing a good imitation of a squeaky mouse.

Sheriff Winslow snatched a pencil from an empty Campbell's Soup can serving as a pencil holder on the corner of the desk and flipped open his pad. "That's Beulah Ackerman? Same last name as the victim?"

"That's right." Ameena pressed her fingers into her knees. "You mean it wasn't Beulah?"

"No, ma'am." He jotted down the name and tapped the pencil point against the desk. Professor Early wasn't going to be happy on his return. "You say she's here at this conference?"

"That's correct. I haven't actually spoken with her personally. But Frank told me earlier that she was here. And I did see her briefly. From a distance, that is."

"When was this?"

Ameena cocked her head to indicate she was thinking. "At the beginning of the opening ceremonies. Come to think of it, I haven't seen her since. Is it important?"

"Were Beulah and Frank married long?"

"Fifteen years, give or take." And there had been a lot of give and take from what she had heard through the grapevine.

"I'd hate for her to hear about her ex-husband's death the wrong way," explained the sheriff. "I'd like to find her and break the news gentle like."

Ameena was not so sure that was necessary given the couple's stormy past but to say so would make her appear catty. "I'm sure someone at registration can give you her room number."

"Right." Sheriff Winslow leaned back in his seat, lacing his fingers behind his stiff neck.

Ameena was still struggling to determine why he had asked to see her. There had to be more that he wasn't saying. Wasn't that the way the police operated?

She was also itching to know what the sheriff had wanted with Matt. "Don't tell me it was Matt who murdered Frank."

"That clueless college kid? No. I thought he might have some information. After all, he is supposed to be in charge of videotaping and recording. I was hoping maybe he'd be of some use. He wasn't."

"That's a good idea. What about security cameras? Was there one in the elevator?"

"No. Only a couple CCTVs outside the main doors. The College of the Alleghenies isn't exactly a high-crime area. Mostly college pranks, like stealing the school mascot or wrapping toilet paper around the chancellor's residence."

She had noticed a statue of the mascot outside the building. It would have been nearly impossible to miss it. A bobcat painted in a patchwork of bright colors sat on a plinth midway up the steps leading to the entrance. Waiting to eat the occasional unwary student, no doubt.

"I already spoke to Ms. Landry about the security setup around here. That wasn't much help either."

"Ms. Landry?"

"She's the lone security officer on duty here at the college right now. More of a caretaker really. With the students and faculty on break, the school figured one security guard would be enough to keep an eye on things."

"Too bad there was nobody keeping an eye on Frank."

"That's not quite true. There was one person."

"Who was that?"

"His killer."

"A man whose name you still haven't told me."

Sheriff Winslow shrugged. "I guess I can tell you. *She* has already confessed to the crime, so I don't see what harm it can do."

"She?"

"A young woman by the name of Giselle Mimieux."

"Who? I don't know her." If she was in the publishing business, Ameena had never heard of her.

"Giselle Mimieux, age twenty-six, drop-dead gorgeous blonde, no pun intended."

Ameena sucked in a breath. "Oh, my word."

"So you do know her?"

"Frank pointed her out to me." The very same woman she had seen pounding angrily on Anthony Mulish's door earlier. He might have dodged a bullet or, in this case, a knife.

"When was this?"

"During TR's reading this afternoon. She was in the audience." Should she reveal to the sheriff that Frank Ackerman had also admitted to once sleeping with the young woman? She decided not to. Doing so would only sully the dead man's image. "You say Ms. Mimieux admitted to murdering Frank?"

"Yep. She says he came on to her a little too strong. She tried to fight him off. She claims she stabbed him in the chest in self-defense because he wouldn't take no for an answer."

"That doesn't sound like Frank," replied Ameena. "And attacking the young woman in a public elevator? That's absurd. The elevator might have stopped any-time. Why would he risk being seen?"

Sheriff Winslow shrugged. "A confession is a confes-sion, Ms. Chowdary. And there's this." He slapped a thick manilla envelope on the desktop.

"What is it?"

He turned the open flap toward her. "A manuscript written by and belonging to Ms. Mimieux. We found it upstairs in Frank Ackerman's room. It was under one of his bed pillows."

"What was it doing there?"

"Maybe he was planning a little bedtime reading," answered Sheriff Winslow. "Maybe he was planning to have the lovely Giselle Mimieux give him a personal reading." His right brow rose, sending his eyeglasses akimbo. "If you get my drift."

Ameena got his drift all right.

12

"Didn't I hear the sheriff call you Mister Mulish?" Dorothy squinted her watery green eyes at Anthony Mulish.

"You must be mistaken." The author tugged at his bowtie. Out of the corner of his eye, he spotted one of the deputies escorting a handcuffed Giselle Mimieux across the lobby. What was that all about?

"Maybe the sheriff meant *mulish* as in like a jackass, Snookums." Alcohol slurred Sharon Crumbie's speech.

Dorothy Hall chuckled with amusement. "No." She wagged her finger side to side. "I definitely heard him say *Mister* Mulish."

"Mulish. Mulish." Sharon Crumbie rummaged through her purse for her smartphone. "I seem to remember..." She called up a web browser and typed. "A-ha! Here we go. Wikipedia. Anthony Mulish." Her eyes flitted across the screen of her phone. "American novelist. Blah, blah, blah. Sixty years old?" She glanced up at the author. "I wouldn't have thought a day under seventy."

Anthony Mulish fumed.

"Let me see." Dorothy twisted her friend's hand around so she could see the smartphone screen. The hair was different but the man in the black and white photo did look a lot like this pompous pile of pudding standing in front of them.

Sharon Crumbie tucked her phone away. "You write those tedious little novels that nobody but pompous twits like yourself read."

Anthony Mulish felt his face heat up. "Those tedious little novels, as you call them, are going to win me the Nobel Prize one day."

Dorothy Hall and Sharon Crumbie together slapped their palms against the table, laughing raucously as a pair of startled hens. "That's a hoot!" shrieked Dorothy.

"You? Win a Nobel Prize? For what? Not literature, that's for sure. And they don't give out a prize for over-inflated egomaniacs."

"True, you'll never win a Nobel Prize for literature."

"I'll bet you've never even read my books," replied Anthony Mulish. "Probably still reading and re-reading your Nancy Drew collection."

"You leave Nancy Drew out of this," warned Sharon Crumbie, eyes narrowing. Nancy Drew and Carolyn Keene were sacrosanct in her opinion.

"You are no Camus or Steinbeck," taunted Dorothy. "And if Hemingway was alive today, he'd probably grab his shotgun and shoot you dead."

"You're not even on par with Agatha Christie or Georges Simenon!" chimed in Sharon Crumbie.

"Heck, he couldn't even begin to fill Eberhart's shoes, rest her soul."

"Who?" Anthony Mulish was growing tired of the tiresome women and this one was babbling.

"Mignon G. Eberhart, you idiot!" shouted Sharon Crumbie. "She was one of the most famous and successful crime novelists in the world!"

"Never heard of her."

"That figures. Look at you. You have no knowledge, no appreciation for the crime writing field." She cursed like a drunken sailor on shore leave. "To think you never heard of an author who, in her day, was as popular as Christie. You don't deserve your success."

"It isn't fair." Dorothy Hall sighed, pushing her face into her hands. "Such a shame that Ms. Eberhart and her work have been nearly forgotten while someone like you revels in the spotlight."

"Boo-hoo." Anthony Mulish saw nothing unfair about it at all.

"And her, an MWA Grand Master."

"Forgotten and good riddance. No doubt the same will happen to the two of you," shot Anthony Mulish. "And, based on the quality of your work, sooner rather than later, I should think."

With a bloodcurdling shriek, Sharon Crumbie hurled herself at Anthony Mulish. She missed, landing awkwardly on the molded plastic tabletop.

She flailed helpless, arms and legs kicking like a beached crustacean. Dorothy Hall grabbed Sharon Crumbie's ankles and pulled her down into her chair.

"And to think you're up for a Poe Award." Dorothy Hall told him, breathing heavily from the exertion of yanking her friend back to earth. "What did you do? Did your publisher bribe the nominating committee?"

"Yeah," Sharon Crumbie rallied. "And then you murdered your publisher to keep everyone from finding out the truth."

"The truth is that Death Gets Cozy is the best mystery novel to come out in a very long time," Anthony Mulish said in his own defense. "Ever, I dare say. TR Ipé is a name to be reckoned with."

"That's tripe! You think we're stupid? T-R-I-P-E. Tripe!" Dorothy Hall waved a pudgy fist in the general direction of his big nose. Spit flew from the corners of her mouth. "And that's what you write!"

"Wait until everybody here learns your nasty little secret," warned Sharon Crumbie. "See who votes for you when they discover what an imposter you are!"

"It doesn't matter. You'll never win, TR," asserted Dorothy Hall. She laid a calming hand over her friend's. "Every other nominee is far more deserving than you."

Anthony Mulish loomed over the table, throwing his shadow over the two hammered woman. Although he had seen the short list of nominees for Outstanding Original Hardcover Mystery Novel of the Year and was not impressed with the competition, it didn't matter. "For your information, I have no intention and absolutely no desire to win a Poe Award."

That was true. He feared it would only sully his literary reputation further. And now, if word got out—and knowing these two women, it would—that he, Anthony Mulish, and TR Ipé were one and the same, his reputation as a serious novelist would be ruined. His life in tatters.

Better to lose than to win such a dubious award.

Anthony Mulish stifled a groan. What had Ameena done to him?

13

"What?" sniped Dorothy Hall. "You think you're too good for us?"

"You!" screamed a woman.

Anthony Mulish turned. He recognized that angry voice with the affected French accent. Sure enough, despite the tight red sheath dress and a pair of ridiculous high heels, Giselle Mimieux came sprinting, albeit awkwardly, across the lobby. Her arms were pulled rigidly behind her back and a jacket was draped loosely over her shoulders.

A frightened deputy ran to catch her. He grabbed her arm as she reached the author. "That's enough of that, miss!" the deputy said sternly.

He wrapped his hands around her handcuffed wrists to keep her from bolting once more. What would the sheriff think if he couldn't handle a little girl like this?

"I shouldn't have spiked your water, I should have stabbed you!" Giselle Mimieux shouted in Anthony Mulish's face. "Nobody turns me down!" Spittle flew from her mouth, spattering his cheeks.

"You spiked my water?" So that why he had collapsed on stage earlier. He had begun to suspect he had some as-yet-to-be-determined fatal illness.

"Yes, that's right. With Clozapine!" the woman shouted loudly and proudly.

Clozapine? Anthony Mulish had an aunt who suffered all her life with schizophrenia. Wasn't that the drug she had been prescribed? The diagnosis certainly seemed to apply to Giselle Mimieux.

Seeing that the deputy had the crazed woman well in hand, Anthony Mulish felt no fear in replying drily, "This is a tough business, Ms. Mimieux. One must get used to rejection. Especially," he said driving home a figurative knife of his own, "one as talentless as yourself."

Giselle Mimieux struggled against the deputy's grip, twisting and stomping like the star attraction at a Texas rodeo. She lost the battle.

"What's going on?" demanded Sheriff Winslow, inserting himself between the weird author, his culprit and his deputy. Sherlock Holmes and Watson snuggled side by side on a small padded bench. Watson watched the action. The attendee dressed as Sherlock read the small print of a mystery magazine with the aid of a very large magnifying glass that looked like a prop from an old Basil Rathbone film.

What was going on in the world? wondered Sheriff Winslow. How had he gotten transported from his sleepy little county in the mountains to this madhouse?

"I see you have had the sense to bind this wild woman," Anthony Mulish said. "She broke into my room earlier today. I was forced to throw her out."

"You threw my manuscript out your window, jerk face!" Giselle Mimieux struggled once again against the deputy's grip on her arms.

"Is that true?" Sheriff Winslow asked her. "You broke into Mister—" He paused. What was he supposed to call him? "This man's room?"

"He invited me." Giselle Mimieux thrust out her perfect breasts. "Then when I wouldn't do what he wanted —ungentlemanly things I might add—he threw me out. My manuscript, too. Out the window!"

Sheriff Winslow bounced his hat against his thigh. "Would that be the same manuscript we found in the victim's room?"

"I had a second copy. And a third. I like to be prepared."

"Like you were prepared to kill Frank Ackerman? How did you come to have a knife on your person when Mister Ackerman attacked you in the elevator as you claim?"

Anthony Mulish stepped out of reach. "*She* stabbed Frank?" Here he thought she was a relatively harmless lunatic with a raging libido and loose morals when it came to advancing her career.

He'd been alone in his suite with the woman. Seeing her in this new light, he realized he was lucky, very lucky, to be alive. What a time to die, now that he was finally making some decent money.

"That's right. I stabbed him." Giselle's eyes glittered as if she was happy to have committed the crime. "Right in the heart. Which is something you lack, TR!"

"About that knife, Ms. Mimieux," nudged Sheriff Winslow.

"I told you, I like to be prepared. The world's a dangerous marble."

"And you're off your marble," Anthony Mulish said.

"It's dangerous, all right, just ask Frank," Ameena said who had come along with the sheriff.

"Any luck finding the weapon, Rogers?" Sheriff Winslow asked the deputy.

"No. We looked all over the grounds where she says

she tossed it. There was no sign of a knife anywhere."

"Damn."

"Found some pages of her book though." Deputy Rogers pulled a soggy wad of paper from his leather jacket. "Soaked."

"Ruined." Giselle Mimieux snarled at Anthony Mulish. "Copy paper and toner are not cheap! I'm sending you the printing bill!"

"I'll get the rest of the men together. Maybe we'll spot something," said Sheriff Winslow.

"The snow is really starting to come down, Sheriff. It won't be easy."

The sheriff looked out the window and nodded. Rogers was right. "We'll have better luck in the morning. Let's get her in the lock-up."

"What about the crime scene?"

"I believe I've *seen* enough," Sheriff Winslow said wearily. "Pun intended."

"Does that mean we are free to use the elevator?" asked Ameena. She was exhausted both physically and mentally. She had no desire to climb five flights of stairs.

"Yeah. I'll tell Landry." Sheriff Winslow excused himself to have a few words with the college's lone security officer.

Eve Landry sagged with relief on hearing that she had been relieved of crime scene duty. The thirty-two year old single mother of two had joined the campus security team expecting, at worst, to play nursemaid to a bunch of high-spirited college kids making the most out of being away from home for the first time, not a dead man.

Definitely not a murdered dead man.

If any of her friends had suggested she might one day

be standing over a dead body on the campus of the College of the Alleghenies, she would have predicted that dead body to have once been the property of one of the randy old professors around here who died suffering a fatal heart attack amidst sexual relations with a gullible young coed. It was not unthinkable. She'd had her share of offers.

Despite the overtime pay she was collecting for sticking around over the school break, she vowed never to volunteer for this duty again. Even shacking up for the week with that cute caretaker looking after the chancellor's on-campus house while he and his wife were in Key West wasn't enough to motivate her to consider a repeat performance.

Dorothy Hall and Sharon Crumbie had disappeared. The last sheriff's deputy left through the main entrance. A couple dozen people formed small groups around the sofas and chairs in the lobby. These people had come for the conference and were going to suck every last minute of joy out of it that they could before returning home carrying their swag bags and credit card bills.

"Let's go, TR." Ameena yawned like a camel at the end of a ninety-nine mile march through a desert sandstorm.

"You go ahead." Anthony Mulish replied. "I have something I need to do."

"At this hour? It's after midnight."

"I'll see you in the morning." Anthony Mulish spotted the young man, Matt, speaking in hushed tones to the security woman outside the elevator door.

Ameena and several other guests entered the elevator and disappeared from sight. The security guard grabbed a heavy blue suede coat from a chair near the water fountain between restrooms. She zipped up her jacket and disappeared out the front door.

Matt took off down the hall toward the room where they had watched the film earlier.

Anthony Mulish hastened after him.

Matt pulled open the door to the theater room just enough to slide inside.

What was the young man up to?

Anthony Mulish moved silently across the dull brown commercially-carpeted floor. He waited a couple of beats before trying the door handle. It wasn't locked. Slowly, he pulled the door open. The overhead lights were dimmed. Wall sconces spaced along the walls emitted a bluish-white glow, like rare, giant blue ghost fireflies.

The screen was dark, which was as it should have been.

The room was empty.

He heard a sound spilling down from above. The theater held a couple hundred seats or more, half of those were above the landing he had entered on, the rest below. At the top of the steep, gray concrete steps stood a solid white door. It, too, was shut.

From the hole through which the movie was projected, Anthony Mulish, saw a faint yellow luminosity. He heard nothing but the sounds of his own footsteps and light breathing as he climbed upward.

Why didn't he call it a night and get some sleep? Something compelled him and he didn't know what it was. Perhaps it was that annoying pair of cozy mystery authors goading him, chiding him.

Perhaps Frank's murder was getting under his skin.

Maybe he was simply nosy and tipsy.

Anthony Mulish tried the door knob. Unlocked. He pushed the door open.

A strong arm locked around his neck and squeezed.

14

"Ughmeph," yelped the author, flailing frantically and futilely at his unseen attacker.

"Oh!" The arm released itself like a dazed anaconda falling out of a kapok tree. "It's you."

Anthony whirled around. "Are you mad? Are you trying to kill me?" He gently rubbed his wounded windpipe.

"I am so sorry, Mister Ipé, sir!" apologized Matt, rapidly wringing his hands. "I had no idea it was you, sir."

"Who the hell did you think it was?" Before the young man could answer, he added, "And why were you trying to strangle them?"

"I-I wasn't trying to strangle anybody." Matt pushed his hands through his blond hair. He moved to the center of the small projectionist's booth, pressing his fingers into the back of a coffee-stained green cloth swivel chair. "I guess I'm just nervous, is all. I mean, after what happened tonight."

Anthony Mulish frowned to demonstrate his displeasure. "Still, you can't go around strangling people first and then asking questions after, Matt. You might have killed me."

"I know, I know. I really am sorry." Matt swung the chair around and threw himself into it. "You won't report me, will you? I could get kicked out of school." His eyes doubled in size. "I could go to jail!"

"All right, all right." Anthony Mulish tossed his arm. "That's enough talk of that." He had the upper hand and knew it. Now how could he use it to his advantage? "Nobody's going to jail. Well, except that Mimieux vixen. The woman is mad. And dangerous."

"Yeah, tell me about it." Matt hung his head.

"You have had some experience with her?"

Matt's pasty white cheeks turned to cherry bombs. "Sort of."

Anthony Mulish cocked his head to one side. "Define sort of."

"We sort of spent the night together."

Anthony Mulish jerked. The woman truly was a slut. "Why?"

"Huh?"

"I mean, why did she sleep with you? That is, I can understand you wanting to sleep with her, she's a sexy young thing. But why her you?"

Matt shrugged. "I dunno. I never thought about it."

"Why am I not surprised?" muttered Anthony Mulish. "Did she want something special from you?"

Matt crinkled his brow. "You mean like something kinky?" He shook himself. "Gross."

"No. Heaven forbid. I mean, are you a published mystery author?"

"No."

"Publisher? Agent? Anything?"

"None of the above." Matt glumly shook his head. "I'm a communications major. Hoping to go into broadcasting. Two more years to go. You sure I won't get in trouble for attacking you?"

"You have my word."

"I mean, it wouldn't look so good me beating up on the guest of honor. And you such an old guy too."

The author simmered but let that last statement pass without comment. Which was hard to do considering the boy had omitted to state correctly that he was the *special* guest of honor.

And what would Giselle Mimieux have wanted with Matt? He could do nothing to further her career. It seemed out of character. "Did she ask you about Frank Ackerman?"

"Who?"

"The dead man."

"No."

Anthony Mulish ran his eyes over a shelf filled floor to ceiling with films, some in canisters, others in videotape boxes.

"Why did you come up here, sir? You aren't still mad at me about the microphone incident, are you? Because it really wasn't my fault. I've been telling the AV Department that—"

Anthony Mulish hit Matt in the side of the head with a metal film canister. It was empty. It couldn't have hurt much. Nonetheless, Matt whined and rubbed his left ear.

"That hurt, sir."

"Sorry." Of course, the boy had had it coming. Matt's incessant yapping was giving him a headache and preventing him from thinking.

The author placed the dented canister on a small table located within easy reach of the chair. The table held a small coffee maker and an open packet of vanilla cream-filled sandwich cookies. He helped himself to one and took a nibble. It was stale but he was hungry.

He chewed it quickly and swallowed. "Speaking of the microphone, did you fix it?"

"Not yet. I'll need to rewire."

"Where is it now?"

Matt seemed to find this a hard question. It was a minute or so before he provided an answer. "I put it in the storeroom."

"And where is this storeroom?"

"There's a corridor behind the room where you were speaking this afternoon. The AV department keeps a small storage room there. You know, cables, mics, what nots. I put the busted mic in an old milk crate on the floor. That's where we toss all the stuff we need to fix up. Why?"

"Did you notice anything unusual?"

"Unusual how?"

"With the microphone." He didn't want to come out and ask Matt if it had been tampered with. That would only lead the young man to questions of his own.

"No, sir."

Anthony Mulish leaned over the top of Matt's head. "How's your ear?"

"Okay, I guess." Matt rubbed his ear and winced. "How's your neck, sir?"

"It's been better. Then again, now I know what it feels like to be choked to death or nearly so." He smiled for the boy's benefit.

"Again, sorry but...with all due respect and everything, couldn't that be helpful? I mean, for a mystery writer like yourself, sir?"

Anthony Mulish tensed. "I am not a—" He hated it when people called him a *mystery* writer. He was a writer, a novelist. He just happened to have written a mystery. A brilliant mystery, of course, but still a mystery.

Anthony Mulish concluded it would do no good to take out his frustrations on the young man. He patted Matt on the shoulder. "Get some sleep."

"Thanks, I think I will." Matt rose and stretched, stuffing his T-shirt down into his baggy blue jeans. "And if there is anything I can do for you, Mister Ipé, sir, you let me know."

"I intend to do just that." Smiling benignly, he waved goodbye. "I'm going to grab another cookie. I'll turn out the lights when I'm through."

Matt seemed puzzled but didn't waste much time or thought on it. He disappeared out the door. Anthony Mulish listened to the slap of the young man's sneakers bouncing down the steps until he could hear them no more.

Ignoring the cookies, he turned to the film shelf. There it was: a videocassette edition of *Throw Momma From The Train*. He had spotted it while talking to Matt. An abomination. A slap in the face of Patricia Highsmith and all that was holy.

Anthony Mulish slipped the videocassette from its case. He dropped the tape to the floor and crushed it under his heel. The film case burst open with a satisfying crunch.

Bending, he picked up the broken case. He tore out the videotape, twisting and breaking it until nothing and no one could put it back together again.

Patricia Highsmith, he was sure, would thank him, wherever she was. He'd read somewhere that the great author had once attended a London cocktail party with a head of iceberg lettuce and a hundred hungry snails in her handbag, claiming the snails were her companions for the evening.

If true, and Anthony Mulish preferred to believe it was, he had to admire her originality. Not to mention, in most cases the company of snails would be preferable to the company of humans.

Scooping up all the broken plastic and torn strips of film, he dumped the bits and pieces behind the shelving unit where no one would ever find them. And, even if they did, the film would be unwatchable.

Wiping his hands on a napkin snatched from a short stack on the side table, he grinned, satisfied that he had done his good deed for the day.

Yes, if Ms. Highsmith was in Heaven, which was right where he himself expected to be ensconced as an esteemed writer-in-residence someday, she'd thank him for his good deed when he arrived. Perhaps with a nice bottle of tequila. Because surely even Heaven wouldn't frown upon a man having a decent drink now and again.

Life after death couldn't possibly be all ambrosia and nectar.

Anthony Mulish flipped off the light in the projection booth as he'd promised Matt. Next, he wanted a look at that malfunctioning microphone.

If Giselle Mimieux was even half as crazy as she appeared in public, there was a good chance she had tried to murder him with it via electrocution.

15

Wandering slowly through the near-deserted lobby, Anthony Mulish noted only Sherlock Holmes and his wife, Dr. Watson, remained, slumped shoulder to shoulder on the blue sofa in the corner.

Entering the lecture room where he had been scheduled for his ill-fated reading earlier, he floundered in the dark until discovering a light switch. Blinking in the sudden austere overhead light, he crossed to the rear of the room.

Truth be told, he was finding it a little spooky wandering around the deserted building where a murder had occurred mere hours earlier.

Thankfully, the crazy French woman was behind bars where she was bound to remain for many years to come, if not the remainder of her promiscuous and obsessively overambitious life.

Behind a heavy black curtain, he uncovered a door. Opening it, he discovered a second door leading to the corridor Matt had described. Unfortunately, he could see very little. The only light came from a fire exit sign a good twenty yards to his right.

The narrow corridor was deadly quiet and still. He paused, back pressed against the wall, waiting for his eyes to adjust to the sparsity of light.

Moving to his left, he opened the next door he came

to. This revealed another classroom, so did the following door. Realizing that this side of the corridor probably provided access only to classrooms, he started checking doors on the opposite side. The first two doors were locked. The third opened a janitor's closet smelling of bleach, citrus soap and damp mops.

"Bingo!" Anthony Mulish whispered as he flipped the light switch inside the next room. Metal shelving filled the small L-shaped space. Projectors, microphones, stands, several dusty laptop computers and other bits and pieces of electronic AV gadgetry crammed the shelves.

A heavy oak desk, sagging under its own weight, sat opposite the door. The assortment of small tools arrayed in a collection of recycled pickle and mayonnaise jars made it plain that this was an ersatz workbench rather than a seat for scholarly pursuits.

A battered black plastic milk carton sat on the gray concrete floor near the desk. Microphones, frayed microphone cables, cord adapters, electrical boxes, a couple of old modems, broken lights and a solitary rust-encrusted harmonica in the key of C spilled from the carton. A jumble of junk jumbo. What was all this?

The mics looking pretty much all the same to him, Anthony Mulish grabbed the top one, hoping for the best. Carrying it to the desk, he flicked on the lamp and stared at the device. Was this the microphone that had almost killed him?

He turned it over in his fingers. Could it have been tampered with? Had Giselle Mimieux tried to murder him with this too? Was she an aspiring poisoner and electrocutioner?

Why?

He scratched his head, deep in thought.

Why would she want to harm him? Why would anyone want to harm him? He was the revered and adored author of Death Gets Cozy. He hadn't an enemy in the world.

The door squeaked.

Anthony Mulish turned but not fast enough...

16

"Mister Ipé?"

"Huhg-mm?" Anthony Mulish groaned. His nose smashed painfully against the concrete floor. And some lout seemed to be hitting him repeatedly in the side of his skull with a sledgehammer.

"Mister Ipé? Mister Ipé?"

Frantic hands shook him. An agitated woman's voice called to him from a galaxy far, far away.

"Sir?"

He felt himself being rolled over onto his back and did his best to accommodate the process. It beat having his face smushed against the cold hard floor.

"Can you hear me, Mister Ipé?"

Anthony Mulish risked opening his eyes.

A frantic, red-faced woman, eyes big as billiard balls, loomed inches from his own face. Her furrowed brow resembled the canals of Barsoom, as described by Edgar Rice Burroughs, who, while something of a pulp writer, Anthony Mulish couldn't help admiring for both his imaginative fiction and business acumen.

She looked vaguely familiar. But this vision was no damsel in distress, carved from the same royal stuff as Dejah Thoris, Princess of Mars.

"Are you okay?" she asked with concern. "Let me give you a hand."

She extended her right hand. He noticed a ring on each finger. You couldn't not notice them. And each fingernail was a different color lacquer. When she pressed her fingers together it was like looking at a rainbow at arm's length.

Anthony Mulish allowed her to take his hand, groaning as he pulled his knees up. He braced himself against the desk. "I know you."

"Sure, it's me, Jenny Garrett. Your editor."

"Ah." His former editor. "Right." Anthony Mulish sniffed cigarette smoke. He looked slowly about, refamiliarizing himself with his surroundings. He was on the floor inside the AV storeroom. "What are you doing here?"

"Me? What are you doing here? It's the middle of the night. I couldn't sleep. Wired, you know? I was wandering around. Spooky old place, isn't it?" She hugged herself then said, "Let me help you to your feet." She thrust out her hand, bumping him in the nose.

"Ouch!"

"Sorry."

Anthony Mulish frowned, rubbing his nose. "I think I'll remain here a minute longer."

"Sure. Suit yourself." Jenny Garrett began fiddling with a pair of stainless-steel slip joint pliers she'd found on the desk, snapping them open and closed repeatedly.

Snap snap snap.

Watching her brought to Anthony Mulish's mind those terrifying, carnivorous, razor-sharp-toothed dolls featured in Roger Vadim's classic, if kitschy, film *Barbarella,* which had been based on the French comic book created by Jean-Claude Forest.

And, now that he thought about it, there was a bit of

Barbarella DNA in that Giselle Mimieux woman.

"I went outside to have a smoke. When I came in, the door was ajar and I noticed the light. Then I found you sprawled out on the floor."

As for Jenny Garrett, she could do some damage with those pliers—and appeared ready, willing and able to do so.

Wincing and groaning, Anthony Mulish pawed his way up from the floor using the wobbly handles of a desk drawer for support.

Head throbbing, he reached a tentative hand into his scalp. Drawing his fingers back and looking at them, he noticed his fingertips were spotted with blood.

His blood.

"Did you faint?" Jenny dropped the pliers with a rattle as they hit the desk. "Can I get you an ice pack? Or a doctor, maybe?"

Anthony Mulish pressed his arms into the desk. There was a space where the microphone he had been inspecting had lain. "What did you do with it?"

"With what?"

"The microphone. Where is it?"

"What microphone?" Jenny Garrett pulled a pack of cigarettes from a hidden pocket in her ankle-length wool skirt, which she had paired with a burgundy and peach striped cardigan and white basketball sneakers. She extracted a cigarette and looked at it with longing.

"There was a microphone here on this table." Anthony Mulish pointed an accusing finger.

Jenny Garrett swung her eyes around the windowless room. "There's plenty of microphones. Here." She kicked the milk carton towards him. "What do you want with one now?" The guy was weird and, the more she dealt with him, the weirder he got.

Anthony Mulish cocked his head and looked her up and down carefully for a moment. He glanced at his watch. He'd been unconscious for twenty minutes or so. "What are you doing here, Jenny?"

"I told you. I saw the light on and—"

"I mean here at Murder Under Cover."

Jenny dragged her eyes away from the author as she spoke, focusing on her cigarette pack, squeezed tightly in her fingers. "Honestly?"

"That would be a pleasant twist."

She squelched a frown. "I was hoping to talk to you. I was hoping maybe you would reconsider letting me edit your next novel."

"There is no next novel," Anthony Mulish said firmly. He sat on the desk. If Frank Ackerman wasn't already dead, he had half a mind to kill him. The book was supposed to be a closely-guarded secret.

Jenny snorted derisively. "Come on, Mister Ipé, everybody at AP knows there is a next novel. Your big follow-up to Death Gets Cozy."

"You are mistaken."

"It's called A Cozy Ending." This time, she ignored campus rules against smoking. Pulling a green disposable lighter from the small backpack-style purse she carried, Jenny lit the cigarette and began puffing greedily. "Nice title, by the way. I dig it."

"I do not care if you *dig it*. You aren't even supposed to know about it."

Anthony Mulish snatched the cigarette from her mouth and ground it under his heel. "No one but Frank Ackerman and my new editor, Polly something—"

Frank had sworn that he would keep the news of the

new novel a secret as long as possible. What if Ameena found out about it? Things could get ugly.

"Dumas."

"What?"

"Polly Dumas. She's your new editor. At least she thinks she is. She's a hack. I can do better." Jenny levelled her eyes on the author, feeling cocky.

"You had your chance and you botched it."

"Yes, sir." Jenny didn't believe for a minute that she had botched a damn thing. But she needed this job. She needed him. She had been demoted and the climb back up was going to be long and hard. "But I learned a lot in the process."

Jenny Garrett stroked Anthony Mulish's arm. "I learned a lot from you." She walked her fingers up to his shoulder and tickled his ear lobe. "You are a wonderful teacher." The arrogant SOB had sent pages and pages, veritable reams of paper excoriating her careful editing.

As she had told her Persian cat, Perseus, one day Anthony Nothing-But-Tripe Mulish would pay. He would pay bigtime.

"Well..."

Jenny smiled. "All I'm asking is that you think about it."

"I'll do that." Anthony Mulish ran a finger inside his collar. His skin was damp. A mixture of perspiration and blood.

Jenny swayed towards the door and opened it. Hand on the door knob, she left him with something more to consider. "With Frank gone, Mister Ipé, sir, wouldn't it be nice to have someone inside Ackerman Publishing? Someone you can trust? Someone who knows you and has your best interests at heart?"

The author twitched his eyebrows. "I suppose."

"That someone could be me." She worked her way back to where Anthony Mulish remained with his butt affixed to the desktop. She took his face gently in her hands. "Let it be me." She planted a kiss on his nose and turned once more.

As she reached the open door, Anthony Mulish said, "With Frank dead, I'm not even sure there will be a book."

That sudden realization struck him cold.

Jenny grinned. "This is the publishing world, Mister Ipé. Death Gets Cozy is a big success. And rightfully so," she hastened to add. "Who knows? It wouldn't surprise me if Frank's death doesn't boost your sales even more. It might even boost the entire Ackerman catalog."

"Hm-m." He'd already accepted the advance money but maybe he could renegotiate a higher royalty rate?

"You going to be okay? Can I escort you to your room?"

"No. You run along. I have some thinking to do."

"Sure. We'll talk later."

Anthony Mulish listened to the soft patter of her sneakers moving with an unsteady beat along the floor, followed by the sounds of a distant door opening and closing.

Jenny Garrett was right. The publicity surrounding Frank's murder could lead to even greater sales. Publishing was a bloodthirsty business.

Anthony Mulish slid off the desk, swaying a little, still dizzy. He dusted himself off. People were ghouls.

A smile crept onto his face. Because at least they were ghouls with money to spend.

17

Anthony Mulish knocked his knuckles against Ameena's door, indifferent to the lateness of the hour. What did it matter? She was his agent after all. "Ameena? Are you awake?"

The author pressed his ear to the door and winced. Whoever had hit him in the back of the head had not been fooling around.

What was the world coming to? He'd been poisoned, nearly electrocuted, practically strangled and now bashed in the noggin.

What was going to happen next?

He heard the sound of movement on the other side of the door and held his breath. What had he been thinking? There just might be a vicious killer lurking on the other side. Waiting to pounce on him. Should he retreat?

A moment later the door cracked open and Ameena stuck her nose out, wrapped in a long black silk robe over fuchsia and sea-blue cotton pajamas. A cloud of jasmine followed her to the door.

He sneezed.

"Anthony?" Ameena suppressed a yawn. And a shudder. This was not the sight she longed for in her dreams.

After a brief bedtime chat with Ravi on the telephone, and his promise to give her love to the boys, who were both fast asleep at that hour, she had fallen into a deep, longed for, and well-deserved slumber.

A slumber fueled not only by her overwhelming fatigue but by the volume of alcohol she'd been imbibing and the Benadryl she kept in her purse along with a travel-sized mace spray dispenser, which not only worked like a charm but every time she bought a replacement, the manufacturer made a donation to breast cancer research organizations.

A cause which Ameena felt every bit as strongly about as she did eradicating overaggressive jerks in bars. She'd discovered that a good dose of pepper spray to the eyeballs was every bit as good as a shot of insecticide on a cockroach's repulsive exoskeleton.

"What are you doing here?" Ameena demanded.

Anthony Mulish's face was drawn, his cheeks drooped and his eyes twitched. Was he drunk?

Was she going to need her pepper spray?

"I need to talk to you."

"Can't it wait until morning, TR? We'll have breakfast. Coffee." Plenty of coffee. Reality didn't set in until after coffee. "We can talk then. Nine o'clock, okay?" She gently eased the door shut.

The author stuck his foot out, jamming the doorway. "We need to talk now."

"It's past two in the morning!" she said a little too loudly.

The door of the room across the hall creaked open. "What's going on out here?" An elderly male in drawstring pajama bottoms inquired, scratching his hairy paunch.

"Sorry," Ameena whispered to the man. She recognized him as the spouse of one of the popular cozy authors. Her author at her door in the middle of the night. This was how rumors started.

She grabbed Anthony Mulish by the wrist. "You'd better come inside."

Anthony followed her into the room.

Ameena flipped on a light switch, illuminating the narrow entry. She moved to her lumpy mattress and sat, indicating that he could have the desk chair.

"This is where you are sleeping?" He took in the spare surroundings, which included a bunkbed, the desk where he now sat, and a black microwave oven atop a mini-fridge. "Not much, is it? I have a lovely suite."

Ameena gritted her teeth. Of course he had a lovely suite while she was being forced to live in what seemed like nothing more than an army barracks in some economically-struggling third world country.

"What is so important that it can't wait until morning, Anthony?" She leaned over, pulling her purse from under the bed. She blew off the dust bunnies and dug a bottle of aspirin out. Could you mix aspirin and Benadryl? Did she care?

She popped three in her mouth and washed them down with a swig from a bottle of complimentary Virginia springs water.

"I was almost killed. Somebody hit me in the back of the head. Knocked me unconscious." He tipped his head forward to show her the proof.

"My god!" She handed him the aspirin bottle. "Are you okay? Did you notify the police? Security?"

"No. I'm fine, really." Anthony Mulish did help himself to a couple of aspirin. He also helped himself to a bottle of root beer in the fridge, guzzling it down in three hearty gulps.

Ameena adjusted the belt of her robe. "Are we talking about Matt the college boy who is helping with the con?"

"Yes."

"That doesn't make sense. Why would Matt hit you?"

"It wasn't Matt." Anthony Mulish paused. "At least, I don't think so. Although," he tapped his fingers along the chair's armrest, "it could conceivably have been him. He did strangle me earlier. And he knew where I was going."

"Matt strangled you?" Ameena took a deep breath, planting her hands on her knees. "Start at the beginning. Where does Matt fit in this story?"

She settled herself. Like an Anthony Mulish novel, his oral tales could be equally long-winded.

"I told you, I was following him."

"Why were you following Matt?"

"I wanted to see what he was up to."

"And what was he up to?" Ameena shook the aspirin bottle, wondering how many more it might be safe to take and wishing she had some vodka to neutralize their effect on her stomach lining. At least, that's what she liked to tell herself.

Ameena considered delusions one of the precious things that made life bearable.

"Straightening the projectionist's booth. He said he wanted to make sure he had put the films away properly. He didn't want to get into trouble."

"And then somebody hit you?"

"You're jumping ahead," complained the author. "I wanted to see the microphone that gave me a jolt this afternoon."

"Yesterday afternoon."

"What?"

"It's tomorrow. I mean, it's today. So you were jolted yesterday."

"Whatever. The point is, I asked Matt if I could see the microphone. He told me it was waiting to be repaired in a storeroom on the ground floor." He described the room.

Ameena opened her mouth to ask for another point of clarification but thought better of it when he glared at her.

"I found the microphone just like he said. The next thing I knew, I was on the floor and Ms. Garrett was shaking me."

"Jenny Garrett?" This was getting interesting. Not quite worth him waking her up in the middle of the night interesting but almost. "What was she doing there?"

"She said she was having a smoke outdoors, came in through the fire exit and saw the light on in the store-room—"

"And you lying on the floor."

"Exactly."

The agent shook her head side to side. "The whole thing is weird but I don't get it. This Giselle Mimieux person stabs Frank to death in the elevator and then you get attacked." She tapped her finger against her lips.

"Maybe Matt and Giselle are accomplices."

"I suppose you may be right. But in what?"

"I have no idea." None of it made any sense.

"The police have Frank's killer behind bars," Ameena reminded him. "Better yet, Giselle Mimieux has confessed in front of witnesses."

"Thank heavens." The woman needed psychiatric

help and a padded cell. One less loony roaming loose. As far as he was concerned, only one in nine persons was even reasonably sane. The rest were, at the very least, borderline certifiable. He had yet to decide whether his agent fell into the former category or the latter.

The agent was doing some thinking. "Maybe no one hit you, Anthony."

"But my head—" His hand flew upward. "You saw it."

"Maybe you passed out. It was late. You had been drinking. It's been a long day. You fainted and hit the desk or the floor," she conjectured. He was no spring chicken.

"Something could have fallen off a shelf and hit you," she continued. "There are a number of possibilities. It could have happened that way, right?"

She'd had a dotty old aunt once who had suffered similar bouts until finally succumbing due to pneumonia after spending a brutal cold winter night outside her Teaneck, New Jersey home, naked, except for her cat sitting on her lap in the rocking chair out on her back porch, determined to watch Sputnik pass overhead.

Never mind that Sputnik had flown in 1957 and Aunt Diya had decided to conduct her ill-fated watch in 1997.

"I was struck in the back of the head. I am certain of it."

Ameena climbed to her feet. "Then I suggest you lock your door tonight and that you tell your story to the police in the morning." She crossed to the door. "In the meantime, let's both get some sleep. We're going to need it."

"I suppose you are right." Anthony Mulish followed her to the door as she opened it.

Hint hint.

"But if Sheriff Winslow has Frank's killer locked up, then why would somebody hit me in the head?" Anthony Mulish wanted to know.

Ameena could think of a million reasons but, remembering her fifteen-percent commission, voiced none of them.

18

Returning to his suite, Anthony Mulish's nostrils picked up the unmistakable aroma of pizza. He was not a fan.

Even more perplexing, while the TV in the sitting area had been off when he left his suite, it was now airing some cable cooking show featuring a plump chef who needed to spend a little less time in the kitchen and a little more time on a treadmill.

He powered off the television set.

A wildly-mustachioed chef embellishing the cover of a large, greasy pizza box on the table smiled at him. He lifted the lid. Only one slice was missing, making the remainder look like a cheesy pepperoni Pac-Man.

The next thing he noticed was that someone had used his laptop. He wasn't too concerned. It was cheap and not much larger than a tablet. Knowing little of the inner workings of computers, and caring even less, Anthony Mulish used the device mostly to communicate via email—a necessary evil these days—and to play the occasional hand of solitaire or Boggle.

Anthony Mulish did his novel writing on a vintage Royal KHM manual typewriter. It was big, black and heavy. Cumbersome, yes, but a thing of beauty. He had seen an old black and white photograph of William Faulkner himself using a similar machine.

Anthony Mulish loved the heft of it, the solid feel of the keys as he pressed down firmly on them with his fingertips. There was substantiality, a reality that could not be conveyed on an electronic gizmo.

Real novels called for real typewriters.

Anthony Mulish had left the electronic device on the desk, off but with the lid up. The lid was now down. He lifted it slowly and the screen came to life.

He was about to investigate further when a sound from the bedroom drew his attention. It was nothing loud, merely a soft murmuring of some sort. Tiptoeing to the bedroom door, he felt like Papa Bear coming home to find a stranger in his house. As he approached, he heard a small rustling within.

Thinking of his publisher's brutal slaying and his own recent bop on the back of his head, and everything in-between, Anthony Mulish searched the sitting room for a weapon of some sort. The best he could come up with was a steak knife in the well-stocked kitchenette.

Not that he would dream of stabbing anybody but he was not in the mood for a second bash on the head. The knife might provide some defense from his earlier attacker, or at least make them think twice, should they be on the premises and try to harm him once more, having failed to kill him the first time.

Returning to the bedroom door and squeezing the knife handle firmly in his left hand, he slowly turned the doorknob with his right.

Giselle Mimieux, self-proclaimed crazed killer, stepped out of the door to the adjoining bathroom. Running a plush white towel over her face, she smiled brightly as she noticed him.

"Hi. I've been wondering what happened to you. In

fact, I was beginning to get a little worried. It's so late."
She was wearing his bathrobe. It gaped immodestly
open, exposing the ample curve of her breasts and her
cute little belly button.

"What are you doing here?" The author clenched the
knife tighter.

"The police had to let me go," she said with a pout.
"Somebody saw me at the upstairs bar after the movie
and said I was there the whole time. Until Mister Ackerman's body was found, that is. The spoilsport." She
turned down the corner of the bedcovers.

"Pity," he replied drily.

"Yeah." The corner of her mouth turned down. As she
fluffed the pillows, one breast popped out. She ignored
it.

He did not.

Was he still unconscious? Lying on the cold, hard
ground of that moldy storage room?

Anthony Mulish gently patted the back of his head.
Had she tried to strike him down? "Where were you an
hour ago?"

"With the police, I guess. Why?" She grabbed a
small bottle of complimentary body lotion that she
had helped herself to from the glass tray beside the
bathroom sink. She squirted some into her palm and
stooped, rubbing it over her legs.

Momentarily distracted, Anthony Mulish shook himself and explained how he had been struck from behind
downstairs.

"That's weird. Who would want to harm you?"

"I know, right?"

"You know, when that nice deputy dropped me off, I
did see Jay Copperfield going up in the elevator."

"Are you sure?" He noticed her dress, bra and thong undies tossed over the blue club chair near the window. The pink, lace-edged panties seemed to speak volumes.

Giselle shrugged. "I think so. I could be wrong."

Copperfield. The man was a thug.

"I'll have a word with him in the morning."

"Yes, you should do that." The aspiring author leaned closer. The white robe's belt hung loosely, revealing a noteworthy gap of flesh, that cute little belly button again, and the fact that she waxed.

"Let me see your head."

Anthony Mulish winced in anticipation, bracing himself for the inevitable pain and discomfort as she probed his scalp.

But she was very gentle, especially for a crazed killer.

"Ooh, that is a nasty bump. Just a sec." Giselle bounced to the bathroom and returned with a warm, damp facecloth. She proceeded to very carefully rinse the wound.

To his surprise, it didn't hurt a bit. And she smelled like fresh soap. He liked the smell of fresh soap.

"There." Giselle faced him and smiled. "All better." She kissed his nose then left to deposit the blood-stained washcloth atop the toilet tank and returned.

She flopped down on the bed and crossed her exquisite legs, sending her robe, his robe, higher. She didn't appear to notice. "The police were really upset with me. Sheriff Winslow says because of me the real killer might have escaped. He warned me that he would throw the book at me if I ever tried anything like that in his county again."

"You did confess to stabbing a man to death."

"Well, sure. I saw an opportunity and I took it. You

can't blame me for that, can you?" She leaned all the way back, extending her arms over her head. The bottom edge of the terry cloth robe slid further upwards.

Anthony Mulish watched, hypnotized.

He was torn. Was she playing with him? Like a female praying mantis waiting for the right moment to bite off her mate's head and eat him?

"I thought the publicity might be good for me," Giselle said as if it was the most sane thing in the world. "That sheriff acts like I'm crazy or something. I mean, come on, you said it yourself, the publishing business is hard." She drew the last word out. "Writing a book is easy compared to getting one published. Am I right?"

Anthony Mulish forced his eyes from her crotch area to her partially exposed breasts, to some bland black and white photograph on the wall behind the bed depicting some long ago Virginia coal mine.

He blinked. "Why are you here in my room again?" Was she a glutton for punishment? Hadn't he made himself clear? "And what were you doing with my computer? I don't like people touching my things."

Giselle frowned. "I didn't touch your dumb old computer. And I do mean old. Even my mom, who is a total Luddite, has a newer laptop than that boxy antique of yours. I don't know how you manage to write a grocery list on it, let alone a novel."

Realizing he was still clutching the steak knife, Anthony Mulish set it carefully on the credenza. Out of Giselle's reach.

"Anyway, the police only let me go a little while ago. I was hungry. I ordered a pizza. Oh, I did turn on your TV."

"Shouldn't you be in your own room?"

"It's all icky."

"Icky?"

"The police were all over in there." She hugged herself. "I feel so invaded, you know? I mean, they totally invaded my privacy. Got their hands all over all my stuff. They even got fingerprinting powder all over the place. That stuff really stains, you know?"

"No, I did not know. But you can't stay here." The girl was oblivious. She had invaded his privacy without a teaspoon of respect for him. An army of Mongols swooping down on the Song Dynasty from northern China might have been less heavy-handed.

"It's just one night. No big deal, right? I'm sure the organizers will be able to find me a new room tomorrow. Unless you want to be roomies?" She batted a pair of extraordinarily long lashes for his benefit.

"I prefer living alone." He didn't even own the obligatory cozy writer's cat.

"Whatever." Giselle flipped over, showing a very becoming rear end that the robe did little to conceal.

Anthony Mulish felt something stir and it wasn't a proverbial Christmas Eve mouse.

Giselle patted the fluffy king-sized pillow beside her. "Come on. What are you waiting for? Hop in. It's getting late. I need my beauty sleep."

The woman was completely bonkers. There was no doubt in his mind.

Completely bonkers.

Anthony Mulish untied his shoes, slipped off his trousers and slid under the covers.

A man who has faced death and survived has nothing to fear.

19

The next morning, slowly prying open one dry eye after the other, Anthony Mulish realized that Giselle had gone. As he pushed his bony white legs into his trousers, he noted that his wallet was gone too.

Nothing remained of the wannabe author but the soapy fragrance of her youth. Wiping the sleep from his eyes, he stared blearily around him. He had forgotten to remove his contacts and the world was out of focus.

Shuffling to the bathroom, he plucked out his old daily lenses. He splashed some water on his face and popped a fresh pair onto his eyeballs.

Anthony Mulish blinked. The world was right again. At least, as right as it ever got.

Happily, he found his wallet lying atop the dresser. Unhappily, one of the two credit cards he normally carried was missing.

Anthony Mulish positioned a pod in the room's coffee maker and dumped a bottle of cold water in the reservoir. With the coffee brewing, he crossed to the desk, determined to get in an hour or two of writing before being forced to endure another day at the conference.

He was working on a new novel, an ambitious project that would interweave the history of the city of Paris from medieval times to modern times via the lives of the philosophers who had dwelt there through its long and colorful past. He'd begun the story at the home of Pierre Abelard and would conclude through the eyes of Simone de Beauvoir as she lay dying in a Paris hospital. His working title was Philosophy of Paris. He was sure that this novel would finally put him on the literary map and secure his place amongst the literary giants.

If this masterwork didn't win him the Nobel Prize for Literature, he didn't know what would. Freaking Bob Dylan had won for concocting three minute ditties with titles such as *Mr. Tambourine Man* and *It Ain't Me, Babe*.

The direction the Nobel committee was moving, the next recipient of the now somewhat dubious honor might be Lady Gaga, whose name he was only familiar with through tacky billboards and whose music he was oblivious to. With a name like Gaga, he knew for certain she wasn't composing symphonic masterpieces.

In his mind's eye, he pictured some gyrating vixen on stage, flaunting an absurd bullet-bra, vomiting mindless pop drivel at teeny-brained teenyboppers.

Anthony Mulish had recently splurged on a 1931 Remington Underwood portable typewriter. While still ungainly by today's standards, the smaller machine came in handy while traveling, which he rarely did. What was the point?

As he snapped open the sturdy carrying case, he noticed that his work in progress, the recently edited version of A Cozy Ending, was nowhere to be found.

He slowly closed the typewriter case lid then opened it once again as if the bound manuscript would appear by magic.

It didn't.

"Hm-m."

Anthony Mulish frowned in annoyance. He was certain he had packed the edited copy. He intended to go over a few points in private with Frank Ackerman while they were both stuck at the conference.

Where had it gone?

Anthony Mulish riffled carefully through his suitcase and searched his entire suite top to bottom to no avail. The manuscript was missing.

A horrible thought struck him.

Had Giselle decided to exact her revenge while he had slept? Had she tossed his manuscript out the window as he had done to hers? An eye for an eye? A manuscript for a manuscript?

Anthony Mulish crossed to the window, threw it open and peered out. Nothing but snow and barren woods. He pulled the window shut.

He remembered that he had been emailed a copy by Ackerman Publishing. He had his assistant, a college girl named Roxanna who lived across the hall, print the copy out for him. That meant the electronic version still existed on the infernal machine.

Opening his laptop, Anthony Mulish stared at the screen a moment in an effort to remember what Roxanna had explained to him. He tentatively moved the pointer icon with his finger and clicked on the folder she had created for him. The folder popped open. He was satisfied but only for the briefest of moments.

The folder was empty.

Had he done something wrong?

He reversed his steps and tried again.

Still empty.

"That's odd," he muttered to the coffeemaker while drumming his fingers on the desk. The coffee maker gurgled a useless reply.

Anthony Mulish hadn't looked at the electronic file in ages. What had caused it to disappear?

The author retrieved his coffee and returned to his seat. He clicked on the file folder once more. Nothing happened. Well, something happened but it wasn't good: Error - File not found.

Anthony Mulish tried again. His laptop repeated its unwelcome reply. A Cozy Ending was missing.

That was peculiar but not a major problem. Ackerman Publishing had a copy of the book too. He made a mental note to ask Frank about it. Then he remembered that Frank was dead.

Maybe he would mention the incident to Jenny Garrett since she was here at the con. He could hardly say anything to Ameena. As far as his agent was concerned, Death Gets Cozy was his first and final mystery novel.

He was absolutely going to mention this to Giselle. She had lied to him. She must have used his laptop and, in the process, either intentionally or accidently, removed the file. She seemed to have made off with the hard copy of the novel too.

To make matters worse, she had robbed him of his credit card.

What game was she playing now?

One more thing niggled at him.

What did she think of A Cozy Ending? Had she read it? Did she like it?

Anthony Mulish finished dressing, a pale yellow shirt to go with the tan chinos, and downed a second cup of coffee with a plastic-wrapped pastry from the gift basket. He threw on his tweed sport coat and left his room.

Downstairs, he found his agent standing in line for coffee and a light breakfast in the hospitality hall that the organization had set up on the ground floor. A couple of indie publishers sponsored the breakfast. That meant hot beverages, cheap fruit and locally-made muffins.

"How's your head?" Ameena helped herself to tea and a banana-walnut bran muffin. She wore a deep purple pantsuit and low-heeled leather shoes.

"A bit sore but nothing I can't power through." With the food line backing up behind him, Anthony Mulish slowly dug through a pile of blueberry muffins until he found one to his liking, firm sides and a broad top with plenty of blueberries and crystal sugar sprinkles.

"You're a real pro, TR," Ameena felt compelled to reply.

"Yes, nothing and no one gets the best of me," Anthony Mulish said smugly.

"That's for damn sure," Ameena muttered into her shoulder. "That's because you've got no *best* to get."

"Did you say something?" Anthony Mulish asked, helping himself to fresh cup of coffee from the urn.

"Nope. Not me. Nothing."

Anthony Mulish filled his mug two-thirds with coffee, saving a third for milk and sugar. Discovering there was no milk, just some powdery milky-white substance in a deep dish that smelled like it had been scraped off the side of a toilet bowl, he settled for drinking his coffee black and sweet.

Large round tables draped with white linens filled the room. The author and agent found a couple of empty seats near the center of the room and settled in.

Anthony Mulish finally noted his agent's drooping face and red eyes. "You look tired."

"I am tired. *Somebody* woke me up in the middle of

the night."

"Really? Who?"

"You!" she said a little too forcefully.

"It was urgent."

She rolled her weary eyes. With Anthony Mulish, anything that concerned him, and everything did, was urgent. "You missed all the excitement this morning." Ameena pulled her muffin apart with a fork and explored the interior.

"Oh? What was that?"

"Giselle Mimieux was seen wandering around downstairs a little while ago. Her appearance caused quite the commotion. People were shouting. Running away. Screaming that there was a killer on the loose." She took a tentative nibble of her muffin. Not bad.

What she didn't mention to him was that she had been one of those people. And not just running or screaming—both. A couple of con attendees found her huddled in the cafeteria kitchen and coaxed her out after the all-clear signal had been given.

"I know."

"You know what?" A line of worry carved its way between her eyes.

"Giselle spent the night in my room."

"She what?" Ameena dropped her fork. She leaned down and picked it up from the floor.

"She spent the night in my room."

"You slept with her?" Ameena gasped. "Are you crazy?" Okay, a rhetorical question. She wiped off her fork with a napkin.

"The police had to let her go. She didn't kill Frank."

"I know that." Her mind reeled with the bomb he had just dropped. "Sheriff Winslow calmed everybody down and explained the situation."

"He's here?"

"Yep. A couple of his deputies are around here someplace too. On top of investigating Frank's murder, Sheriff Winslow is one of the guests."

"At a mystery conference? Whatever for?"

"He's scheduled to give a talk. There are often criminal justice experts and the like at these things. See that woman with the red shawl at the next table?"

Anthony Mulish turned to see a broad-shouldered woman with long gray hair tied in a tightly wound ponytail held together with a black leather skull and crossbones thingamabob. "What about her?"

"That's Queenie Arthur. She's an expert on poisons. They call her the Poison Queen. She's a regular speaker at events such as this all across the country."

Anthony Mulish gazed at the woman's back. "And people attend her classes?"

Ameena noticed the woman's shoulders tense up. "Keep your voice down, TR."

"I mean, how hard can it be to dream up a scenario for poisoning someone?" He continued unabated. "Anyone who has seen an episode of Murder She Wrote knows what to use and how to use it."

Ameena winced.

Queenie Arthur turned stiffly in her chair. "I agree, Mister Ipé." Her words flowed on a thick Arkansas drawl. "It's a whole lot easier to poison a body and get away with it than most people realize. That's what I teach."

Queenie smiled but Ameena noticed that her smile never reached her eyes. "Oh, who's that over there?" She pointed toward the front of the room. "Is that Janet

Evanovich?"

Author and agent dutifully turned to look. "I don't see anybody special," Anthony Mulish said.

Ameena nearly leapt from her seat. If she could get Janet Evanovich as a client, it would be the coup of the century. She'd be famous among agent circles. But she'd seen the famed author's face on many a book jacket. The woman coming through the door didn't bear even the vaguest resemblance to the best-selling writer.

"My mistake." Queenie Arthur dabbed the corners of her mouth with a balled up napkin. "Back to poisons, it's simple really. That's what I tell everybody. In fact, if a soul had a mind to, they could poison somebody right here in this room."

"Highly unlikely," Anthony Mulish retorted.

"In the blink of an eye, when the victim wasn't looking. With something virtually untraceable, using off-the-shelf products." There was a pregnant pause before Queenie Arthur added, "Slip some poison in their drink, for instance. And no one would be any the wiser."

"Theoretically speaking, I suppose," the author said with a shrug. "What is your point?"

"No point." Queenie Arthur smiled evilly at her companion, a rail-thin woman in blue jeans and a navy sweatshirt. "Just making conversation. How's your coffee, TR?" Her eyes fell on his mug.

Anthony Mulish gripped the mug tightly in his hands and pulled it to his lips. "Perfect," he said defiantly.

Only his agent noticed that he had not actually taken a drink. He set his mug down and pushed it far away. "Tell me, Ameena, what is the good sheriff supposed to be enlightening attendees on?"

"Sheriff Winslow is giving a lecture on crime scene

investigation this morning."

"Ha! The way he botched the investigation into Frank's death last night, it seems to me he ought to be *taking* a class in crime scene investigation, not teaching one."

"I'd like to see you do better," challenged a familiar voice.

20

Anthony Mulish and Ameena turned their heads. Sheriff Winslow sat at the table behind them.

"Good morning, Sheriff Winslow," Ameena said weakly. "I didn't notice you sitting there."

"No kidding." The sheriff crossed his arms over his chest and glared across at Anthony Mulish. "I know how to do my job, sir. We took the young lady into custody because she confessed to the crime."

Nearby attendees eyeballed the action. Ameena wished she could disappear. There was plenty of space under the table. Maybe if she slowly oozed underneath and pulled the tablecloth over herself, the world would go away?

"You should have known better than to take Ms. Mimieux's word for it, Sheriff," replied Anthony Mulish, not backing down or even dreaming of apologizing. "It's been my experience that in cases such as these—"

"What experience?" hissed Ameena, grabbing Anthony Mulish's arm, looking at him in alarm. He'd written one damn murder mystery and he'd never left his tiny apartment to write it.

Anthony Mulish brushed her off. "It has been my experience that in murder cases there are always a few unstable sorts who confess to these crimes. Attention seekers. Sad, desperate people seeking notoriety. It is your job," he went on, apparently oblivious to the fact that Sheriff Winslow was becoming more and more livid, "to separate the killers from the kooks."

The sheriff fought to contain himself. He'd had next to no sleep and that had come on a foldout cot in the den that he and his wife had been forced to sleep on when the blow-up mattress sprang a leak.

But he was up for reelection next year. Insulting a visiting guest of honor, let alone taking out his forty-five and shoving a bullet between the author's eyeballs, wasn't going to help his chances of winning the popular vote.

Of course, if they'd met the jackass, it just might lead to his landslide victory.

Sheriff Winslow's fingers squeezed the edge of the table although it was TR Ipé's scrawny neck he was imagining between his fingers. "Yes, sir. I will try to remember that. Thank you, sir."

Why was he being so polite? Most voters in these parts had nothing against justifiable homicide.

It had taken all his strength and every drop of his willpower to get the words out. He felt exhausted. And humiliated. Ashamed even. When he found the real killer, he prayed it would prove to be this guy.

"By the way," Anthony Mulish wasn't going to let up. "Before you go, I'd like to file a report."

"About what?" Sheriff Winslow said through a tightly locked jaw.

"One of my credit cards has been stolen."

The sheriff snorted. "Call your credit card company." He pushed back his chair, drained his coffee and stomped out. "I've got a class to teach."

"That was rude," Ameena told him.

"What was?"

"The way you talked to him. The sheriff's only doing his job. And you should have told him that you were attacked last night."

The author picked up his coffee mug, glanced at Queenie Arthur, then set it down quickly without drinking. Drat that woman. "The sheriff is not doing his job very well. There is a killer, possibly roaming around loose yet and, instead of hunting him down, he's giving a lecture on how to catch a criminal. That's a bit rich, don't you think?"

"What about finding out who hit you last night?"

"I have some ideas of my own," Anthony Mulish replied enigmatically.

"Care to share them?"

"Not at this time."

Ameena decided not to pursue the matter. There was no winning with him. There never was, even when she was clearly right. "So what is the deal with you and Ms. Mimieux?"

"Deal? There is no deal. I found her in my room last night."

"Again?"

"I'm afraid so."

"Why?" This was getting to be a habit for the odd French woman. What if the police were wrong? What if the witness had made a mistake? What if Giselle Mimieux really was the killer?

The goose that had laid the golden egg could become a dead goose.

Anthony Mulish gave Ameena the explanation that Giselle had provided to him as to why she was in his suite once again.

"I don't like it. I don't like it one bit," she replied after he finished. "Remember, TR," she said, waving a chunk of bran muffin in front of his nose, "a copy of one of her manuscripts was found under Frank's pillow. I think it's too early to discount her as a suspect. But, even if she's innocent of murder, mark my words, the woman is up to something." She dropped a chunk of muffin on her tongue and chewed slowly.

"I asked her about that. She told me she had given Frank a copy of her manuscript and he had agreed to take a look. Perfectly innocent, if stupid, on Frank's part."

"What do you mean?"

"I read the young lady's manuscript, remember? She couldn't write a decent grocery list, let alone a novel."

"I wonder how she is at writing obituaries." The agent sipped her tepid tea, her mind wandering to home. The boys would be up now. Hopefully, Ravi remembered that they had a gymnastics class this morning. "Did you ever stop to think that this Giselle might also be the person who attacked you last night?"

"She couldn't have. She was with the police."

"Are you sure?"

Anthony Mulish frowned. He was pretty sure but that wouldn't satisfy her.

"And what about Matt? Have you talked to him? What if he followed you there and struck you down?"

"You suggested that earlier. I can't imagine a scenario that—" The author froze.

"What?"

"Matt did mention that he and Ms. Mimieux had had relations."

"As in sexual relations?"

"Yes."

Ameena reapplied her lipstick. "All I can say is, I hope you've had your shots." She rummaged around in her purse for her hairbrush.

"Not funny."

"It wasn't meant to be, TR." A couple had joined them at their table, taking chairs at the opposite side. She smiled a greeting then whispered, "She's a groupie, Anthony. Can't you see she's using you?"

A ghost of a smile reshaped his face as he realized she could be right. "Yes, isn't it great?"

Ameena sighed. How many times did that make now that she had sighed wearily since meeting Anthony Mulish? It didn't bear thinking about. The answer would probably break her heart. "I hope the sex was good at least."

"Sex? I did not have sex with her."

"You told me you slept with her."

"And I did."

"You mean slept slept?"

"Of course. What do you take me for?"

Ameena clenched her hairbrush, forcing it through her knotted hair. Answering that question would only stir up a hornet's nest of trouble.

Besides, there wasn't enough time left in the world to do the question justice. She wasn't going to spoil what remained of the weekend trying to provide even a summary conclusion.

21

Ameena rose from the table. "I think I'll go check out some of the panels."

She had some time to kill before her agent-author pitch duties. One of the agents scheduled to attend Murder Under Cover had dropped out at the last minute. She'd agreed to fill in for him. That meant listening to a dozen or more five-minute pitches from hope-filled aspiring authors. It was her job to crush those hopes. Drudge work but the organizers had promised to comp her registration fee in exchange.

One always has to pay the piper.

"Speak of the devil," Ameena said under her breath, sinking back into her chair.

"What?" Anthony Mulish spun around. Giselle Mimieux, his lunatic overnight guest, came riding in on a patchouli-scented cloud.

"There you are, *TR*." Giselle winked complicity. She slapped his missing credit card on the table and set a small brown paper sack beside it. "How is your boo-boo, baby?"

"What's this?" He peered into the bag as her fingers explored the back of his head.

Boo-boo? thought Ameena. Baby?

"A new razor and shaving supplies." Giselle opened the bag for him. "You mentioned last night that you had forgotten to pack yours, silly. Plus, some antiseptic and cotton swabs for your wound. I hope you don't mind, I borrowed your credit card. Mine's a little maxed out at the moment," the blonde added sheepishly.

Ameena gawked. Ms. Mimieux stood several inches taller than her. And as far as cup sizes went, she didn't want to know. The young woman had squeezed herself into a pair of skinny jeans. A crisp white shirt hugged her chest and disappeared under the waistband of her jeans, accentuating her impossibly skinny waist. A black bomber jacket with a fleece collar completed the look, such as it was.

Anthony Mulish stuck his nose inside the bag. A disposable razor and a bar of organic, all-natural shaving soap made with shea butter and coconut oil. He took a whiff and inhaled a woodsy, musky scent with a trace of sandalwood. His favorite. "How did you know?"

Giselle beamed with pleasure. "Lucky guess." She ran her fingers through his hair. "I know my man." She looked at Ameena as if seeing her for the first time.

Sure, thought the agent, because the last time Giselle had seen her she had been running like a scaredy-cat in the opposite direction.

"I'm Giselle." She extended her hand.

"Ameena Chowdary, TR's agent."

"Yes, I know exactly who you are. You are so lucky. What an honor to have TR as your star author. I mean, you must be pinching yourself."

"Believe me, I'm practically slapping myself." This was the weirdest dream I have ever had, thought Ameena. Then she had a profound revelation. Maybe the problem wasn't like her husband suggested. Maybe her problem wasn't that she was drinking too much...

Maybe, just maybe, she was drinking too little. She couldn't wait to test her new theory and hoped the bar opened early.

"So are you taking any new clients?" Giselle batted her eyelashes hopefully.

"Well..."

Anthony Mulish clutched the bag. "Where did you get all this?"

"At one of the shops across the creek."

"There are shops nearby?" He hadn't noticed anything on the way to campus.

"Uh-huh. Right across the bridge, on the left. Not much really, a few little stores."

"I see."

Ameena wondered if one of those shops included one selling beer or wine. This being Virginia, anything harder such as liquor, would only be available for sale at state-run stores.

"It's a short walk," Giselle said. "Good thing. Some creep stole my car but no big deal. I walked. It was nice."

"Somebody stole your car?" Ameena asked.

"Yeah, some creep," she said once again.

"Did you report it to the sheriff?"

"Should I?"

The agent blinked at her in speechless awe.

Giselle flashed her brilliant white teeth. Probably the only brilliant thing about her, thought Ameena, cruelly.

"Say, maybe I can get a ride home with you guys at the end of the conference?"

"Where do you live?" Ameena asked uneasily.

"Where do you live?" Giselle turned the question back on her with a vacuous smile.

"I live out on Long Island. But I'm dropping TR off

first."

"I live in the city," Anthony Mulish explained.

"New York City?" Giselle cupped her face between her hands. "Me, too!" She squeezed his shoulders. "This is perfect."

"Yes, perfect," Ameena managed to reply. Share a long drive home with this ditzy, and quite possibly deadly, blonde and her pompous client? She could only pray the world ended before that became necessary.

"Would you excuse us a minute, Ameena?" Giselle took Anthony Mulish's hand. "Let's go clean up your little boo-boo."

Ameena's mouth hung open long and wide enough for a swarm of wasps to build a nest inside.

Giselle led the compliant author to the ladies room where, to the dismay of startled onlookers, she applied antiseptic to his wound. "There. It looks better already." She planted a kiss atop his head and led him back to the table.

Anthony Mulish wore a silly grin on his face as he returned to his seat.

Ameena couldn't stop staring. Not only had the young woman dressed his wound she had stylishly combed his hair. Frankly, he'd never looked better. Or stupider, but life is all about give and take.

"I can see you two are busy. I'll let you get on with your meeting." Giselle told Ameena what a pleasure it had been to meet her and sashayed toward the exit.

The agent shook herself and waved goodbye, still not quite certain what she had just witnessed.

Anthony Mulish carefully sliced his blueberry muffin into quarters and popped a piece in his mouth. "I think I'll go too."

"*You* want to attend a panel?" The last thing she wanted right then was his company. Besides, if Anthony Mulish showed up at Sheriff Winslow's lecture, the sheriff was likely to use her biggest bread-winning author for demonstration purposes. A demonstration the author might not survive.

"No, I think I'll get some fresh air."

"Good idea." They strolled out to the lobby together.

Stan and Reba stood side by side in the corner near the entrance with their backs to them.

"He's coming!" Peggy shouted from her spot at the registration table.

Stan spun around, red-faced. He tapped his partner on the shoulder and she turned too. They pressed their shoulders together.

"Good morning, TR." Reba's face was the color of a ripe strawberry. She shot Stan a troubled look and stiffened her jaw.

"I hope you slept well, TR." Stan smiled weakly. He wore a puffy green-and-blue knit sweater and jeans. Reba wore a dark skirt and a thick navy turtleneck shirt.

Ameena rolled her eyes so far back in her head she thought they'd lodge there permanently. If Stan only knew how and with whom Anthony had spent his night.

"Fine, thank you."

Reba ran a nervous hand through her hair. "I do hope you understand that last night's disturbance was not the norm. I mean," she giggled nervously, "far from it."

So that was going to be the party line, thought Ameena, calling Frank's brutal murder a disturbance?

The author pinched his eyebrows together. "I should hope so. A man was stabbed to death."

"Right," said Stan. "A sad thing that."

"A real tragedy," agreed Reba.

"I take it the conference will be continuing?" Ameena asked. So far, things seemed to be operating nearly as expected except for the occasional whispers and nervous looks on some of the participants' faces. Talk all morning had been centered on speculation that the remainder of the con would be cancelled.

"Yes, after an emergency meeting this morning, the committee has decided to continue," explained Reba.

"In Frank's honor," added Stan.

"Besides," Reba said, sounding apologetic, "we can't cancel. There are people here who saved up all year to attend."

"I'm sure Frank would have wanted it that way," Ameena replied. "Have you talked to his ex-wife?"

"Yes, she's given us her blessing."

"I wonder if she gave Frank the knife," Anthony Mulish blurted.

His companions gasped.

"You don't think Beulah Ackerman had anything to do with Frank's death, do you, TR?" Reba asked.

"Somebody stuck a knife through his heart. Frank admitted to me that there had been a great deal of acrimony between himself and Beulah."

"I don't know," Stan told him. "Beulah has offered to donate one thousand dollars to help establish a memorial fund in Frank's honor."

"We're thinking of using the money to promote the most promising debut cozy mystery author each year," Reba said.

"With an annual award—"

"The Frank Ackerman Award—"

"In his honor."

Reba rubbed her hands together. "Perhaps you would care to contribute, TR?"

Dead silence.

"You can count me in," Ameena said to fill the space where her author should have piped up. She poked him in the ribs.

"I'll talk to my accountant," Anthony Mulish said, deflecting the suggestion. He didn't have an accountant. Nor did he plan to hire one.

"We are planning a memorial for tonight," Stan told them.

"We're hoping you will say a few words, TR, seeing as how Frank was your publisher."

Anthony Mulish nodded solemnly. "He was more than my publisher. He was my dear, dear friend. I shall miss him."

If Ameena's eyeballs weren't still stuck in the recesses of her head, she would have rolled them once more. "Of course, let us know what we can do. TR and I will help in any way we can. Isn't that right, TR?"

Ameena couldn't help noticing that every time she said TR, Stan and Reba shared troubled looks. What was going on?

Anthony Mulish noticed too.

"Step aside, please," insisted Anthony Mulish, inserting his hand between them.

Reluctantly, Stan and Reba split apart like two halves of a stubborn atom.

Anthony Mulish gasped. Ameena chuckled, thought better of it, and smothered her titters with her fingers.

The easel held a blow-up photograph of himself. Anthony Mulish had seen and admired it on their arrival to the college. TR Ipé, Special Guest of Honor was written above his image in gold letters.

He was planning on taking the poster home as a souvenir at the end of the event. He envisioned hanging it on his bedroom wall where no one but he would ever see it.

However, someone had taken a permanent marker and savagely scribbled *Anthony Mulish* across his chest in red. Another someone, judging by the differences in penmanship, had scrawled *jackass* across his mouth.

"Animals," Anthony Mulish hissed through gritted teeth.

"We are so sorry," blurted Stan.

"We apologize profusely," agreed Reba. "We were about to take it down."

"It must have been some college kids." Stan planted his hands on his hips, shaking his head slowly side to side. He grabbed the poster and savagely broke it into two pieces over his knee. "Their idea of a joke."

Anthony Mulish wasn't buying their explanation. Across the lobby, he spotted Dorothy Hall and Sharon Crumbie giggling like immature conspiratorial school girls.

He may not have known yet who had murdered Frank Ackerman or struck him on the back of the head but he knew exactly who had butchered his picture.

22

The sky was a fuzzy blue-gray blanket. Snow fell lazily from above. Anthony Mulish pulled his collar tighter, wishing he had thought to pack a heavier winter coat.

Regardless, it felt refreshing to get out-of-doors and away from that claustrophobic mystery conference. What was it Giselle had said? Across the covered bridge that spanned the creek and then a short walk to the shops?

As his breath came out in little-engine-that-could puffs, he thought first that he would look for a bookstore. Whenever he visited a town, he always liked to see if they carried any of his novels. His real novels.

His serious novels. His Anthony Mulish novels.

Alas, on all his combined travels he hadn't discovered a single bookstore with a single copy of a single title of his in stock.

Once, when he was visiting Toronto, he had stopped in the library. He'd been delighted to log onto their computerized library catalog and discover that they had a copy of his novel of a decade ago, titled *Is It Any Wonder, I Wonder*. No one had checked the work out in years.

To make matters worse, some crass library user had written a caustic review of the book in the library's on-line system, calling it the work of a talentless hack who had all the panache of a lemur and the face of a slow loris.

That review still rankled. And he looked nothing like a loris, slow or otherwise.

Anthony Mulish slipped twice crossing the bridge, slick with compacted ice. The creek below was frozen over.

Following a hard-packed dirt road lined with barren trees he found what was no more than a hamlet nestled along the creek whose name he did not know.

The scattered shops had a Germanic flavor, the local shop owners' association's attempt to give the shopping area some much-needed flair. Only a few vehicles, most lightly dusted with snow, lay in sight. The handful of stores and eateries clearly were intended to appeal to the denizens of the college. Cheap food, cheap new and used clothing and cheap entertainment.

A cinema calling itself, rather unimaginatively, the Bijou Theater occupied a space that had once been a drugstore and offered five dollar-seats anytime day or night. The Onion Bookstore sold mostly secondhand college textbooks along with some classics such as Herman Hesse, Aldous Huxley and John Steinbeck. He couldn't find a single Anthony Mulish title. To be sure, he had asked the bored sales clerk perched on a stool behind the register reading a Steven King novel.

To add insult to injury, the clerk had asked him twice to spell his last name for him.

To make matters worse still, Death Gets Cozy stood in a place of honor in the display window in front of a poster advertising Murder Under Cover.

"That book is going to haunt me for life," Anthony muttered, staring glumly at it through the glass from outside the store.

With the cold seeping into his toes and climbing his ankles, he went searching for something hot and someplace warm to enjoy it. Options were few and, of those, only two were open. Signs taped to the entrances of many of the establishments announced that they were temporarily closed due to the school break.

Anthony Mulish chose the Brew & Chew. It was an idiotic name but it was the closest, it was open, and he was very, very cold.

Inside, he unbuttoned his coat as he approached a wan college-aged fellow in need of a shave and a haircut. The fellow looked like he'd been mauled by a bobcat in those blue jeans of his with those silly, trendy rips up and down the legs, that the young seemed to favor these days.

The only thing remotely presentable about the young man was the long-sleeved T-shirt bearing the shop's name. A row of silver earrings ran the length of his right ear. The youth greeted him, revealing a single silver ball that penetrated his tongue.

Anthony Mulish winced visibly and very nearly lost his appetite.

The strains of some unidentifiable pop music pouring from the speakers placed strategically in the four corners of the room weren't helping either.

"What's good?" the author inquired, looking at the black menu board.

"McDonald's," the kid was quick to reply. "But you'll never see one in this one-horse burg." He tapped the counter impatiently. "Our specialty is the French roast coffee. At least, that's what the boss tells me to tell the customers."

Anthony Mulish detested French roast coffee. The very name conjured up visions of Joan of Arc being burned on the stake and her remains ground into a fine brew. Gross.

Legend had it that the nineteen-year-old girl's heart had survived the fire and was still out there beating in a secret location deep in some hidden recess of an obscure French abbey.

There was a novel in there somewhere. Maybe he'd write it someday.

"You know what you want yet, mister?"

"Huh?" Anthony Mulish pulled himself back to reality. After studying the chalkboard menu, he settled on hot cocoa made with real Belgian chocolate and a small slice of pumpkin strudel. The counterman promised to bring everything to his table.

As Anthony Mulish's eyes raked over the tables, a familiar face broke into a smile and waved to him.

"Mister Ipé, sir. Please, come join us." The man was sitting with two others.

The author skirted between several occupied tables and pulled out a battered wooden chair at the table in the bay window where the three men were seated. As much as he disdained sitting with strangers and making small talk, this would give him a chance to do some sleuthing.

"Ulaf Ulafsson. We met the other day at the con. Remember?"

Anthony Mulish shook the proffered hand. He did not remember the meeting, only that he'd seen the fellow at the con. "Of course," he lied. The young man appeared about as memorable as a slice of white toast.

The other two men turned out to be Nate Saget

and Chad Long. Chad had flat black hair and even flatter looking gray eyes. His face appeared to have been squeezed in a vise. His clothes were stark, simple and black from his trousers to his down jacket. He smelled of cheap motel soap.

"It's an honor to meet you, sir," gushed Chad Long. He half-rose and offered his hand as well. "I've read Death Gets Cozy three times."

"Three times?" Anthony Mulish couldn't help feeling flattered.

"Yes, I like to study the masters. That's how I learn." He smiled. "I hope to be published one day, just like you."

"Time and patience, Chad. That's what it takes. Time and patience."

Anthony Mulish nodded an acknowledgment to the counterman as he set a mug of hot cocoa and plate of warm strudel on the table for him. Tiny marshmallows floated on the creamy surface of the cocoa.

"Are you an author too, Mister Ulafsson?" Anthony Mulish inquired as he pulled apart his strudel and tasted.

Two houseflies struggled vainly against the grimy window, neither seeming to understand the concept of glass.

"Oh, no, sir. I'm a fan. In fact," said Ulaf, "I am your biggest fan. Nate's a published mystery author." He pointed to their other companion.

"Are you, now?" said Anthony Mulish benevolently.

"Yes, a first-timer," Nate said with pride. "Like you." He blushed. "Well, except I'm no bestseller. I wrote a cozy, first in a new series. It's about a children's librarian at the Detroit Zoo who is an amateur sleuth. I write as

Lee Walters."

The words suddenly flowed as if a dam had burst. "My publisher thought it was best to use an indeterminate pen name. My protagonist is female. I'm not." He forced a laugh. "Some readers object to that."

"Ignore them," was Anthony Mulish's advice. It suddenly struck him that he had run into this Ulafsson character in the men's room the other evening.

"We were just talking about the murder." Nate slowly dragged a spoon through his earl grey tea. "You must have some thoughts. Being such an expert and all."

"Yes." Ulaf scooted his chair closer. "Tell us, who do you think killed your publisher?"

"And why?" added Chad Long.

Anthony Mulish stretched his neck, stared at the tin ceiling a moment, like an actor on the stage, revelling the attention. All eyes were on him, awaiting his weighty thoughts.

Sadly, he had few and would have to keep his ideas rather vague. "I believe," he began, solemnly looking at each man in turn, "that the local constabulary, if they can find the killer at all, will learn that the person who murdered Frank was a disgruntled author."

All three men bobbed their heads in agreement.

"Makes sense," said Ulaf.

"It is a tough business," Nate said. "Authors build up lots of frustrations."

"You think maybe the killer was somebody whose novel Frank rejected?" asked Chad Long.

"Yes, or whose contract Ackerman Publishing recently cancelled."

"Wow," said Nate. "I hadn't thought of that. I just got my first contract. I confess, I'd be pretty upset if my publisher suddenly dropped me."

"It happens," said Anthony Mulish.

"Now that you mention it," cut in Ulaf, "the day I arrived I saw Mister Ackerman arguing with Jay Copperfield."

"Really?" Anthony Mulish asked. How he would love to prove that Jay Copperfield had murdered Frank. "What about?"

"I can't be certain. I didn't hear them exactly. But the minute Mister Ackerman arrived, Mister Copperfield made a beeline for him. The next thing I knew, they were arguing."

"Interesting. This Copperfield does have something of a temper." Anthony Mulish had witnessed that himself.

Nate cleared his throat. A patch of red grew on his forehead. "I don't know if I should be saying this." He stirred his tea, stalling for time.

"Spill it," commanded Anthony Mulish.

"Well, TR," he shot his eyes up at the author, "can I call you TR?"

"Yes, yes." The author motioned for Nate to continue. "Get on with it."

"Well, TR, you see, my agent is Beulah Ackerman."

"Ah, Frank's ex-wife."

"Yeah. And she's been great to me and everything. She got me my first publishing deal. Not with Ackerman but with a real nice small press out of Chicago, HHL Books. Have you heard of them?"

Anthony Mulish shook his head in the negative.

"Anyway," Nate hurried on, noting the impatience in TR Ipé's eyes, "she really hated her ex, Frank. She said he was a real louse."

"Did she ever threaten him any physical harm?" asked the author.

"Yeah," said Ulaf, with a frisson of excitement. "Did she ever say anything about wanting him dead?" He pumped his arm like he was driving home a blade. "Sticking a knife in his chest?"

"Yes, that's just it." Nate chewed his lower lip. "She told me over drinks one night that if she thought she could get away with it, she'd stab him in the face with a pair of sewing shears."

"Why?" demanded Anthony Mulish.

"To get even with him for stabbing her in the back," Nate told him.

Ulaf whistled softly. "A pair of sewing shears?"

"Yes, she was very specific about that. Beulah likes to make her own clothes in her spare time," Nate added, as if sewing and stabbing went hand in hand.

"Did you tell Sheriff Winslow this?" Anthony Mulish steepled his fingers. Women were the deadliest of the species as far as he was concerned.

The deadliest, most dangerous and most devious.

"No." Nate shook his head. "I couldn't do that. I mean, what if she found out I told on her? She's my agent. She could drop me. Then where would I be? What would I do?"

"You really must tell them, Nate," Anthony Mulish told him.

"I suppose." It was clear the newbie author loathed the idea. "I'll think about it."

"Gee," Chad Long fondled his brie-filled baguette. "I had no idea the publishing world was so cut throat."

"Does it make you want to change your mind about being a published author?" asked Ulaf.

"Are you kidding? A published novelist is all I've ever wanted to be. I'd kill to—" Chad Long glanced around the table in dismay. "I mean, I'd do anything to get published." He shoved his sandwich deep into the cavern of his mouth, cutting off further comment.

Nate broke the stunned silence. "I know this is somewhat presumptuous, TR, but would you blurb my next book?"

Anthony Mulish turned his attention to his pumpkin strudel. Breaking off a small piece with his fork, to keep from getting his fingers sticky, he dropped the piece in his mouth and chewed.

The strudel tasted every bit as dismal as it had sounded. He washed away the chalkboard flavor with the hot cocoa. The server hadn't managed to ruin that. The drink was sweet and chocolatey. He slurped up a few gooey marshmallows and ran his tongue over his lips. "Yes."

"You mean you'll blurb me?" gushed Nate, his hands clutching the table in his excitement. Having a blurb from TR Ipé on the cover of his next paperback would be a real feather in his cap!

"Yes, it is presumptuous of you to ask." Anthony Mulish slid his unpaid bill to the center of the table, leaving it for them to deal with as he headed back out into the cold.

23

Ameena cornered Sheriff Winslow at the end of his lecture. She had waited patiently until the last of his listeners had asked the last of their questions. Mystery writers often had lists of questions for law enforcement officials.

"That was a lovely talk, Sheriff. I enjoyed it immensely."

"Thanks, Ms. Chowdary." Sheriff Winslow plucked his hat off the lectern and placed it on his head.

"Call me Ameena, please."

"Barney." He lightly touched the brim of his hat.

"Have you ever thought about writing a book yourself, Barney?"

"Me? What would I have to write about? I can't come up with stories like these people. I have trouble lying to my wife."

Ameena had given it some thought. "Maybe a combination of things. Some how-to, small town crime-solving, mixed in with some colorful local stories. You're a good storyteller. A natural."

The sheriff laughed. "Are you kidding? This is a small, tight county. If I started telling tales out of school about my colleagues, friends, family and neighbors, I'd at the very best get ostracized and, at worst, shot."

"I suppose. But think about it. If you change your

mind, contact me." Ameena handed the sheriff her business card. "I'll be happy to take a look at anything you send me. I'm always looking for interesting new clients."

"Speaking of interesting clients, I'm beginning to understand why someone might have wanted to knock this TR Ipé or whatever he wants to call himself—I can come up with a few choice names for him myself—upside the head," said Sheriff Winslow. "Not that I am condoning the action, of course."

"Of course," Ameena agreed. "I didn't know you were aware of the attack on TR."

"I heard about it from Jenny Garrett."

"I see."

"She told me she found him snooping around in some storeroom behind the classrooms late last night."

"Did you check it out?"

"Yeah. There was no sign of foul play. In fact, the only sign that anything went on there at all is the supposed bump on the back of your author's head."

"There is no supposed about it. It's there, all right. I suggested to Anthony, I mean, TR, that he might have slipped and bumped his head without any outside help at all. Maybe even passed out and hit the floor or the corner of the desk he mentioned."

"You're probably right. If I was gonna hit the guy, I'd want to make sure he never woke up." Sheriff Winslow blushed darkly. "Again, only joking. And I'd appreciate it if you wouldn't repeat my little joke to anybody."

Sheriff Winslow's eyes darted across the lobby. His wife was always telling him that one day his jokes were going to land him in trouble.

"You have my word," said Ameena.

"Thanks." Sheriff Winslow approached a glass water cooler set up on a round table in the lobby. Lemon slices and ice cubes bobbed along the water's surface. He helped himself to a paper cup and offered one to Ameena.

She declined. "Do you think we are safe here now?"

"Here at the college? I'd say so. In cases like this, the murderer is probably hundreds of miles away by now. If that crazy Mimieux woman hadn't sidetracked us with her confession," he put air quotes around the word, "that she murdered Ackerman, we might have had a chance to catch the real perp."

He drained his glass then refilled it, drinking quickly. "But not now."

"That might be bad news for you but, frankly, I'm relieved."

"I think our killer escaped in a stolen car," offered the sheriff.

"What makes you say that?"

"We had a report of a missing vehicle early this morning. A little blue Fiat convertible. Trust me, Frank Ackerman's killer is long gone. My deputies and I have searched every room thoroughly. We even checked the chancellor's residence.

"We've come up empty-handed." Sheriff Winslow crumpled his cup and tossed it in the trash can beneath the table. "I'd say our man is probably half way to Mexico by now."

"I hope you're right."

The sheriff zipped up his coat. "I'd better get back to the station."

Ameena walked him to the exit. "Tell me, was it Giselle's car that was stolen?"

"What makes you ask that?"

"She told us her car was stolen."

"She didn't say anything to me about this. When did she tell you?"

"This morning, at breakfast."

"That's funny." The sheriff looked thoughtful. "I'm not even sure she owns a car, let alone that it was stolen. Maybe I'll ask her brother about that."

"She has a brother?"

"Yep."

"He's not here, is he?" Her head darted side to side. "One crazed, self-confessed killer on the premises is quite enough, thank you very much."

"Sure. You didn't know? Matt Mimieux. He's enrolled here at the college."

"Matt?" She gave Sheriff Winslow a description of the young man helping the investigation.

"That's right. You saw him in the office when I interviewed him last night after the murder."

Matt was Giselle's brother? "But..."

"What is it?"

"Matt told TR, I mean, Anthony, that he and Giselle had had a thing."

"A thing?" The sheriff tipped his hat. "You mean like a sexual thing?"

"That's what TR seemed to imply. Or rather, that was the impression that he says Matt gave him. Maybe TR misunderstood."

"I'd say so."

"He does have a tendency to hear what he wants to hear." She pushed a loose strand of hair behind her ear.

"I can believe that."

"Still, if Giselle Mimieux has a brother on campus,

why did she spend the night in Anthony's room rather than bunking with him?"

"Those two crazies spent the night together?" Sheriff Winslow cleared his throat. "I mean, no offense."

"None taken." Ameena smiled. "There is something very strange going on at this conference besides murder. I only wish I knew what it was."

"If you see or hear anything, anything at all, you let me know." Sheriff Winslow pulled off his hat, adjusted the divot and reattached it to the top of his skull with an accompanying sigh.

"What is it?"

"Sorry. The in-laws are expecting me to take them sightseeing this afternoon." His eyes cut to the great outdoors. "If the snowstorm doesn't hit, which, my luck, it won't. Oh the joy."

He reached for the door handle. "In the meantime, I'll see what I can turn up. But when it comes to Giselle Mimieux, there's no telling what's true and what's make-believe. And to tell you the truth, Ameena, I'm not sure even that girl knows the difference her own self."

Ameena didn't doubt that for a second. She definitely needed to talk to Anthony about this.

"You might want to warn that author of yours to keep on his toes around her."

"I'll do that." Ameena did not need Anthony Mulish's death on her hands.

Speaking of the devil in cozy clothing, Anthony Mulish plodded up the steps as Sheriff Winslow bounded down them. They passed like two ships in the night, each barely acknowledging the other's presence.

Anthony Mulish shouldered the door open. He liked

to avoid germs as much as humanly reasonable. "Ameena, just the person I was looking for." He rubbed his frozen limbs for warmth.

"What's up?"

"I have an idea."

The agent stifled a groan. Whenever Anthony Mulish announced he had an idea, it generally resulted in her needing to pop a couple of Advils. Followed promptly by a stiff shot of single malt scotch.

"Tell me," she said, in this case meaning, please shut up and leave me alone to suffer through the day in relative peace.

"I went for a walk. You know, it's an excellent activity to get the brain functioning. You should try it sometime," he said, unbuttoning his coat.

"Yes, of course. I'll do that." Ameena held her temper. She had developed a somewhat thick skin when it came to his barbs. Skimming a little extra in commissions helped to ease any residual pain. "Come to the point. What's your idea?"

"I believe I know where we might find the murder weapon."

Ameena took a step backward, jostling a passerby. "Sorry," she called. Turning to her author, she whispered, "What are you talking about?"

"I think I know where we can find the knife that was used to stab Frank."

"You do, huh? If that's the case, why didn't you tell Barney?"

"Who?"

"Barney Winslow, the sheriff. You just passed him on the way in."

Anthony Mulish snickered mean-spiritedly. "Is that

Barney Winslow or Barney Fife?" He gazed out the window at the retreating squad car as its wheels bounced over the covered bridge. "I'm not only going to find the weapon that was used to commit this nefarious crime, I am going to catch Frank's killer," he boasted.

Nefarious crime? Who talked like that? she wondered.

Only Anthony Mulish, that was who.

"Great. You do that." She reached up and patted his shoulder. "I think I'll catch the end of another session. Afterward, I've got some critiques to suffer through."

"No." Anthony Mulish clamped his hand over her narrow wrist, stopping her. With a withering look from her, he quickly let go. "You are coming with me."

"What? Why?"

"Because you are going to be my witness."

"No. I have no intention of going with you while you play amateur detective. I'm your literary agent. Not your partner in crime solving." She tried once again to leave. "Find somebody else to play your Watson."

Despite his better judgment, Anthony Mulish again latched onto her wrist. "Think of it, Ameena. Can't you see the headline? TR Ipé Solves Heinous Murder Of His Beloved Publisher."

The agent yanked her wrist free, rubbing it thoughtfully. She could see the headlines. The New York Post, for sure. Maybe the Times.

Sales of Death Gets Cozy, already strong, would go through the proverbial roof.

Much to her chagrin and against her better judgment, she felt herself caving, being suckered in by the lure of publicity. And money.

"What makes you think you can find the murder

weapon when the sheriff and his men can't? They've searched the college and grounds exhaustively."

Anthony Mulish grinned. It was a rare and somewhat ugly sight. "Like they say, hide the evidence in plain sight."

"Meaning?"

"Meaning follow me."

24

"Where are we going exactly?" Ameena quickened her pace to match her author's. Trepidation followed her like a second shadow.

"I'm looking for the kitchen," replied Anthony Mulish, pulling open door after door. "In a place this size, there must be one here someplace."

Ameena blew a loud sigh. "Why didn't you say so?" That morning, she had run blindly straight into the cafeteria kitchen in her hurry to get away from Giselle Mimieux whom she thought had escaped from police custody and might be on a vengeful, murderous rampage.

In retrospect, perhaps she had overreacted a bit. Then again, one couldn't be too careful. Why, just being in the vicinity of her wrath-inciting client could put her in harm's way, should he rub someone the wrong way.

And, with Anthony Mulish, there was never, ever a right way.

Ameena stopped in a space where three hallways merged to get her bearings. "It's this way," she said, after a moment. "Follow me."

In minutes, they reached the cafeteria. It could hold two hundred students easily. Plastic tables and chairs filled the space. Strips of fluorescent lighting hid behind opaque panels. Only two lights in the center of the room were now lit, creating a cold and eerie atmosphere that any Hollywood set designer would have been proud of.

Footsteps echoing across the tile, they moved behind the serving counter. Two swinging doors with windows at eye-level—eye-level if you weren't as short as Ameena—separated the cafeteria from the kitchen. She pressed her palm against the right-side door and entered.

The kitchen was cold and empty too. Polished stainless steel equipment lined the long, narrow space.

Anthony Mulish paused inside the entrance and rubbed his hands together. "Keep your eyes open, Ameena. We are looking for a knife."

"Thanks, I didn't think we were searching for a Celtic spear." The agent shivered and it wasn't merely from the near-freezing temperature. Did she really want to find a knife with Frank's blood on it?

"My, my. Testy, aren't we, Ameena?"

"Yes, *we* are," Ameena hissed. "I didn't come to Virginia to play gumshoe."

"And Frank Ackerman didn't come with the intention of being murdered."

The corners of the agent's lips did a sudden downturn. The only thing worse than being berated for lack of sensitivity was being thus berated by Anthony Mulish. "Let's get on with this."

She helped herself to a tiny packet of salted crackers piled in a stainless steel bowl, tearing the cellophane open with her teeth when her numb fingers refused to cooperate.

"I'll check this side of the kitchen. Why don't you look over there?"

Again, Ameena didn't know which was worse, being

left alone or getting away from Anthony Mulish. Shoving the dry crackers into her mouth, and two extra packets into her pocket, she moved slowly to the right as he had asked.

A soft glow spilled down from canned LED lights mounted in the ceiling.

Anthony Mulish coughed, his coarse bark bouncing off the pale yellow-tiled walls and stainless steel and aluminum industrial-grade restaurant equipment.

Ameena flinched seeing a row of knives spread out on a white towel next to a prep station. Long, neat and deadly looking. If any one of them had been the murder weapon, it had been carefully wiped clean because there wasn't a spot of blood on them. Leastwise, not to the naked eye.

However, she'd seen enough TV shows to know that the police could find blood on just about any item, if they had a mind to. Sheriff Winslow and his deputies would have tested and removed them if they were remotely of interest. If the murder weapon was in the room, which she very much doubted, it wouldn't be hiding in plain sight like Anthony had suggested.

"Find anything?" she whispered across the room.

At the moment, Anthony Mulish had his head inside a cold gas oven. "Nothing so far," came his muffled reply.

He moved past the ovens to the grills. Peering through the sooty, black slats, he wondered, could the killer have left a knife down there? "Bring your cellphone over here."

"What is it?" Ameena wasted no time scurrying over. To her surprise, Anthony Mulish's company was preferable to the eerie silence at the other end of the long kitchen.

It was a good thing that Frank Ackerman's killer had stolen a vehicle and was long gone, elsewise she was on the verge of being long gone herself. Anthony Mulish could fend for himself and find his own ride home. He and Giselle could share a Greyhound bus for all she cared.

"You've got one of those flashlight doohickeys, don't you?" Anthony Mulish held out his hand, waving his fingers impatiently.

"It's not a doohickey," argued the agent, as she rummaged in her purse and pulled out her phone. "It's called an app. And I don't know why you don't join the twenty-first century, the twentieth for that matter, and get yourself a cellphone."

She swiped the phone's screen and pressed the flashlight icon, shooting a beam of bright white LED light into her eyes as she twisted the phone around to see that it was working properly. When was she going to learn?

"Just hand it over." Rather than waiting, he grabbed the phone from her hand, aiming the narrow shaft of surprisingly bright light over crusty slats of the black cast iron grill.

Ameena watched impatiently as her author slowly moved the beam of light up, down and sideways. Her knees took comfort in the padded kitchen mat under her feet. "Do you really expect to find something in there? Besides fishbones?"

"Shh. I think I see something," he said excitedly. "Here, hold the light."

Ameena rolled her eyes. "Fine, I'll take it but be quick about it. The battery is low as it is and I've got calls to make." She had forgotten to charge the phone's battery overnight. That was his fault too.

"Here." Eyes mere inches from the face of the grill, Anthony Mulish pushed the phone into her fingers. Unfortunately for the both of them, though more so for the owner of the phone, the agent hadn't been ready.

"Hey!" shrieked Ameena watching her twelve-hundred-dollar phone slip noisily through the grates. Her hands leapt at the grill, fingernails striking hard and breaking.

She cried out in pain, cursing Anthony Mulish in several different languages as she pawed through the grating for her phone. "Look what you made me do!"

"I told you to take it." Anthony Mulish and his agent peered down into the abyss of the grill. The cellphone light flashed once, blinked twice then went dark. The phone disappeared from view.

Ameena shoved him out of her way. "That cellphone cost me a bundle. Help me move these grates."

With effort, the pair lifted a heavy section of greasy black grating and set it down with a clatter atop the grate beside it.

Ameena rolled up her sleeve, squinched up her face and plucked her cellphone out of the muck. Thick dark brown oil coated her month-old phone.

"Gross." She held it in her extended fingers. Was it salvageable? Would the rank odor ever disappear?

Like she wished Anthony Mulish would?

"Stop overreacting," Anthony Mulish said, handing her a white dish towel he'd grabbed from a shelf.

She wiped her poor phone as best she could.

"It's only a phone. You can buy another one, for goodness sake."

"Right," she said through gritted teeth, rubbing hard.

And she'd take the cost of it out of his next royalty check.

Anthony Mulish handed her another towel that she used to wrap her precious phone inside like she had once swaddled her infant sons all those years ago.

Even so, it was like locking the barn door after the horse had run off. What was the point?

Her smartphone was waterproof but it was not greaseproof. And it sure as hell wasn't Anthony Mulish-proof.

"There's nothing else down there." Anthony Mulish poked his nose into the black gaping hole.

It was all Ameena could do not to give his big nose the same treatment he had given her expensive cellphone.

"Are you satisfied now?" she said harshly, holding her swaddled phone in her tight grip.

Anthony Mulish, as per his wont, ignored her anguish. "No." He wiped his fingers on her towel. Pausing only a moment, he sauntered over to a steel-clad wall to which magnetic handled knives were attached.

The agent remained where she was, far from the knives and Anthony Mulish, afraid she might be tempted to use one of them on the lout.

As much as his continued existence was a bane to her own, his demise, no matter how satisfying, could lead to a long prison sentence. While a short vacation from Ravi and the boys could be a good thing, twenty years to life behind bars with no possibility of parole—or alcohol —was unthinkable!

Fuming, she stuffed the greasy carcass that was once a miracle of the modern age into her purse.

Ignorant of Ameena's plight and mental state, Anthony Mulish carefully studied knife after knife, leaning in and peering silently at each deadly blade, as if one of them would confess to the crime.

Deciding that none was of interest, he turned in a three-sixty. "What's in there?" He pointed to a large box constructed of embossed, galvanized steel panels and a heavy steel door. A digital thermometer next to the door told them that it was a balmy 35 degrees Fahrenheit inside the box.

"A walk-in refrigerator or freezer, I expect." Her kid's school had a similar one. Two, in fact. She'd seen the one at her children's school when she volunteered.

"Let's see what's inside."

"Forget it. Nothing in there but fruits and vegetables. Maybe some fresh beef and fish." The agent gave herself a bear hug. "Besides, I'm not going in there. It's cold enough out here."

"Maybe Barney Fife felt the same way. Maybe he and his deputies didn't check inside the walk-in at all. Maybe," the author continued chiding the absent sheriff, "that's where we'll find our murder weapon."

Ameena glared up at him. "Fine. But if I find the weapon first, I'm taking all the credit." At this point, she didn't care whether Anthony Mulish liked it or not.

Ameena yanked angrily on the cold polished chrome handle. "And if Sheriff Winslow hears you call him Barney Fife, I'd duck if I were you."

The door remained shut, unmoved by her efforts.

Meager human, go away, it seemed to chant.

Riled by its stony resistance, Ameena tugged on the handle once again, squeezing with both hands.

With a whoosh of cold air, the thick door flew open, sending Anthony Mulish backwards into the sous chef station. Two heads of iceberg lettuce tumbled to the tiled floor, landing with dull thuds.

"Out of the way." Anthony Mulish dove at his agent, pushing her aside. Like Hillary climbing Everest or Armstrong landing on the moon, if credit was to be claimed for being first, he wanted it to go to him. "I'll go first."

Straightening his jacket, he took a cold, deep breath. "You keep a look out."

"For what? The abominable snowman?" If there was a yeti, the author was probably about to enter the beast's lair and be eaten. So be it. Who was she to interfere with natural selection taking its natural course?

"Just stay here and make sure I do not get locked inside." Anthony Mulish had a fear of tight, enclosed spaces.

Especially those from which there was no escape.

"Don't give me any ideas," Ameena said under her frigid breath.

Anthony Mulish flicked the light switch to his left. A steel-caged light in the ceiling of the walk-in blinked on.

Dusting off his trousers, he stepped inside.

25

Pulling his coat tighter, breath flying out in short cloudbursts, he carefully examined his surroundings. Sturdy floor-to-ceiling steel wire shelves bulged with row after row of wooden crates, clear plastic bins of all shapes and sizes, commercial-size canned goods, and canisters covered with aluminum foil or cellophane wrap held in place with thick rubber bands.

Blowing on his fingers for warmth, he opened box after box. Nothing but food and half of that looked inedible. Was this the stuff he'd be forced to eat at the banquet?

Prying open a box of cantaloupe that had been loosely folded shut, his eyes widened in surprise. In the middle of a pile of fruit, a thin, black composite-handled knife had been plunged through the tough netted rind and into the center of a ripe melon.

"The murder weapon! I've found it!" Anthony Mulish beamed. "Wait until I tell Ameena. Wait until I tell that fathead sheriff."

He rubbed his hands gleefully. Wait until Murder Under Cover's attendees found out. He'd be even more famous! More beloved!

"Who are you talking to?" demanded Ameena from the other side.

Anthony Mulish ignored her. He let the cardboard lid

slip from his cold fingers. It was time to notify the authorities. Picking up the box to carry it away in triumph, he suddenly stopped, realizing it would be best to leave it in place. Evidence and all that.

He set the heavy box back exactly where he had found it. More or less. There was nothing he could do about the fingerprints he was bound to have left but that was of no import as far as he was concerned. At least, not compared to his great discovery.

Giving the box a final nudge to get it just so, something caught his eye. He shoved the box aside, no longer caring about preserving the crime scene in his haste to get a better look.

Something seemed not quite right.

Taking a quick breath, he peered between the boxes. "What the devil?"

Anthony Mulish jumped backward, banging the shelf behind him, sending a ten-pound sack of carrots to the floor.

"What's going on in there?" Ameena called through a crack in the door.

"There's a body in here!"

"What do you mean a body?" shrieked the agent. "A human body?"

"I mean I see a hand."

Ameena's head appeared. "What kind of a hand?" Her teeth chattered like a wind-up pair of plastic teeth.

"A human hand," he hissed at her.

"A what?" She gulped. "Is it, you know, attached to anything? Like the rest of its body?"

"How should I know?" The author shoved his own frozen hands under his armpits. "All I could see was a hand and his side. And a patch of dark clothing."

"Where?" Ameena dared to extend her neck into the walk-in fridge, relieved that the hand seemed to be connected to a body.

"Down there," pointed Anthony Mulish. "Behind those boxes."

"What is it doing there?"

"Again, how should I know?"

"Are they dead?"

The corpse's hand had been a hideous, bloodless white. "If you were alive, would you lie down for a little nappy in a walk-in refrigerator box?"

"Who is it?"

"I forgot to ask them," snapped Anthony Mulish as he came tumbling out of the walk-in. Propelling Ameena out of his path, he barreled through the door and into the relative warmth and safety of the kitchen. "Perhaps you would like to ask them yourself," he grumbled, rubbing himself up and down.

The agent wasn't going to dignify the snide remark with an answer. "Are you sure it's human? Maybe it's a cow or a pig? Something on the menu."

Anthony Mulish's right brow rose to the crown of his head. "If *that* is on the menu," he pointed, "I am going on a hunger strike."

"What should we do?"

Anthony Mulish's hands clung to the stainless steel counter. His breath came out in short, sharp bursts. The room seemed to be spinning at an odd angle. "You stay here," he commanded, laying his hands on his agent's shoulders. "I'll get the authorities."

"Oh, no, you don't." Ameena pulled herself free of his grip. "You are not leaving me alone with a dead body. We go together!"

"What about him? Or her?"

"I'm sure he or she can take care of themselves for a few minutes. What's the worst that could happen?"

"Well..."

Ameena tilted her head at him. "Unless *you* would like to stay with the corpse?"

"Don't be silly." He shoved the heavy door shut. "Call him."

"Here, you dial." Ameena unwrapped her grease-soaked phone and flung it at her biggest client—biggest earning, biggest windbag and biggest jerk.

Striking him square in the chest, the phone bounced to the floor, landing on the greasy towel.

"Fine," he said, dusting himself off, ignoring the fallen ball of cloth and her oily, dead phone. "We'll go together."

They started off at an even, steady pace. Before long, this increased to quick strides. By the time they reached the opposite side of the cafeteria and the nearest exit, they were running for their lives.

26

Dorothy Hall and Sharon Crumbie were the first people they encountered.

"What are you both running from?" said an amused Sharon Crumbie.

"Yes, what's wrong? Are your critics after you, TR?" chided Dorothy Hall. "Or should I say Anthony. Anthony Mulish."

Anthony fumed, torn between his dislike of the two women and his haste to announce his discovery.

"Yes." Sharon Crumbie and Dorothy Hall joined shoulders. "Let's call him Anthony Mulish, Snookums. It is about time the world knows who you really are."

"Ladies, please," urged Ameena. "It's time to set aside your petty differences."

"Petty? There's nothing petty about it at all. Your author has been quite insulting."

"Quite," agreed Dorothy.

"There's been another murder!" blurted Ameena.

"Another murder?" Sharon Crumbie and Dorothy Hall shared a look of puzzlement. "Are you sure?"

"Yes! I mean...I think so?" Ameena looked at Anthony. Doubts crept in. This was Anthony Mulish, after all. Was her imagination getting the best of her?

"Of course, we're sure," snapped Anthony Mulish. "I saw it with my own eyes."

"Who?" asked Sharon.

"Where?" demanded Dorothy.

"In the kitchen," replied Anthony Mulish, inserting himself into the conversation. "I found the body myself. Now, if you don't mind, we need to find security and call the sheriff." And the news media.

"*You* found him?" Sharon blinked in disbelief.

"That is correct. In fact, I also found the weapon."

"You did?" Ameena asked in surprise.

"Yes. Inside a box of melons."

Ameena bit down on her lip. Things were moving too fast and too wrong.

"So, go ahead," Anthony Mulish said loudly, shooing his hands in their direction. "Announce to the world who I really am. I have found a second victim and the murder weapon that was very likely used in the commission of both crimes. If there are fingerprints on it, we'll have our killer's identity in no time. My name will spread like wildfire."

"Or horse poop," Sharon told him.

Anthony Mulish held out his hand. "May I?"

"May you what?" snarled a now-deflated Dorothy.

"Borrow one of your phones, of course."

The two women shrugged at one another.

"Mine's in my room," Dorothy stated.

"Fine." Sharon Crumbie dug into a teal purse the size and shape of a bowling ball bag and brought out a pink-cased smartphone stickered with a graphic of her latest book cover on the backside. "Here."

Anthony rolled his eyes at the phone and punched the screen. "How do you work this infernal thing?"

Ameena returned the eye roll and snatched the phone from his hands. "Let me do it." Shivering and dripping with sweat, she wiped the back of her hand against her brow before dialling 911.

Nothing.

She squinted at the phone. "No reception. We'll have to move nearer the entrance for a better signal. Come on."

"You two go ahead," said Dorothy. "We'll wait right here."

Sharon Crumbie questioned her friend with her eyes but stayed put. "I had better get my phone back," she grumbled, driving daggers into Anthony Mulish's backside as he and his agent scurried down the hall like a pair of rats fleeing a sinking ship. "And in one piece."

As Anthony and Ameena reached the lobby, he snatched the smartphone from her hands. "I've got this." He had watched her tap the phone to life and repeated the procedure himself. He hit the redial button and was immediately transferred to an operator.

He blurted out who he was, giving his name, and location. The emergency operator asked him calmly to explain the nature of his emergency.

"I've solved a crime."

"Solved a crime?" came the firm voice on the line. "Sir, this line is dedicated to reporting emergencies only. Do you have an emergency?"

"Aren't you listening? I told you. There's been a crime and I've solved it."

The woman at the other end frowned. It was too early in the day to be getting calls from drunks. "Okay." She tugged at her earpiece. "What is the nature of the crime?"

"I have discovered the instrument that was used in the commission of the extermination of Frank Ackerman."

"Extermination you say? You got bugs?" The emergency operator stifled a yawn with the back of her hand and looked longingly at the coffee machine out of reach at the other side of the small, windowless room she was confined to for the length of her shift. Monkeys in cages had it better. At least they got a view through the bars. And plenty of fresh air.

"I've got the weapon. It's stuck in a melon."

"A melon?"

"Correct." Turning to Ameena, he stage-whispered, "Just my luck, the phone's been answered by a dimwit."

"Wait, did you say Frank Ackerman?" That was a name she knew. That was the dead guy in the elevator at the College of the Alleghenies that all her colleagues were talking about. She had not been on duty when that call had come in. No, she had to be on call for a guy who wanted to report a melon with a knife stuck in it. "What's he got to do with a melon?"

"A cantaloupe to be precise," furthered Anthony Mulish, trying desperately to get through to the slow-witted emergency operator. "Athena variety, I believe."

"Sir, like I tried to explain, this line is for emergencies only. I'm going to hang up now." It was a good thing this telephone call, like every other, was being recorded. Nobody was going to believe this one, and she was definitely going to be telling this story at the watercooler for days to come.

"I told you," Anthony Mulish's voice rose, "this *is* an emergency."

Ameena tugged at his elbow and mouthed a few words.

Reading her lips, the author added, "Oh, and I've discovered another body."

"You mean another melon?" the emergency operator asked with growing impatience. "Whadyacallit, Athnea?" She was stressing and her Tennessee accent was exposing itself.

"That's Athena. But I am not talking about cantaloupe. I am talking about a person—Homo sapiens!" Anthony shouted into the smartphone. "When will you stop talking about melons? Have you got melons for brains?"

He shrugged off Ameena's angry, incessant tugging at his sleeve.

"Stop insulting the woman," Ameena pleaded.

"Me? The woman's a Neanderthal!"

"Sir, calm down, please." The emergency operator's temper was rising and her patience sinking. Nothing in her sixty hours of job training had prepared her for this. If this jerk didn't stop insulting her, she was going to take one of those melon ball scooping doohickeys to his brains. "You were the one talking about melons, sir. Can you put whoever it is you're talking to on the phone for me, sir?" His keeper, probably. Mental patients shouldn't be allowed the use of telephones, she'd been telling her boyfriend that for years.

"No, I will not." Anthony Mulish dug his fingers into the fleshy palm of his hand and took a deep breath. "Listen to me, very carefully. I have found a dead body here at the college."

"The College of the Alleghenies?"

"That is correct."

Was that what this was? A college prank? Some frat gag? She thought the student body was on break now.

"The body, I don't know if it is a man or a woman,

is stuffed in the cafeteria kitchen's walk-in refrigeration unit. I suggest you send Barney Fife—"

"Anthony!" Ameena hissed in dismay.

"I mean, Sheriff Barney Winslow, as soon as humanly possible." He stabbed the screen, cutting the connection. He handed the smartphone to his agent. "What incompetence."

Ameena looked forlornly at Sharon Crumbie's phone. A large jagged crack crossed the screen. That hadn't been there before. How was she going to explain this to the woman?

She dropped the phone in her purse. It was a minor problem compared to the major ones that seemed to be raining down on them like bus-sized meteorites.

27

"Let's wait outside," suggested Ameena. A crowd had gathered at a distance, their interest piqued by Anthony's loud and wild telephone conversation. Their unwavering, curious eyes were giving her the jitters.

"Good idea."

They walked midway down the steps to the marble bobcats and sat on the cold, hard stone.

Peggy came up the steps, balancing a square cardboard box in her arms. "There you are, TR." She blushed as she peeked at him from behind the box. "It is all right that I call you TR, I hope?"

She wore an ankle length forest green wool skirt and a thick white sweater. Her brown hiking boots were striped with a ring of damp mud.

"What?" Anthony Mulish's mind was on other things. Far more important things. The murder of Frank Ackerman, this second murder, if indeed the body in the refrigerator had been the victim of a murder, and his rising literary future.

"I asked if it'd be okay if I call you TR." Peggy blushed.

"Of course. And you are?"

Ameena winced. "Peggy is one of the volunteers. You remember." She smiled for Peggy's benefit. "TR is only teasing. He's a big joker." Peggy could take that one way. She herself had meant it a whole other way.

"Aren't you, TR?" Ameena's not-so-gentle elbow nudged him between the ribs.

"Yes. You must forgive me. My funny bone is a bit dulled at the moment. Finding a dead body does that to one."

"A dead body?"

"That's right."

"Another one? Here?" She stared at the building as if it was evil incarnate. "Who is it?"

"We aren't sure yet," said Ameena. "We're waiting for the sheriff."

"Yes. Where is he?" complained Anthony Mulish, twisting his watch and tapping the crystal. "He should have been here by now."

"I don't understand. I thought the sheriff had the killer in custody." Peggy said.

"You mean Giselle," the agent answered. "Didn't you hear? Sheriff Winslow had to let her go. She lied about being responsible for Frank's death."

"Lied? Why would she do that?" Peggy's mouth gaped. "Why would anybody do that?"

"Because she's wacko," replied Ameena.

"That's rather unkind of you to say, Ameena," said Anthony Mulish. "I'm surprised at you."

"You're defending her?"

"Of course not. Although she did buy me my favorite shaving soap."

"With *your* credit card, TR. The one she snatched from *your* wallet."

"Oh, dear." The two bickered like an old married couple, realized Peggy. Yet, she had asked around, discreetly. TR was unmarried and his agent was married and had two children. "Is it safe to go inside the building?"

"Of course," replied Anthony Mulish. "Off you go."

"You might want to stay out of the kitchen," cautioned Ameena.

"Okay..." Peggy took a step, stopped, clearing her throat. "Actually, before I go, TR, I had been looking for you." She lowered the box to the plinth that hosted one of the bobcats. "I was hoping for a word." She glanced towards his agent. "In private."

Ameena uncrossed her legs and made to rise.

"Stay, Ameena. You can say anything you want to me in my agent's presence. She's heard it all."

Sadly, thought Ameena, that was true.

Peggy gulped a steadying breath. "Well..."

"Yes?" Was she going to ask him to do even more unpaid work at this conference? Wasn't he already doing enough? Wasn't his mere presence here more than enough?

"I was wondering if you would care to join me for dinner tonight. At my table." Peggy stared at the steps, avoiding eye contact.

There was a moment of terrifying silence.

"No, thank you." Anthony Mulish stood. "Is that a siren I hear in the distance?"

"No?" Peggy melted.

"Sorry, no. False alarm." He scanned the distance. The only thing moving was a young man on a red bicycle wobbling his way across the snow-covered bridge.

"I'm afraid our seating arrangements have already been made for us, Peggy," Ameena said, trying to lessen the blow to the woman's shattered ego. It wasn't a lie. Besides, who knew if they'd even make the banquet? They might be tied up answering the sheriff's questions all night, in which case they'd miss the banquet entirely.

"Of course, I knew that." Peggy laughed to cover her embarrassment. "Silly me. What was I thinking?" She picked up her box and trudged up the steps.

Ameena shook her head at Anthony Mulish. "That was mean."

"What was? What did I do?"

"Dismissing Peggy like that. Can't you see she likes you?" Though why, Ameena didn't know.

Anthony glanced up the steps. Peggy fought to push herself and the box through the entrance. "Her? She's old."

"She's ten years younger than you. Easily." Probably not that much older than Ameena herself, truth be told.

Anthony frowned, thrusting his cold hands inside his coat pockets. "What's your point?"

Ameena turned and marched up the steps.

Anthony Mulish watched her go. The woman was inscrutable.

"Everything all right?" Nate inquired, coming up the steps with Chad Long.

"Women," was Anthony Mulish's curt reply. "They are impossible."

"Amen," said Nate, raising his hand for a high-five.

Anthony Mulish ignored the gesture. Barney Fife had arrived.

Sheriff Winslow pulled his squad car to a stop at the bottom of the steps and gazed upward. TR Ipé slash Anthony Mulish slash one humongous pain in the butt, stood on the steps smirking down at him.

When the emergency operator had radioed him to report the author's call, he hadn't known whether to laugh or to cry. When she had gotten to the part about cantaloupes, he was convinced she was pulling his leg. She had insisted she was not.

She had also asked the sheriff to shoot Anthony Mulish squarely between the eyes the minute he saw him. Sheriff Winslow agreed to at least give the idea some consideration.

If this buffoon really had found another dead body, plus the knife used to kill Frank Ackerman, Sheriff Winslow was going to hang up his badge.

What would he do next? It was too early for retirement, he was only in his late-thirties. Maybe he could go back to school, learn a trade.

Something that wouldn't require him to work with the public in general, mystery writers in particular.

28

The black clouds soaring above the chancellor's house seemed to double in size then double again. A storm was coming and it was going to be a big one.

"What's going on?" Sheriff Winslow snapped. Climbing the steps left him out of breath. It was a good thing the county had no annual physical fitness requirement.

"It took you long enough," was Anthony Mulish's reply.

"I was halfway across the county." The sheriff unzipped his leather jacket. "And unless you can give me a good reason for wasting my time coming back here, that's exactly where I'm heading. Again." Even an afternoon playing tour guide to the in-laws was preferable to five minutes with Anthony Mulish.

Ameena stepped between the two men. "There's been a second murder, Sheriff."

Sheriff Winslow frowned. "That's what the emergency operator said you were claiming. Although she wasn't real clear on things. I was hoping you had confused her and were talking about the Ackerman case."

"No," replied Ameena. "I'm afraid not."

"However, there is a good chance the two murders are related," claimed Anthony Mulish.

"Right," Sheriff Winslow said with a lack of interest.

He had been listening to a college basketball game in his cruiser. He had a five-dollar bet on the game with his father-in-law and it was coming down to the wire. He was going to miss the end of the game because of this guy and his dumb phone call. "I never thought I'd hear myself say this, but what's this about a melon?"

"Follow me," commanded Anthony Mulish. He turned and marched up the steps. Ameena and Sheriff Winslow had no choice but to follow him inside.

"Where are we going?" whined the sheriff.

"You'll see." Anthony Mulish waved him into the cafeteria. Ameena trailed after them.

Dorothy Hall and Sharon Crumbie smiled benignly, seated at a cafeteria table.

"Hello, Sheriff." Sharon Crumbie wriggled her fingers in their direction.

Dorothy Hall snickered. A colorful ball of yarn sat in front of her, bouncing about on the tabletop as she steadily worked a pair of pink knitting needles.

"Ignore them," said Anthony Mulish. This was his shining moment. Pushing through the swinging doors to the kitchen space, he stopped in front of the walk-in cooler. "The body is in here."

"In there?" Sheriff Winslow eyed the walk-in refrigerator dubiously. This wasn't your usual murder scene. Husbands and wives caught in the wrong beds or quick-tempered, short-fused bikers at one of the bars out near the Interstate. That was more the norm in his county.

"I'll show you." Anthony Mulish reached for the door handle.

"Stop!" Acting on instinct, the sheriff threw up his hand. "Don't touch anything. Fingerprints."

"We've already touched it," replied the author.

"Repeatedly," confessed Ameena.

"And now I'm telling you to stop touching it." Sheriff Winslow roughly pushed the author aside. "If there is a dead body in here, we need to preserve the scene."

He waved a finger of warning at Ameena and Anthony Mulish. "You two don't move."

"Of course." Ameena bobbed her head and laced her fingers over her belly.

Slipping on a pair of black nitrile gloves, Sheriff Winslow checked out the light switch next to the door. It was in the on position. Using two fingertips, he pulled open the door and went inside.

Anthony silently fumed as several minutes went by. "What is taking him so long?"

Ameena shrugged, glancing at Dorothy Hall and Sharon Crumbie, whispering back and forth and behaving all too strangely. What was up with them?

The heavy refrigerator door suddenly popped open.

Sheriff Winslow stamped his feet against the floor as he unpeeled his gloves from his hands. "Get in here."

"Me?" asked Anthony Mulish.

"Both of you." Sheriff Winslow stiff-armed the door to keep it from closing as agent and author stepped inside. He did not sound happy. "Where's the body?"

"What are you talking about?" grumbled Anthony Mulish. "It is right—" He bent at the waist and peered into the recess of the refrigerator where he had seen the dead body.

Nothing.

Nothing but empty space, that is.

29

Spinning around to look at Sheriff Winslow, Anthony Mulish blurted, "I don't understand."

"Neither do I." Sheriff Winslow planted his hands on his hips. "You've wasted my time and the county's gas. I ought to send you a bill for both."

"I can assure you, there was a dead body right here only minutes ago."

Ameena dared a peek. "Are you sure, TR? About the dead body, I mean?"

"What? Of course, I'm sure!" The author jostled a box of melons. "What about this?" He thrust the open box at Sheriff Winslow.

The sheriff tilted his head and looked inside. "I see a cantaloupe with a kitchen knife stuck in it. I don't know what the laws are in your part of the world but in this county, stabbing a melon isn't considered murder one. Heck, it isn't even a misdemeanor."

"But this could be the same knife that was used on Frank," pressed Anthony Mulish.

"I doubt it. If it was, my men would have found it yesterday."

"Maybe." The author was unconvinced. "Maybe not."

Sheriff Winslow bristled.

"Couldn't you have it tested, Sheriff?" suggested Ameena. "It couldn't hurt, could it?" She was reasonably certain Anthony was going bonkers. She had read some-place that it was best to humor people in such cases.

"I suppose." Sheriff Winslow sounded rather dubious.

Anthony Mulish thrust the cumbersome case of melons at him. "What about those two?"

"What two?" demanded Sheriff Winslow.

"Those two women out there. Dorothy Hall and Sharon Crumbie. They knew about the murder. Ask them. Go ahead, ask them."

"They did?" The sheriff blinked stiffly. His eyelids were freezing to his eyeballs.

"That's right, they did," Anthony Mulish replied. "And they were alone with the body."

"You think those two harmless-looking women out there murdered someone, dragged them into this walk-in, and then dragged them out again after you discovered it?"

"Exactly." Anthony Mulish folded his arms over his chest. "Arrest them, Sheriff. I demand it."

"You demand it?" If Sheriff Winslow had not been holding a half-case of cantaloupes awkwardly in his icy, numb fingers, he just might have socked the guy in the jaw.

"Can we talk about this outside?" suggested Ameena, inching her way to the open door. "It's freezing in here."

"Good idea," Anthony barreled past the sheriff. "You can interview our suspects, Dorothy Hall and Sharon Crumbie."

"*Our* suspects?"

"Go ahead," said the author, slamming the walk-in door shut behind them. "Ask them what they are doing here."

The two cozy mystery writers eyed the approaching trio with expectation.

"Excuse me, ladies." Sheriff Winslow placed the box of fruit on the table between the women. Feeling every bit the fool. "Did you notice anything unusual while you were sitting here?"

Dorothy Hall shook her head firmly in the negative.

"Not a thing," agreed Sharon Crumbie.

"How long have you been here?"

"Five minutes or so," replied Dorothy Hall, her hands working her knitting needles.

"Maybe ten," Sharon Crumbie said.

"And you didn't see anything unusual? Anything at all?"

"Nothing," stated Dorothy Hall, hesitating only slightly.

"What about the dead body?" demanded Anthony Mulish, certain the two were up to something.

"You tell us, TR. You see, Sheriff," Sharon Crumbie said, "Mr. Mulish here told Dorothy and me that he had found another dead body."

"This time, in the walk-in cooler," chortled Dorothy Hall.

"So we came to see if it was true."

Sheriff Winslow looked at the melon in the box. Ooze seeped slowly from the knife wound. He was really going to take a ribbing for this one when he got it to the forensics people down at the state lab. "You went inside the walk-in refrigerator?"

"Yes, I admit, we did," replied Sharon Crumbie. "I am sorry."

"We wouldn't have gone inside if we had thought there really had been a dead body inside," Dorothy Hall added meekly in their defense.

"And what did you find?" Sheriff Winslow wanted to know.

"The same thing you did, Sheriff." Dorothy Hall's face bore a world-class grin. "Absolutely nothing."

"That's impossible!" shouted Anthony Mulish. "They moved it!"

"Why?"

"To confound me."

"Confound you? I gotta admit, you're sorta confounding me." Sheriff Winslow scratched the back of his neck.

Dorothy Hall and Sharon Crumbie chuckled with delight. "This is funnier than a Parnell Hall novel," quipped Sharon Crumbie.

"I'm telling you, Sheriff, those two will do anything to make me look bad." Anthony Mulish pointed angrily at the two women.

Ameena clamped her hands on Anthony Mulish's arm and pushed it down to his side. "Please, Anthony—"

"I'm beating them at their own cozy game and they do not like it. Not one bit."

Sheriff Winslow sucked in a breath. "I'm telling you, Ameena," he bent to the level of the agent's ear and whispered, "I'd like to beat this guy, myself. Get my drift?"

Ameena nodded. "Remember," she whispered back. "He suffered a bump on the head."

"Right." Sheriff Winslow paced, composed himself. He was a professional, after all. "Has anyone else been in or out of this cafeteria since you've been here, ladies?"

"Not a soul," came Dorothy's reply.

"Living or otherwise," added Sharon Crumbie. She

giggled and that set Dorothy Hall off as well.

"This isn't funny." Anthony Mulish turned in desperation to his agent. "You saw it, Ameena."

"Actually," mumbled Ameena, coloring slightly. "No."

"No?"

She shook her head. "No. I mean, I peeked into the walk-in but I didn't see the body. If there was a body," she added softly.

"What? *If* there was a body? Of course there was a body. I saw it myself."

"Listen, Mister Ipé, I heard all about that bump on the head you suffered," interjected Sheriff Winslow. "Maybe you are experiencing some sort of, I don't know," he scratched the nape of his neck, wondering how to phrase this without getting sued. "Repercussions."

"Repercussions?" Anthony Mulish flamed. "Don't patronize me, Sheriff. I know what I saw." He slammed his fist into the palm of his opposite hand. "And what I saw was a dead body."

Sheriff Winslow chewed on his upper lip. "Male or female?"

"I don't know."

"Young or old?"

"I couldn't tell."

Sheriff Winslow thrust his hands into the back pockets of his trousers. "What can you tell me?"

"That he or she was dead. Ice. Cold. Dead."

Ameena and Sheriff Winslow exchanged a look.

"By the way, I'd like my phone back." Sharon Crumbie extended her hand.

"Of course." Ameena slowly removed the writer's phone from her purse and carefully handed it to her upside down.

Sharon Crumbie immediately flipped it over. "It's cracked. There's a large crack in it!" She thrust the evidence under the agent's nose.

"Really?" Ameena pressed the woman with her most sincere smile. "Why, so there is. I am surprised you never noticed it before. A crack that size."

"But—" spluttered Sharon Crumbie.

Dorothy Hall stood and grabbed her friend by the elbow. "Never mind. Come on, Sharon. We have a panel. Besides, I think we've squeezed all the entertainment value possible out of this turnip." She jerked her thumb in the direction of Anthony Mulish, standing to one side looking befuddled.

"I'm telling you, Sheriff. There has been another murder. Those two women, whom you are now allowing to escape, probably had something to do with it." He watched sourly as the two women shuffled off.

"Come on, Mister Ipé, you can't possibly believe those two are killers."

"They are mystery writers. They kill for a living."

"So do you," shot back Sheriff Winslow. "I suggest you get some rest, Mister Ipé. Take a nap. There's a doctor in town. Maybe he can prescribe you something for your nerves."

"There is nothing wrong with my nerves," fumed Anthony Mulish.

"No? How about your eyesight?" *Or your sanity.* Sheriff Winslow had had enough. He grabbed the box of fruit in both hands. The sides of the cardboard box caved in under the pressure. "I'm out of here."

Sheriff Winslow paused at the cafeteria exit. "Do me a favor, Mister Ipé?"

"What's that?"

"If you find anymore murdered fruit, cantaloupe or otherwise, phone the FBI. That's their bailiwick. Leave me out of it."

Anthony Mulish was happy to see the man go. "What a poor excuse for a law enforcement official."

"Sheriff Winslow's doing the best he can, TR. He couldn't have done more than he did. There was no body. Maybe what you saw was a side of beef or something. Or maybe, like the sheriff suggested, you're simply overtired."

"I am telling you, Ameena, there is a dead body floating around here somewhere and I am not going to rest until I find it." He looked madly around the room.

Ameena patted him on the shoulder. "You do that." She left without another word. Because, really, there was nothing more to say.

30

Outside, Sheriff Winslow hopped in his squad car. He drove slowly around the building until he was certain he was out-of-sight. He stopped, opened the back door of the cruiser, dragged the box of melons from the rear seat and tossed it in the dumpster.

He listened with great satisfaction to the sound of melons bouncing around inside the deep steel bin—— imagining each and every one had Anthony Mulish's fat, conceited face on it.

Not quite as satisfying as shooting the moron, but shooting meant paperwork and Sheriff Winslow abhorred paperwork.

31

"Fingerprints be damned." Anthony Mulish threw open the door of the walk-in refrigerator. A body had been in here. He had seen it with his own two eyes. "Bodies do not simply disappear."

That raised the questions: Where had it gone? And who had done the taking?

He stomped up and down inside the walk-in. Nothing.

Anthony Mulish's money was still on Dorothy Hall and Sharon Crumbie. At the very worst, they were murderers, partners in crime. At the very least, they were hiding something. Anthony Mulish knew people. He could read them as easily as reading a book.

Determined to track the pair down and wring the truth out of them, he headed to the lobby. He spotted Ameena chatting with one of the organizers at the opposite end.

He studied a map and conference schedule standing on an easel near the registration tables. According to the listing, several panels were now in progress. Most down the corridor to his left.

Dorothy Hall and Sharon Crumbie had said something about attending a panel. He smiled and went searching for his quarry, running into Jenny Garrett along the way as she stopped to drink from the water fountain.

"Jenny. A word with you, please," Anthony Mulish said.

She wiped her mouth with the back of her hand. "Sure. What's up? Have you given some thought to what I said?"

"Yes," he lied. "In fact, you could help me now." Glancing around to make sure they couldn't be overheard, he said, "I cannot find my copy of you-know-what."

"You know what?"

He dragged her to the wall. "A Cozy Ending. I am certain I brought a paper copy with me. It was the edited version," he whispered. "Now I can't find it. Not even a copy on my laptop."

"Hmm. I'll be happy to look into that for you. Ackerman Publishing doesn't keep regular hours on the weekend but I'll reach out to some folks and see if I can't get you a copy ASAP. Anything else?"

"No, that will do."

"Fine." She ran her fingers up his arm. "Remember, I'm here for you, TR."

Anthony Mulish gulped and hurried off. Why was it every time he talked to Jenny he felt like he was dealing with the Devil herself?

Anthony Mulish moved quickly past draped tables lined up on either side of the narrow hallway. An author sat at each table, having concluded speaking on his or her panel, waiting and hoping to sign copies of their latest releases.

Tented name cards at the edge of each table identified the authors. A copy of each of their books stood on acrylic stands beside them. Hopeful, please-come-talk-to-me-and-buy-my-book-before-

I-die-of-embarrassment smiles frozen on each writer's face.

At the first table Anthony Mulish passed, a young woman in a flowery blue-and-red dress sat stiff as a board behind a small stack of novels, the cover of which featured a cocker spaniel popping out of a sewing basket. Sewing Up Death was the novel's cutesy, whimsical title.

He stopped.

"Hi, Mister Ipé." The young woman said perkily. Her nametag identified her as Gloria Meecham.

"Hello."

Wait till she told her friends that TR Ipé had asked for a copy of her latest mystery novel. They would be utterly and completely jealous. Maybe the author at the next table would take a photo of the two of them together with her phone. She could post it on social media. What a coup that would be!

"Are you a fan?" Gloria Meecham held her pen at the ready, expecting to autograph a copy of her novel for him.

Anthony Mulish rummaged around in the crystal dish of tiny wrapped chocolates she had set out as an enticement to get passers-by to stop. "Of chocolate?"

His eyes lit on two special pieces, dark chocolate with almonds. He palmed them. "Yes."

Gloria Meecham's heart sank as, without another word, TR Ipé turned on his heels and entered Hall A in search of his prey. A panel was already in progress. Nearly every seat was filled.

Standing in the rear, he scanned the heads. Dorothy Hall and Sharon Crumbie were not present, neither speaking up at the raised dais or seated out in the audience.

Slowly unwrapping a chocolate and popping it on his tongue where it melted down in a sweet, gooey mass, he exited and tried Hall B. The room was an exact copy of Hall A. Only the individual faces in the audience and at the speaker's table had changed. A speaker droned into a microphone in a voice barely audible about the short-story writing process.

Anthony Mulish felt like interrupting but refrained. Short stories were a waste of time, in his opinion. If it was worth saying, it was worthy of being a novel.

That was his motto.

He stared at the talking face, memorizing it, so that he could enlighten the speaker at another less pressing time. Removing the foil from his remaining chocolate, he dropped it slowly onto his tongue, savoring each moment of sweet pleasure.

Hall C was next. Queenie Arthur stopped mid-sentence as he barged into the room. She sat alone at the front of the room, addressing her rapt audience.

"Don't mind me," said Anthony Mulish, spotting his quarry, Sharon Crumbie and Dorothy Hall, two rows in from the rear. They sat near the center of the row with Sharon Crumbie to Dorothy Hall's right. The chair to Dorothy's left was unoccupied and held a Murder Under Cover tote bag and her ubiquitous ball of yarn.

Queenie Arthur tugged at her ponytail, skimmed her notes then continued talking about the merits of strychnine.

Hunching over, Anthony moved slowly up the center aisle and pushed his way down the row. Sharon Crumbie glared at him and refused to move her legs. He was forced to climb over her, balancing himself by planting his hands on the chair in front of her. That chair and its occupant keeled forward.

Buzzes and murmurs ensued.

"Excuse me," Anthony Mulish grunted. Dorothy Hall hissed in annoyance as he grabbed the handles of her tote and tossed it under her seat. With a flick of the finger, he sent her ball of yarn after it. The ball did what balls always do—it rolled and rolled, leaving a multicolored trail three rows up and four seats over.

Friendly hands rolled it back the way it had come. Dorothy Hall yanked up the loose strands of yarn in her fingers and swore. "You did that on purpose, Ipé," she snarled.

Dorothy Hall also gave him a jab between the ribs with one of her knitting needles. She would have done it again if Queenie Arthur had not shot her a look of warning. She shoved her knitting in her tote bag and scooched over as close as possible to her friend and as far as possible from TR Ipé.

"Quit that," snarled Anthony Mulish. He rubbed his side. "This is an expensive jacket."

"Ha! Looks like something the Salvation Army rejected, if you ask me."

"I did not ask you."

"And those stitched leather patches on the elbows?" She pinched his elbow. "Those went out with the Hoover administration."

"I'll have you know—"

"Is there a problem here?" demanded Queenie.

Anthony Mulish and Dorothy Hall swung their heads around. Queenie loomed at the end of the row. If the steam coming out of her nostrils and the fire in her eyes was any indication, she was not a happy camper.

"I'm so sorry, Queenie," Dorothy Hall told her. "It won't happen again."

"What about you?" Queenie aimed her finger at Anthony Mulish.

"I am all ears." Anthony Mulish passed his fingers across his lips, zipping them. The woman reminded him of his mother. She was scary too—and prone to boxing his ears if he so much as questioned her wisdom about even the slightest thing.

Like the time his mother insisted that there really was a Santa Claus and he had replied that, even if there ever had been such a semi-godlike creature as Santa Claus, he most surely would have passed away centuries ago due to complications of obesity and diabetes after scarfing down all those Christmas cookies that his believers insisted on baking and leaving out for him on Christmas Eve, much to Santa's detriment. "Those children are enabling him," he'd said, earning him another cuff to the ear.

"See that you are." Queenie gave them each a dose of evil eye. "All of you. You do not want to make Queenie angry." With that threat spoken, she plodded back to her position at the front of the room.

"See what you did? You made Queenie mad." Dorothy Hall whispered in his ear. Queenie was a valuable resource. She often messaged the poison expert with questions when she was stuck trying to come up with a new and delightful way to kill somebody. She could not afford to make her mad. Dorothy Hall snatched her knitting and began unraveling the mess Anthony Mulish had made.

He stared at the yarn. "If you spent more time fashioning your stories rather than knitting kitty daywear, your sales would improve dramatically."

"This isn't for a cat, numbskull."

Sharon Crumbie leaned over Dorothy Hall's lap and shushed them both.

"What is it then? Some new outfit for that little alien sidekick from your little novels? What was its name? Kinky Boots?"

"I've told you, that's *Kikiyu*," Dorothy Hall replied with gnashing teeth. "My fans adore him."

Anthony Mulish chuckled maliciously. "All two of them?"

Dorothy Hall whipped out a knitting needle and aimed it at his soft belly.

"Don't. He's not worth it, Snookums." Sharon Crumbie's hand on her wrist stilled her. "Let's go," she urged.

Anthony Mulish sucked in his stomach, afraid to breathe or move. Dorothy Hall held the needle an inch from his navel.

"Fine. Consider yourself lucky." Dorothy Hall withdrew the knitting needle and jammed it in her tote.

"That's my girl," said Sharon.

"Stay away from me," Dorothy Hall said, her hot breath tickling his ear as she climbed to her feet and gathered up her things. "Or you will be next."

Only when Sharon Crumbie had successfully dragged her angry friend away did he dare breathe again.

"What a disagreeable and unstable woman that Crumbie creature is," Anthony Mulish muttered to the man seated nearest.

32

Queenie Arthur took a last question and ended her talk. Anthony Mulish couldn't wait to escape. Bored to the point of despair, he hadn't dared leave before then for fear of Queenie's reaction.

He moved quickly through the lingering crowd and exited. No sign of Dorothy Hall or Sharon Crumbie.

Jay Copperfield, swaddled in a frumpy gray sweatsuit, slipped into the auction room. Giselle had seen Copperfield getting on the elevator late last night *after* the deputy had returned her to the college.

What had the portly and short-tempered cozy author been doing wandering the building at so late an hour?

Probably up to no good.

"Time to ask him just that." He found the pretentious man standing beside a plethora of cat-inspired gifts occupying a half-yard's worth of black-draped table space.

Copperfield eyed the bidding sheet.

"People are actually offering to pay for this?" Anthony Mulish said over his shoulder. "You couldn't pay me enough to haul this assortment of trash away."

Jay Copperfield had supplied that assortment. This included a sheepskin-lined cat bed, a sack of organic catnip tied in a red ribbon, three cans of premium cat food—tuna, turkey, and mackerel—a pair of paw-sized black-and-white fake mice, and something labelled DJ

Phat Katt. This absurd product looked like one of those silly phonographs that were popular with DJs at hip-hop parties. However, in this case, rather than a vinyl record, a cardboard scratching pad in the shape of an LP sat on the fake turntable.

"The bid's up to one-fifty." Jay Copperfield proudly jabbed a long fingernail at the line near the bottom of the sheet. Damp red hair tamped down atop his skull. Water and mud decorated his brown oxfords.

The man was a slob.

"Nice to see that you have dressed for the occasion," Anthony Mulish quipped. "Tell me, how are you planning on dressing for dinner tonight? Argyle socks, bib overalls and an I Heart Kittens T-shirt?"

"Go away, Tripe. Disappear."

"That's TR Ipé."

"That's Anthony Mulish. And I looked you up on Wikipedia. Your claim to fame is being the least successful literary novelist in modern history. And, brother, that's saying something."

"Very funny." Anthony Mulish knew the man was lying. There was only a small stub of a posting on Wikipedia concerning him. And he had written that himself.

Actually, he had written a much longer piece but every time he posted it, some Wikipedia troll took it down. To his consternation, they also kept inserting his real age.

Jay Copperfield moved away but it was no use. Anthony Mulish followed. "What were you doing wandering the building late last night?"

"Who says I was?"

"You were seen."

"By who?" Copperfield paused beside Cherie Maraschino's matchstick masterpiece.

"Giselle Mimieux."

"That fruitcake?"

"That fruitcake is a lovely young woman. In fact," Anthony Mulish bragged, "I believe she is rather fond of me."

"I rest my case." Jay Copperfield ran his pink tongue across his upper lip.

"Someone actually bid one hundred dollars for this match and glue monstrosity?" exclaimed Anthony Mulish, his eyes scanning the bid sheet. Ulaf Ulafsson's ninety dollar bid had been surpassed by the hundred dollar bid of one Emily Jonas.

"It's a work of art," Copperfield declared.

"It is a three-alarm fire waiting to happen," deadpanned Anthony Mulish.

Copperfield gaped at him. "What are you doing here, Mulish?"

"Talking to you."

"No, I don't mean now. I mean here here." He waved his fat arms. "I mean, you are not one of us. You don't seem to like anything or anybody. So I don't get it, why come to a conference for mystery lovers? Why not a conference for gasbag pseudo-intellectuals instead?"

Anthony Mulish found the question baffling. "Because I was invited. I am the special guest of honor." His chest swelled with ego and pride.

"You're a blowhard and a phony."

Anthony Mulish loosened a matchstick from one corner of the house and picked at it with a fingernail. "It was you who struck me down last night."

"Brother, if I hit you, you'd know it." Copperfield pounded a fist into his palm.

"I was in the storeroom last night. Someone came in when my back was turned and knocked me unconscious."

"For real?" The cozy author took a step back and studied his accuser. "If you find out who clobbered you, let me know. I'll give them a free autographed copy of my latest book."

Anthony Mulish ignored the other author's jibes. "What were you arguing with Frank Ackerman about?"

"Frank's dead, remember?"

"You were seen arguing with Frank earlier that day. Why? Because he dropped you? Cancelled your contract?"

Jay Copperfield's eyes narrowed to slits. The tops of his cheeks visible above his beard burned with anger. "Are you spying on me? Having me followed?" He jabbed his index finger into Anthony Mulish's chest.

"I am simply trying to find out who murdered Frank and why."

"This isn't one of your lousy books, TR. Leave solving murders to the professionals."

"I would, if there were any professionals to be found. I don't think there is one within a hundred miles of this dreary spot." His faith in the sheriff, after the debacle in the cafeteria kitchen, had never been lower. "Between you and me, there has been a second murder."

"What? Who is it this time?"

"I am afraid I am not at liberty to say," said Anthony Mulish, sidestepping the question.

"You are not accusing me of this second murder too, are you?" flared Copperfield.

"Where were you about an hour or so ago?"

"Out taking a walk. I like to hike."

"In this weather?" It was cold and dreary out-of-doors the last time Anthony Mulish had taken a peek.

"Living in the Bronx, I find this refreshing."

"You weren't in the kitchen?"

"Kitchen? What kitchen?"

"The walk-in refrigerator to be exact?"

"I don't know what you are talking about."

"Somebody moved the body. Was it you?" Jay Copperfield certainly looked strong enough to have done so. But he couldn't have moved it far. Not without help. "How are Dorothy Hall and Sharon Crumbie mixed up in this? Are they your accomplices?"

Copperfield eyed the crowd following their conversation. "I'm warning you, Tripe. You keep flapping your pie hole and I'm gonna sue you for slander."

"Did they help you move the body?"

"What body? You say there's been a second murder? That's bull. Where are the police? Huh? Answer me that!"

"You still haven't accounted for your whereabouts last night."

"And I do not have to. Not to you."

"He was with me," a woman's voice declared.

Both men turned to discover the speaker.

"B-Beulah," stuttered Copperfield.

"Hello, Beulah. So sorry for your loss." Anthony Mulish bowed slightly at the waist and extended his hand.

Wearing an ankle-length dark blue dress, brown hair pulled tightly behind her ears, Beulah's green eyes flashed at Jay.

"Beulah, I was just looking for you."

She eyed him dubiously. "So I see." She fingered a tiny matchstick doghouse sitting on a fuzzy patch of green in the front yard of the bigger dollhouse. "Don't tell me, you thought I was hiding in Cherie's quaint creation."

"You and Jay are already acquainted? I didn't realize," said Anthony Mulish.

Jay Copperfield swallowed hard. "Beulah is my—"

"Agent," inserted Beulah Ackerman.

"Right," agreed Jay Copperfield.

"Leave us," Beulah said. Turning to Anthony Mulish, she asked, "Why are you questioning Jay?"

"Because, in case you have forgotten, somebody stabbed Frank to death. And," he added, his hand moving to the back of his skull, "somebody hit me in the back of the head when I decided to investigate the murder."

"You?" Amusement danced in Beulah's eyes. "Investigate a murder? That's rich."

"I happen to be very good at such things. I have a talent for finding clues, reading people."

She rested her painted fingernails on Anthony Mulish's shoulder. "You should really stick to writing books, Anthony. You do have a talent for that. Searching for a killer could get you killed."

Anthony Mulish noted her eyes were as lifeless as stones. "Is that a threat, Beulah?"

"Of course not, Anthony. You do have a tendency to overdramatize. In fact, if I were your editor, I would do something about that. Your writing is rife with it."

The author held his temper at bay. Remembering what Nate had confided to him in the café across the river, he said, "You were seen arguing with Frank yesterday."

"Whoever told you that was lying," Beulah said, a little too quickly and too forcefully, thought Anthony Mulish. "Who was it?"

"Nate," he replied.

"That toad?"

"That toad is one of your authors."

Her eyes narrowed to snakelike slits. "Not for long, he isn't."

Anthony Mulish realized too late that he probably should not have mentioned the novice author by name. "Tell me what you were arguing with Frank about?"

"Why should I want to do that?"

"Because if you don't, I'll have to tell Sheriff Winslow about it." A complete bluff. Telling the doltish sheriff anything would be a complete waste of time. Nothing short of dropping the killer in the sheriff's lap would do any good at all.

"Fine," she said with a sigh. "We were having a discussion, not an argument, about money." She pulled a tube of moisturizer from her purse and traced her lips with it.

"What about money?"

"The same old story. He owed me money. I wanted it. It was part of our divorce settlement." She capped her moisturizer and let it fall into her black leather purse. "Frank owed everybody money."

Beulah ran her hand up Anthony Mulish's lapel. "I wouldn't be surprised if he didn't die owing you money. If so, I wonder if you will ever get it now that he's gone."

"Nonsense. I have a contract."

"With a dead man."

Could Beulah Ackerman be right? Would Frank's death cause him financial loss? "I'm sure my agent has everything under control," he said with false confidence. First chance he got, he would ask Ameena about that.

"Ah, dear, dear Ameena. Tell me, what does she think of you taking your sequel to Death Gets Cozy directly to Ackerman Publishing?"

Anthony Mulish blanched, eyes darting nervously across the room. "How did you know about that, Beulah? It was a secret. Frank swore to me he wouldn't tell a soul. Until publication, of course."

"That's your problem, *TR*, you are naïve. Secrets are meant for telling. And Frank?" She paused dramatically. "Frank had no soul."

Beulah extracted a silver cigarette case from her purse and eyed it hungrily. No Smoking signs hung everywhere—no smoking allowed indoors or within twenty-five feet of any of the buildings on campus. "It seems to me you had as much a reason to murder Frank as anybody."

To Anthony Mulish's dismay, the woman was getting the best of him. "You still haven't told me where you were late last night."

"Weren't you listening earlier?" Her mouth formed a smile. "I was with Jay."

"How convenient."

"And pleasurable," Beulah Ackerman quipped. She glanced at a slender platinum watch locked around her equally slender pale wrist. "I have a meeting with a client. Be careful, Anthony." She took two steps, then turned. "And speaking of editors, I hear that Jenny Garrett is none too fond of you."

"Jenny Garrett?"

"You were responsible for her demotion."

"I simply told Frank that I did not find her editing satisfactory."

"Costing the young woman a demotion in title and pay."

Anthony rubbed under his chin. "Jenny was the one who found me unconscious on the floor of the storeroom after I had been struck last night."

Beulah Ackerman's smile increased. "Now that is convenient, isn't it?"

Yes, it was, thought Anthony Mulish as she disappeared around the corner. He would have another word with Jenny Garrett as well.

He moved to the basket that Ameena had contributed on his behalf. Peggy Wethering had opened with a bid of fifty dollars. A handful of others had offered five-dollar increments above that. Ulaf Ulafsson had upped the ante to seventy-five. Peggy had countered with one hundred.

Not bad, but still far below Jay Copperfield's current high bid.

He would mention to Ameena that she must enter a larger bid, two hundred dollars say, under a fictitious name.

She could afford it.

Moving back to Copperfield's donation, he lingered, waiting for the right moment when no one was watching. He slid Copperfield's bidding sheet under the table to the floor.

That would put an end to the Jay Copperfield bidding.

33

Having worked up a well-earned appetite, Anthony Mulish proceeded to the first floor hospitality banquet hall where he was told that a free buffet lunch would be available between the hours of twelve and one thirty.

He still hadn't looked at any of the manuscripts he was supposed to critique during the con. There would be time for that later. He found he always worked best on a full stomach and a slaked thirst.

Besides, Ameena was supposed to deliver copies of these manuscripts to him. She had not yet done so. If he was late or remiss in his duties, it would be her fault, not his.

Balancing a big plate of food in his left hand, he confronted Dorothy Hall and Sharon Crumbie seated at a round table near the center of the room. Both of their plates were piled high with ham and cheese finger sandwiches, salad greens and pumpkin pie topped with generous swirls of whipping cream.

"What did you do with the body?" he demanded.

"Are you crazy?" Sharon Crumbie leaned forward, protecting her plate. She angled her fork in the direction of his big, fat nose.

"You may have fooled that country bumpkin of a sheriff, but you do not fool me." A sweet potato fry dropped from his plate into Dorothy's hair.

"Hey, watch it!" she squealed, plucking the greasy fry from atop her skull.

"Leave us alone before we have you arrested for stalking." Sharon Crumbie's eyes darted to a woman in a security guard's uniform. "Shall I call security?"

"No need," interjected Dorothy Hall. "Here she comes."

"You're bluffing."

"See for yourself." Sharon Crumbie pointed.

Anthony Mulish turned and stiffened. She was not bluffing. The security guard was approaching with a soldierly stride. Straight for them.

As she neared, he noticed that her blue eyes were puffy and pink. "Hi, I'm Eve Landry. Am I interrupting?"

"Hello, Ms. Landry. Mister Ipé here was just telling us that, in his opinion, your sheriff was nothing but a...what did you say?" Dorothy Hall asked caustically, knowing full well what he had said.

"Country bumpkin," interceded Sharon Crumbie.

"That's right, thank you, Sharon. Yes, Ms. Landry, TR was just telling us what country bumpkins *all* you members of law enforcement are. Again, his words, not mine." She batted her eyelashes at him. "Weren't you, TR?"

"We," assured Sharon Crumbie, indicating her and Snookums with a flamboyant wave of the hand, "are certain you and the sheriff are doing everything in your power to catch Frank Ackerman's killer."

Anthony Mulish felt suddenly like murdering both of them.

Ms. Landry's left eyebrow rose. "Might I have a word with you, Mister Ipé?"

"Now is not a good time." Anthony Mulish cleared his

throat uncomfortably. "I was about to eat my lunch." He held up his full dish as proof.

"I promise," pressed the young security officer. "It will only take a minute of your time."

"I'll hold your plate for you, TR," said Queenie Arthur, sliding into a seat to the right of Sharon Crumbie. She wore a sweet-yet-deadly smile as she extended her hand, palm up.

He frowned at her. Those eyes of innocence hid a heart of darkness the likes of which Joseph Conrad had never seen. She'd probably lace his lunch with some nasty, untraceable poison.

He was not about to die here and now. At a mystery conference, of all places.

"That won't be necessary." Anthony Mulish scanned the busy room. "There's a table with a couple of seats over there." He bobbed his head in the intended direction.

"I'd rather we talk in private, Mister Ipé."

"In private?"

"Yes, sir. Please?"

"Well…"

"Look, there's one of those little tables over there. We can take it over to the window and pull up a couple of chairs. What do you say?" She was chewing some fruity-scented gum, opening and closing her mouth, revealing a gap between her two front teeth.

"Fine," agreed Anthony Mulish, seeing that there appeared no way to get rid of her.

The security officer carried the small table meant to hold dirty dishes over to one of the windows overlooking the chancellor's house. Next, with Anthony Mulish looking on, she brought them each a chair.

Satisfied, he rested his lunch on the table and sat. He unfolded his plastic cutlery from the napkin it had come wrapped within.

"What's this all about then?" He dug his fork into some sort of mystery meatloaf. There had been cantaloupe in the buffet line. He had carefully avoided it like the Black Death. Meatloaf, sweet potato fries, a bread roll and two servings of chocolate mousse would have to see him through the afternoon.

"First," Eve Landry began, swirling a paper cup of coffee with her hand, "let me say that I really enjoyed your book."

Anthony Mulish paused, a forkful of ugly brown meat inches from his maw. "You read it?"

"Oh, yes. Death Gets Cozy is really great. So refreshing, you know?"

Anthony Mulish beamed. Oh, how he knew. "That's very kind of you. I can autograph it for you, if you like."

"I'd love that. But I've got the book at home," the security guard told him. "I'll bring it with me next time. In fact, I posted a review of it on my blog. Landry's List. Maybe you've read it?"

"I'm afraid not but I'll be sure to have a look if you'll send my agent the link."

"Thank you. I only post reviews of books that I've enjoyed. Life's too short. I like to share the books I love and don't see much point dissing the books I don't. To each his or her own, right?"

"Completely right." Anthony Mulish chewed his meatloaf thoughtfully. Maybe he had misjudged bloggers with too broad a stroke. "This is all very pleasant but why did you want to speak to me privately, Ms. Landry?"

Eve Landry gazed out-of-doors as she took a sip of coffee. Snow was falling hard. "I heard you were trying to find out who murdered Frank Ackerman."

"Who told you that?"

The security guard's cheeks colored as she said, "Sheriff Winslow mentioned something to that effect." His exact words had been unprintable and unflattering. *Country bumpkin* was kind compared to some of the names the sheriff had had for the author.

"I see."

"I want to help you."

"You do?" Anthony Mulish pushed a bread roll into his mouth and chewed slowly.

"Yes. You're an expert. I'm not."

"But you are a security officer," the author said, after washing his bread down with some tea.

"Face it. I'm a babysitter to a bunch of college kids." She tugged at her shirt. "This uniform is a joke. You want the truth?"

"Of course."

"I applied to the sheriff's department. Twice." She held up two fingers. "Rejected both times."

"I see."

"We could help one another," she pressed on eagerly. "I know this campus. You know people and murder."

Anthony Mulish considered. "Tell me, Ms. Landry. What is in this for you? Aren't you worried you could get in trouble with Sheriff Winslow for meddling in police business? Worse yet, get fired by the college?"

Eve shrugged her bony shoulders. "It's a risk I'll take. This is a dead end job. I've got two kids to raise. Alone. I'd like a chance to show the sheriff that I've got what it takes to be a real cop." She pointed to his empty cup.

"Want some more?"

"Thank you."

She took both cups and went to refill them, leaving him with his thoughts.

"Do we have a deal, Mister Ipé?" she said, sitting back down.

"I don't see why not." He licked his lips, having polished off both dishes of chocolate mousse in the guard's absence. He had also had time to mull things over. The sheriff did not believe him. Eve Landry did. He could use an ally. "So long as you do not share any information I give you with anyone else."

"Of course, not. I'll keep anything you find out in my confidence."

"Good. In fact," he hunched over the small table, "there has been a second murder."

"There has?"

"Yes. I discovered the body in the kitchen earlier."

"That's funny." Eve leaned back into her chair. "I didn't hear anything about it." She scratched behind her ear. "And with the kitchen workers in there, I don't see how it's possible."

Anthony Mulish frowned. "There was no one in the kitchen when I was there."

"You must mean the cafeteria kitchen then."

"Is there another?"

"There's a small kitchen on the other side. Mostly, it's used for smaller special events and private functions. Like this. That's the one being used now. When classes start up again and the students swarm the campus, the main cafeteria will be open for breakfast, lunch and dinner service."

"I see. Sheriff Winslow thinks I imagined the whole

thing. It is his dubious theory that whoever murdered Frank is long gone. But I believe the killer is still here and has killed a second time. Who knows? Our killer may strike yet again."

"I believe you."

"Thank you. In fact, I further believe the killer must have been watching me. They saw that I had discovered the second victim, and so they moved it when I went to report this to the sheriff."

"That jibes with something I recently discovered."

"What's that?"

"When you're finished, I'll show you."

Anthony chugged his tea. The trail was getting hot, he could sense it. He couldn't take the chance of it growing cold. "I'm ready now."

"Okay." She jumped from her chair. "Come with me."

34

"If the killer is on to you," remarked Eve Landry as she and Anthony Mulish rode the elevator upward, "you could be next, Mister Ipé."

Anthony Mulish tensed. While he had not seriously considered it, the thought had crossed his mind. Did he really want to be the target of some madman or madwoman? Catching a killer could be hazardous to his health. Did he really want to be snuffed out before his time? Deprive the world of his greatest works yet to come?

"As a matter of fact, my agent, Ms. Chowdary, was with me at the time of the discovery," he decided to add, figuring there was safety in numbers. Let the killer go through her if they wanted to get to him.

"Is that a fact?" The security guard led him down an empty corridor. The heavy bunch of keys dangling from her belt jingled as she grabbed for a brass key and shoved it in a lock.

"What is this?" Anthony Mulish asked.

"This is, was, Frank Ackerman's room." She pushed the door open wide and urged him to enter first.

"Why are we here?"

"See for yourself."

Anthony Mulish wavered. What if Eve Landry was the murderer? No one knew where he had gone. She could easily do away with him and no one would ever know.

"Is there a problem, Mister Ipé?"

Anthony Mulish forced himself forward, putting one foot after the other, stepping into the room. It was a near-image of Ameena's small dorm room, only Frank's room boasted a narrow window with a view of the parking lot and a cluster of buildings at the opposite side. White vapor billowed steadily from two tall concrete stacks built atop a concrete block bunker.

The door to the bathroom stood open. At the other end of the bathroom was a closed door.

"Each dorm room sleeps two and shares a bath with an adjoining room," explained the security guard. "No locks. Except for the outside doors leading to the hallway."

Sharing a bathroom? How utterly third world, thought Anthony Mulish.

"And there's no way in from the window. No fire escape and we are several floors up."

"Interesting." Anthony Mulish scanned the tiny space. Drab cinderblock walls painted industrial gray and a beige vinyl-tiled floor. "Why did you bring me here?"

"Are you kidding? Look at this mess." Eve toed a mattress leaning atilt, one end on the wall, the other the floor.

"So I noticed. Not to speak ill of the dead, but Frank was a slob. You should have seen his office. Garbage everywhere."

Anthony Mulish stepped over a pile of books and peeked in the bathroom. Damp and mildew clung to the walls. A soggy towel lay in a wrinkled lump on the tile floor.

"That's the thing," explained the security guard, with the smack of her chewing gum. "It wasn't like this before."

"It wasn't?" The bathroom smelled awful. Anthony Mulish retreated to the relatively clean sleeping quarters.

"No. I was here after the police were through with it. It wasn't like the room was neat as a pin. I mean, things were disorderly but not like this."

She pointed to the beds. "The bunk beds have been taken apart. The bookcases have been torn apart too."

"What about Frank's personal belongings?"

"Over there in the corner."

Anthony Mulish spotted the edge of a red suitcase half-hidden by a tatty navy blanket. He lifted the blanket. The suitcase was open and clothing and personal items spilled out. "Why would the killer ransack Frank's room after he was dead?"

"Good question. If it was the killer." Eve leaned in the bathroom doorway. "Maybe it was somebody else."

"Looking for the same thing the killer was looking for," postulated Anthony Mulish.

"Maybe."

"And now our killer has committed a second murder. Maybe because whatever it is they are after is still to be found."

"Or the killer committed the second murder because they feared discovery," suggested Eve.

"Yes. Perhaps our killer was seen by the victim and they tried to blackmail them." That would make a delicious plot twist. The thought suddenly struck him that the murders, as unfortunate as they were, may work in his favor. Add a dose of realism to his next cozy mystery novel. Because there was no doubt in his mind that, if his follow-up novel, A Cozy Ending, did even nearly as well as Death Gets Cozy, he would be writing another.

The dilemma he would face would be how to keep his real name out of the picture. There were a lot of big mouths and loose lips out there. How was he going to shut them up?

Especially big mouths like Dorothy Hall and Sharon Crumbie out to ruin him.

Of course, with luck, they would prove to be guilty of murdering Frank Ackerman. Arrested and imprisoned, with their reputations ruined, they would be, if not silenced, at the very least judged as unreliable and unbelievable storytellers. Let Kinky Boots get them out of that jam.

"Blackmail?" said Eve. "You could be right."

"Yes, the second victim got greedy and now they are dead. Did you tell Sheriff Winslow about this?" He waved at the disarray.

"No."

"Why not?"

"Like I told you, Mister Ipé, I'm hoping we can solve this crime ourselves. Besides, Sheriff Winslow would probably write this off as the work of pranksters. Maybe even accuse me of setting it up myself."

Alarm bells went off in Anthony Mulish's head. The truth was, he didn't know this woman at all. Perhaps she had done all this herself in an effort to worm her way into the sheriff's good graces. Maybe she was using him for her own devious purposes.

The radio clipped to the security guard's shoulder chirruped. She pressed a button to answer. "Landry here."

"Someone or something has set off the alarm on the gymnasium doors," alerted the scratchy voice on the other end.

"I'm on it." Landry signed off. She stopped at the door. "Coming?"

"You go ahead, officer. I'll only be a moment."

She nodded. "Are you sure you don't know who this second body might have been, Mister Ipé? Any idea at all?"

"None," he confessed. "I only saw a bit of whoever they were."

"I see. If you stumble upon anything else, please let me know first." Her eyes were steady and unblinking.

"Promise." He crossed his fingers. There was something very unsettling about Eve. "One thing before you go."

"What's that?"

"You are well-acquainted with the college and the grounds. Tell me, where would a killer hide a body if one had a mind to?"

Eve smiled, exposing the gap in her front teeth. "I can think of a million places. Most of the dorm rooms are empty until next week. Plus, there are thousands of acres of forest out there."

She gestured towards the tiny window. "Not even the great Sheriff Winslow could find a body if a person knew what they were doing and had a mind to hide one."

With that, she opened the door and disappeared down the hall to the sound of her jangling keys. Leaving Anthony Mulish to wonder what Eve Landry would be capable of if she had a mind to.

Anthony shut the door behind her and walked over to Frank's suitcase for a second look. Why had someone ransacked his room?

"You found another body, TR?" Giselle asked breathily as she appeared as if by magic from inside the tiny closet on the opposite wall.

"Don't do that!" Anthony Mulish's hand went to his heart as he swung around. "You about scared me to death. What were you doing hiding in the closet?" He grabbed the closet door handle and peered inside the shallow cluttered space. "Any other surprises in here?"

"I heard voices. I was scared so I decided to hide." Giselle touched her warm fingers to his forehead. "Are you okay, TR?"

"Yes, fine." He cleared his throat. "What are you doing in Frank's room?"

"I was looking for my manuscript."

"The police confiscated it, remember? When they arrested you."

"Right. The sheriff said he would get it back to me." She fumbled through a stack of papers on the desk. "I thought maybe it might have been brought back here."

"I doubt that. Tell me, how long had you been having an affair with Frank?"

"I never had an affair with Frank!" Giselle managed to look horrified. "Never! I only asked him to read my book." She pouted. "What kind of a woman do you take me for?"

There was no good or gentlemanly way to answer that. So he didn't. "Did you ransack this room?"

"No. It was like this when I came in. I only got here a couple of minutes before you. Why?"

"The security officer who came in with me, Eve

Landry, suspects that someone, Frank's killer, tore this room apart looking for something."

Giselle bounced her index finger off her pouty pink lips. "Eve Landry. That name sounds familiar." She blinked twice. "I remember now. There was a typed manuscript of hers right here on this desk the afternoon I dropped my manuscript off. He told me to just add mine to the pile."

"How curious."

She raked a fingernail along the desktop. "Mister Ackerman said she had dropped it off and asked him to read it. He said he took one look at it and that it was rubbish."

"Funny," said Anthony Mulish, "I don't see it here now."

Giselle shrugged. "How is your boo-boo?" Her gentle fingers massaged the back of his scalp.

"A bit sore," Anthony Mulish confessed. He yanked open the desk drawers one by one. The only contents seemed to be those valueless odds and ends that students collected.

"What are you doing?" She placed her hand on his arm and glanced over his shoulder giving him a full dose of patchouli.

"Searching Frank's room for clues."

"Can I help?"

"Watch the door. Make sure no one disturbs us."

"I can do that." She smiled confidently.

As he riffled through his publisher's things on the floor, he asked, "How did you get in here, anyway?"

From the door, which she held open just enough to stick her nose out, Giselle explained, "I still have a master key." She turned around from her position long enough to say. "Sorry. I guess it was wrong of me to keep it."

"Yes," Anthony Mulish agreed, focusing his attention on his task, rummaging through one unremarkable article of clothing after another, and a leather toiletries kit. Several mystery novels, including one by Jay Copperfield, had been tossed out of the suitcase and rested beneath it. "One cannot simply go around willy-nilly entering other people's rooms without their permission, Ms. Mimieux."

"Giselle, please. Call me Giselle." She hung her head. "You are right. I suppose I should turn it in."

"Well..."

"Yes, TR?"

"Since you already have the master key, it seems to me that there is no real harm in keeping it a little longer. It could come in handy." He waved his finger at her. "But you must tell no one that you have it and you are to use it only with my express permission."

Giselle's face broke into a smile. She danced over to him and planted a wet kiss on his lips.

He blushed like a red balloon. "Mind your post." He shooed her off.

Anthony Mulish straightened his jacket. Frank's belongings contained nothing unusual at all. The only thing he'd seen from his fishing expedition, and he'd known this already, was that the publisher had an extremely poor taste in dress.

With Giselle keeping a lookout, he peered in the dorm's tiny fridge and microwave. There were things living in there hitherto unknown on earth.

He stuck his nose in the bathroom, a hotbed of germ-breeding activity capable of producing anything from athlete's foot to the bubonic plague. "Thank goodness my university years are behind me."

Anthony Mulish held a master's degree in English literature. He had considered attending Ole Miss, as had William Faulkner, but feared he would hate the climate. Besides, Faulkner had dropped out early on. Anthony Mulish settled on Stanford, which boasted John Steinbeck as an alumni, even though he also had dropped out early.

"Someone's coming!" Giselle warned.

35

"Close the door," urged Anthony Mulish.

"Right." Giselle quietly pulled the dorm room door shut and stepped away. Anthony Mulish turned out the light. She took his hand in hers as an unseen hand jiggled the knob from the other side.

They held their collective breath as the unknown person on the other side rapped on the door. "Hello? Anybody in there?" squeaked a woman's voice. And it was vaguely familiar to the author.

Giselle gasped as they heard the sound of a key being inserted in the lock. Her fingers tightened around his. "Quick, let's hide!"

"What?" Somebody had nailed his feet to the floor or so it seemed.

Giselle dragged the author to the bathroom, quietly shutting the door behind them. "In here." She pulled him into the damp-tiled shower and slid the opaque glass into its metal frame attached to the wall, concealing them inside. The scent of cheap lime aftershave assaulted his nostrils.

Anthony Mulish wrinkled his nose. His spine pressed against the scummy tiles. Giselle's breasts pushed softly against his chest. Her breath came out in sweet, small puffs, countering the ill-effects.

The author started to speak but Giselle shushed him

with a finger to the lips. "Shh."

They heard the sound of the outer door being opened and bouncing off the wall. "Hello?" After a beat. "What a mess."

Anthony's heart thumped madly. Was it the killer? Was it somebody with a camera? Face it, everybody with a smartphone had a camera now. And everybody had a smartphone.

Except himself.

In his expert opinion, the so-called smartphone was only making mankind all the dumber. He witnessed examples of that each and every day.

Anthony Mulish held his breath, pushing his teeth against his lower lip. How would it look to be discovered hiding in a college dorm shower stall with a mad woman?

What would it do to his literary reputation? Would the Nobel Prize judges hold it against him? Would it nix his chances of one day joining the rarified ranks of Camus, Faulkner and Hesse?

Anthony Mulish smothered a groan of lament. How had he gotten into this embarrassing, if not deadly, predicament?

His mind raced like the greatest supercomputer and spat out an answer: This was all Ameena's fault.

Giselle and Anthony Mulish jumped out of their skin as the unseen woman prowling about rapped on the bathroom door. "Yoo-hoo. Anybody in there?" After a moment, she added, "Last chance. Speak up or I'm coming in!"

Before either could decide whether to reply, the door suddenly swung open. The overhead bathroom light shot on.

Dead silence followed. Giselle and Anthony Mulish huddled, eying one another nervously.

A dark shape snaked towards them. The sliding glass door was thrown back.

"Mister Ipé!" exclaimed Peggy. Her arms flew from her sides. "What are you doing here?" She stepped back, slipping across the wet and banging her hip bone against the sink.

Anthony Mulish and Giselle sheepishly removed themselves from the shower stall.

"And you!" Peggy's eyes grew large and judgmental as she took in the unwelcome sight of the voluptuous young woman holding hands with the illustrious author. "What are you doing here? And with Mister Ipé?"

Peggy grabbed for the author's hand as if to rescue him. "Are you, okay, TR?"

"Yes, yes. Fine." Anthony Mulish noticed that Peggy Wethering's face now bore the signs of far more makeup than she had been wearing when last he had seen her.

"What are you doing in Frank's room? And in the shower?" Peggy dabbed at her face with a hand towel she'd grabbed from a chrome ring beside the basin. She dropped the towel in horror when she saw the black mold growing all over it like a creeping plague straight out of the Middle Ages.

"We were, uh..."

"We heard somebody coming," Giselle said, coming to the author's rescue. "I told TR we should hide."

"That's right." Anthony Mulish freed himself from both women and adjusted his shirt collar. He quickly exited the bathroom, fearful that he'd already picked up some hideous bug from being cloistered in the unhealthy space and fetid atmosphere far too long.

"But I still don't understand what you two are doing in Mister Ackerman's room."

"TR is looking for clues," boasted Giselle.

"Clues?" Peggy followed on the author's heels as he planted himself in the middle of Frank's room.

"TR is going to solve Mister Ackerman's death," Giselle explained. She gently wiped tiny bits of wet crud and soap from the author's sleeve and backside.

"Wow. You are?" The volunteer looked on with distaste at Giselle's unwarranted familiarity with Anthony Mulish. "How exciting."

"Yes." The author cast a look of annoyance at Giselle. How could he conduct an investigation if she blabbed about it to everyone?

Going on the offensive to fend off any further questioning, he asked, "What are you doing here, Miss Wethering?"

"I came to collect Mister Ackerman's personal things. His ex-wife, Beulah, asked me to take care of it for her. The sheriff gave her permission to remove everything."

Peggy ran her hands over the sides of her face. That icky black mold seemed to have clogged every pore in her face. "She said she didn't feel up to the task. I volunteered to gather everything and take it all down to her."

"I see." Anthony Mulish walked over to Frank's open suitcase. "This is pretty much everything."

Peggy swept up the loose clothing and zipped the suitcase shut. She held the weighty red suitcase suspended at her side. "I guess this is it. Coming, TR?"

"In a moment. You go ahead."

The eager and doting volunteer scraped her teeth along her lower lip, wishing she could instead scrape her fingernails across the slut's face. That would put a stop to her smiling.

"Okay." She glanced skeptically at Giselle, hovering possessively near the author. "If there's anything else you need or that I can do for you, TR, please, don't hesitate to ask."

"I won't. Thank you." Anthony Mulish slid his gaze towards the door.

"Sure. I mean, I would do anything for you. Anything."

"I appreciate that, Debbie."

"It's Peggy."

"Right, of course, Peggy."

She smiled at his use of her first name. "I'd better get this to Beulah. But I'll see you at dinner tonight. I was able to score a seat at your table."

"Wonderful. Tell me, did Frank have no children? No next-of-kin?"

"I'm not sure. Beulah didn't mention to me that there were any children."

"I see. That will be all."

The volunteer nodded silently to them both and left, closing the door behind her.

"That was weird." Giselle was the first to speak.

"Yes. Thank goodness, she did not ask us how we got inside Frank's room."

"Right. Hey, what's this?" Giselle pointed to the pile of books that had lain beneath Frank's suitcase.

"What?"

"That bit of paper sticking out of that book there."

"Probably a bookmark."

Giselle moved to the corner of the room where the stash of books lay. She pulled a white envelope from the middle of one of the books. "It's a letter."

"Let me see that." The author took the wrinkled envelope from her hand and read. It had been addressed to Frank Ackerman at the Ackerman Publishing address in New York City. The sender had been Jay Copperfield.

Anthony Mulish extracted the folded letter and read.

"What does it say?"

"It seems Mister Copperfield feels quite strongly that Frank had cheated him out of his due."

"Huh?"

"Copperfield claims Frank or his accountants cooked the books and owe him tens of thousands of dollars. Copperfield is threatening to hire a lawyer and take him to court." He thwacked his fingers against the flimsy paper. The uncouth man hadn't even used a decent stationary, settling for cheap copy machine quality paper.

"Can he do that?"

"He can threaten to but it's an idle threat. Most authors do not earn enough money to afford lawyers and protracted legal cases."

"So what do they do?" Giselle asked.

"Grumble and move on with their lives," Anthony Mulish remarked.

"Or maybe take somebody else's life," suggested Giselle, her fingernails digging gently into his arm.

"There is that," agreed the author. Could Copperfield's accusation be true? Could Ackerman Publishing have been cheating him of his share of the royalties from his books?

That was an unsettling thought. If AP had cheated one author, they could have been cheating others. Including himself.

He might need to have a conversation with Ameena

about the matter. Although, under the circumstances, that could be tricky, considering that he had cut her out of her agent's share of the sequel he had sold to AP.

"What do you suppose the letter is doing here?"

Anthony Mulish slid the letter into the envelope and the envelope into his jacket for safekeeping. "I imagine Frank wanted to discuss the issue with Jay Copperfield. Surely, both were aware that they were each attending the con."

"You sure are smart, TR." Giselle rubbed his back. "Brilliant, really. It is no wonder you are such a great writer."

Anthony Mulish swelled with pride. "Let's go." He took her hand and she didn't complain.

"Where to?"

"To see a man about a letter."

36

Ameena's brain resembled a boiled, gray oatmeal-like mush. Maybe she couldn't see it but she could sense it. A sticky softball-sized lump swelling her cranium and threatening to burst out her ears.

Suffering through two solid hours of manuscript critiques was almost, almost, as tiresome as reading one of Anthony Mulish's novels. Even Death Gets Cozy, his single commercial success, she found derivative and overly twee. She also considered the protagonist both too improbable and of the too-dumb-to-live variety.

She liked the little hermit crab though. Hermie was cute. Reading about his adventures made her think she might like a funky little crab for a pet. And she might have been tempted to follow up on the amusing thought, except it was already trouble enough taking care of the two boys and her husband.

Crabs gotta eat too. What, she didn't know. But they had to eat. And damned if she was going to have to feed it—especially her good blue fin tuna sashimi.

As for Death Gets Cozy, despite her misgivings and much to her amazement after slogging painfully through the story, and laughing in all the wrong places, she had sent the manuscript out to several editors. It had been snatched right up. She didn't know who had been more surprised by that, herself or Anthony Mulish.

Now here they were, the celebrated cozy author and the long-suffering agent who wanted nothing more than to be cozy in her own king-sized bed in her own little eight bed, nine bath house in the burbs.

Stifling a yawn with her knuckles, she forced herself to say to the author of the drivel in her hands, "Yes, that's very nice. Send me the first fifty pages after you've made your revisions."

"Yes, ma'am," replied the eager young redhead across the table. "I listened to every word you said. I'll get right on it." She looked at Ameena as if she were some New York City demigod.

"There's no hurry," the agent said quickly. "Take your time." A couple of years minimum. She was going to need that long to recover from this weekend. "And don't be afraid to make revisions." A million of them, at least.

"Here's my card." Ameena handed out yet another business card from the dwindling pile at her side.

The oatmeal that was her brain screamed in protest. But what could she do? She was duty-bound to be nice to these unpublished authors as they pursued their dreams of publication and best seller's lists.

"Tough day?" asked a man, casting a shadow over the table.

"I'm sorry." Ameena pointedly ignored the speaker as she reached for her purse tucked under the chair. "My time is up and my throat is raw."

Ameena plopped her purse in her lap. "You weren't on my assignment sheet, were you?" She knew the answer to that because she had dutifully and gratefully crossed each name off as they had come and gone. Her crosses to bear.

"No. I'm not here for a critique. I was hoping to talk to

you though." The young man smiled. "Maybe I can buy you a drink? Something to ease that sore throat?"

"Why, thank you, Mister Walters," Ameena said, glancing at the young man's name badge. "I see you are an author." Authors appearing on panels could be identified by green ribbons running along the bottom of their badges. Gold lettering on the ribbons let attendees know that the specimen they were examining and, in many cases worshipping, was a featured author.

This author was short of stature, only a few inches taller than she herself. His light brown hair was parted stiffly to one side and he had a weak chin. He looked like he might tip over at any moment.

"Actually, my real name is Nate. My pen name is Lee Walters." He swept a hand across his forehead. "My editor's idea. She thought it sounded better. Plus, Lee is gender neutral." He grinned an unnecessary apology. "My first cozy mystery came out a couple of months ago." He deftly pulled a card from his pocket and handed it to her.

The front displayed a four-color image of his novel, Murder in the Lion's Den. The graphic artist hired to design the cover had chosen to depict a sated lion resting in its thick-barred cage next to a pile of very human-looking bones.

Ameena found the picture rather unsettling. She didn't like lions, or cages. And she very much did not like the idea of being eaten by a caged lion.

The back of the card contained his social media information. "You can call me Nate," the author suggested.

Ameena smiled and dropped the card into her purse. How many times had she had to do that so far this weekend? Not only was she putting on weight, so was her Gucci handbag.

She could only hope it, and the man standing between her and her first drink at the bar, would somehow miraculously disappear.

"Let's stick to Lee, shall we? Trust me, you need to build your brand."

The newbie author beamed at her, revealing a dimple the size of a meteor strike site. "You see, that's the sort of thing I need to hear."

"You can hear more if you buy me that drink you promised me." If she couldn't get rid of him, the least he could do was spring for the booze.

They found an empty table in the second floor hospitality suite and continued their conversation.

Two drinks closer to heaven, Ameena fondled her wine glass—it was a remarkably good vintage for a California merlot. "Cut to the chase, Lee. What did you want to talk to me about?"

He had talked about the weather, his first published novel (ad nauseam), his dog, his cat, his mother and his girlfriend. How lonely was this guy? How hard up was he for friends?

"I talked to TR this morning."

"Oh?" Ameena braced herself. This was the way many a tale of woe and indignation began.

"Yeah. I ran into him at Brew and Chew. That's a little café in the village across the bridge," he added on noting her confusion.

"Was there a problem? Because if there was—" Ameena signaled for the barman. He splashed more wine into their glasses. It seemed she spent half her time apologizing for Anthony Mulish whenever they went anywhere together in public.

J.R. RIPLEY

She spent the other half of her time drinking and pretending she didn't know him, but that was neither here nor there.

"No, no. Nothing like that," Nate hastened to add. "I mean, I did ask him to blurb my second novel. He said yes. But I think he meant no."

That sounded like Anthony. "Not to worry. I'll have a word with him." Not that she was making any promises.

"Thanks. That would be swell. But, you see, we got to talking about Frank Ackerman's murder."

"You knew Frank?"

"No. I never met him. I'm published by HHL Books. I saw Frank here at the con but we never had a chance to speak. His ex-wife, Beulah, is my agent."

Ameena stiffened. "I see."

"There's more."

"Please continue." Before I fall asleep and plant my face on this table, she left unsaid.

Ameena stifled a yawn. It was mid-afternoon, her brain had coalesced into that soggy oatmeal substance, with an equivalent amount of brain power, her body was limp as a wet dishcloth and she was on her third glass of merlot. What she needed was a nap. And soon.

"I told TR that Beulah really hated Frank. She thought he was a total toad."

"Did she ever make threats against him?" asked Ameena, her brain suddenly kicking back to life or at least a near-life form.

"That's exactly what TR wanted to know." Nate snapped a bite-sized pretzel in half, popped a piece atop his tongue. "Beulah said to me that if she thought she could get away with it, she'd stab him with a pair of sewing shears to get even with him stabbing her in the back."

"A pair of sewing shears?"

"That's right."

"Frank was stabbed with a knife, I believe."

"If you say so."

"Why did Beulah claim Frank had stabbed her in the back?"

"I have no idea. Still, kinda the same thing, wouldn't you say?"

"I suppose." Ameena drummed her fingernails on the table. "I'll ask Sheriff Winslow if the medical examiner is certain of the type of weapon used. Not to say Beulah couldn't have opted for a knife. Just as good or better than a pair of shears."

Beulah was a cut-throat agent. Would she take things a giant step further and start cutting throats, figuratively speaking?

Nate alias Lee was warming to his subject. "I believe Beulah might be the murderer. She's unstable. Crazy even, maybe. Did you know she took out life insurance policies on all her authors?"

"I had no idea." Ameena was stunned. It was unethical. It was immoral. It was totally unacceptable and against all the tenets that the Association of Authors' Representatives stood for. And yet...

What a brilliant idea!

Sign up enough authors, take out a life insurance policy on each. One was bound to kick the bucket now and then. Especially considering that many writers were now starting their careers in their retirement years.

With only a modest investment, she might earn more collecting insurance payouts than she did in residuals with the bulk of her author clients. More money, less work.

Ameena couldn't wait to tell her husband, Ravi. He would be delighted at the concept.

Beulah might be unstable and she might be a murderer, but there was no doubting her financial genius.

"Does Beulah have other authors here at the con besides Jay Copperfield, Lee?"

"I'm not sure. Not that I am aware of. Beulah didn't say. I'll ask around. Do you think that's important?"

"I'm not sure. How large a policy does Beulah carry on you?"

"Fifty thousand dollars."

That was not exactly chump change even for a chump like Beulah. Ameena wondered what a policy like that might cost. Ravi might know. "Why are you telling me all this? Have you told the sheriff your suspicions?"

"That's just it," said Nate. "All I have are suspicions. Nothing solid. TR suggested I tell the sheriff, too. But I can't even prove Beulah ever threatened her ex. If I go to the sheriff and he confronts her, and Beulah finds out I ratted her out, she'll drop me."

"If not stab you with a pair of shears," the agent added with a chuckle, which she regretted the instant she saw the mortified look on the young man's face.

"You don't think—"

"No, of course, not," she replied swiftly, although not surely. The image of fat little bundles of bills totaling fifty thousand smackers swam enticingly before her eyes. Fifty grand could restock the wine cellar, whose reserves had a way of dwindling quicker than one might think.

"I don't mind telling you, Ameena, Beulah scares me."

Nate gripped her hand in his. "Would you consider taking over as my literary agent?"

"Oh, dear," gasped Ameena. "Look at the time." She pulled loose and waved her watch between them. "I'm late for my next meeting. Thank you, Nate. Good talking to you. And thanks for the drinks. I'll be in touch."

She hurried from the hospitality suite on wobbly, wine-filled legs, leaving Nate to deal with his deflated ego and the over-inflated bill for five glasses of merlot.

If what Nate had said was true, she had to wonder if Anthony Mulish could be right, after all. The killer could still be amongst them and may kill again.

Maybe already had.

When it came to believing impossible things, it was becoming easier by the minute. Ever since Anthony Mulish had not only written but successfully published Death Gets Cozy, life had taken on a surreal turn.

She felt like Alice through the looking glass. If Anthony Mulish could become a successful author, who was she to say that he couldn't be right in his wild theories about Frank's murder?

Who was she to think that he couldn't also have been right when he said he had spotted a dead body in the cafeteria's walk-in?

Maybe Anthony really did see a second dead body and it was another of Beulah Ackerman's over-insured authors. Was Beulah crazy? Had she developed a taste for blood after having murdered Frank? Was she going to cash in on her authors' insurance policies until she had no authors left and was sunning herself on some beach in the Caribbean, enjoying the fruits of her ill-gotten gains?

Ameena did not know what to believe but she was

certain of one thing—Beulah was a very dangerous woman.

And smart, don't forget smart.

37

Anthony Mulish and Giselle rode down side by side in what the author had overheard con attendees now referring to as *The Elevator of Death*, since Frank's unfortunate and untimely demise.

Outdoors, the gray sky had morphed to a deep charcoal, the color of briquets. Snow was falling. Fast and hard.

Jay Copperfield, dressed in his favorite leisure suit and Cuddles T-shirt, signed a copy of his latest book for an admirer in a red felt hat near the registration tables.

Anthony Mulish's young fan, Ulaf, chatted with one of the seated volunteers, his con tote bag draped over one shoulder.

"Shall I handle this, TR?" Giselle locked her fingers over Anthony Mulish's right shoulder and whispered softly in his left ear. "I know how to handle men."

Anthony Mulish shivered as if both ends of his anodes had been jolted with a twelve-amp current. "I have no doubt," he replied. "But let me handle this. You wait here."

He took two steps towards his target and paused. What was happening? Was he experiencing a twinge of jealousy at the idea of Giselle making even feigned overtures towards Jay Copperfield?

No. He was not the jealous type. Especially not of

men like Jay Copperfield. Besides, Giselle herself was a mere curiosity. A character perhaps in his next novel.

Nothing more.

"Beat it, Mulish," snapped Jay Copperfield on the author's approach.

"You lied to me."

Copperfield manufactured a chuckle. "Give me a break. You lied to everybody. Claimed to be someone you are not."

"It is done all the time. It's a pen name."

"Yeah, to hide the fact that you are a loser." Copperfield thumped Anthony Mulish in the ribcage with his thumb.

"Do I detect more than a hint of jealousy?" Anthony Mulish asked with a raised and mocking brow.

"What you detect," said Copperfield, annoyed at how much taller the other author was and that he had to bend his neck up at him to look him in the eye, "is not jealousy. What it is, is more than a hint of distaste and disregard."

Copperfield continued. "You're not only a fraud, you're a bag of foul wind that somebody should have deflated years ago. You can't write. And you dress like some amateur stage director's image of a sixties' novelist."

Copperfield swivelled his eyes to Giselle. "And that little playmate of yours you hang around with has all the morality of a Mata Hari."

"Let's leave the young lady out of this, shall we?"

"I do have to hand it to you, Mulish. What Ms. Mimieux lacks in brains, she more than makes up for in the looks department. Tell me, you getting any yet?"

"Getting any?"

"Yeah, you know." Copperfield nudged Anthony Mulish with his elbow.

"I have no idea what you mean."

"Right. I should have known." Copperfield rolled his eyes. "Look who I'm talking to. You wouldn't."

"Let's get back to business," urged Anthony Mulish.

Copperfield stepped aside. "I'm leaving. You've wasted enough of my precious time. Besides, I have no business with you."

"Maybe not," retorted Anthony Mulish, imposing himself between Copperfield and his escape route. "But you had business with Frank, didn't you? Unfinished business."

Jay Copperfield stared up at him.

"Or is that *finished* business now that Frank himself is finished?"

"Just what are you getting at, Mulish?" Copperfield's forehead colored a blotchy purple. That large blotch, just right of center, looked oddly like the Peloponnesian peninsula.

Why, Anthony Mulish realized, in his mind's eye he could see the ancient city-state Sparta situated right there along the Eurotas River. This was, in actuality, an especially deep crease in Copperfield's forehead.

"According to you, Ackerman Publishing cheated you out of your fair share of the royalties on an entire series of mysteries you had contracted for with them."

"Nonsense," scoffed Copperfield. "Where did you hear that?"

"From you."

"Excuse me?" Copperfield balled his hands into fleshy fists. "If you don't shut your lips, I just might shut them for you."

Anthony Mulish slowly removed the letter from his inside coat pocket and confronted Jay Copperfield with it. He extracted the letter from the envelope and snapped it open with a flourish.

"Give me that!" Copperfield lunged for the letter. "That's private property."

"Maybe but it is not *your* private property," gasped Anthony Mulish. Jay Copperfield launched himself at Anthony Mulish, the fingers of his right hand on a trajectory for the incriminating letter.

The letter went flying as both men went tumbling into the registration table. Stan and Peggy struggled to pull them apart.

"Everything okay here?" panted Stan, shirttail dangling and fresh scratch marks on the back of his hand.

"Yeah, just having an editorial disagreement," snarled Copperfield. He forced a smile. "Sorry. Let's talk over here, shall we, TR?" he said with feigned sweetness.

"Is there anything I can do to help settle this?" offered Ulaf, jumping valiantly into the fray. "You dropped this, sir." To Jay Copperfield's dismay, he returned the letter to Anthony Mulish who couldn't resist smirking.

"Thank you." He shook the crumpled letter under Copperfield's nose. It was all the author could do not to punch him in his nose.

"Your assistance will not be necessary, young man," Anthony Mulish told Ulaf.

"Excuse me, Mister Ulafsson," interrupted Reba, baffled by the shenanigans and unsure whether it had all been in good fun or not. "I'd been looking everywhere for you. I have your official badge printed up."

"Thank you, Ms. Lonnegan." Ulaf removed his handwritten nametag, crumpled it up and stuffed it down his trouser pocket. He replaced it in the lanyard with the freshly-printed one. "Sorry to be so much trouble."

"No trouble at all. The registration process can be chaotic. I don't know what happened to your original badge. Everything has been such a challenge," she said, tugging at her wrists. "Mixed-up registrations, not enough tote bags."

"I'm sure you're doing your very best," said Ulaf.

Reba returned to her station at the information desk and Ulaf introduced himself to Jay Copperfield.

"Are you a fan?" inquired Copperfield.

"I'm embarrassed to say, I haven't read your work, sir. But I'm sure I'll love it," he hastened to add.

"No time like the present. My latest is on sale in the bookroom. It's called Fur Whom The Bell Tolls. Give it a read and see how a *real* mystery novel is constructed. Not the trash like TR here pounds out on that ancient typewriter of his."

"I'll keep that in mind." The young man turned to TR Ipé. "Buy you a drink, Mister Ipé?"

"Thank you. That would be most kind."

"I'm afraid he's busy," interjected Jay Copperfield. "Come on, TR. We have some unfinished business to conclude."

Anthony Mulish allowed himself to be pushed along to an alcove behind the stairs. Removed from the sight of witnesses, he was more than a little concerned for his safety.

Out of the corner of his eye, Anthony Mulish saw Giselle scurrying after them at a distance, like a remote shadowy bodyguard or a ninja. That was something.

Although the young woman was completely unpredictable. And he was dubious of what real help she might provide.

"Okay." Copperfield planted his hands on his wide hips. "Where did you get that?" He gestured towards the crumpled letter once again sticking to Anthony Mulish's fingers.

"I discovered it in Frank's room. Tell me, is this letter what you were looking for? Is this why you killed him?"

"What are you rambling about? Are you crazy?"

"Somebody murdered Frank. Somebody ransacked his room."

"It wasn't me."

"Then, who?"

"How the heck would I know?"

"Is it true that Frank cheated you?"

Jay paced narrowly for a moment before answering. "Yeah. It's true. So what? That doesn't mean I murdered the jerk."

"It is a good motive."

"Guess what, Sherlock, you can't collect from a dead man."

"No," agreed Anthony Mulish. "But one can get a certain...satisfaction, shall we say, in knowing that the person who has cheated you is no longer among the living."

Copperfield narrowed his eyes at his accuser. "Just because Frank cheated me doesn't mean I'm the reason he is no longer sucking up air. My agent and I had a plan to cook his goose, all legal like."

Both men paused as an elderly woman made her way awkwardly up the stairs with the assistance of a silver-tipped cane.

"Besides," Copperfield continued once the coast was clear, "you might say I got even with Frank for cheating me by cheating on him with his wife."

"You and Beulah?" This put an entirely new spin on things. And no less reason for Copperfield having wanted Frank dead.

Or vice versa.

"Tell me again," demanded Anthony Mulish. "Where were you at the time that Frank was stabbed?"

"In my room. Writing."

Anthony Mulish's brow shot upward. "I thought you said previously that you were with Beulah."

Copperfield colored. "I was. I was with Beulah. She was watching TV. I was writing. Now can I have that letter?"

Anthony Mulish shoved the letter back into the envelope and held it aloft. "How much did Ackerman Publishing owe you?" He himself was due a royalty statement soon. He would insist that Ameena examine it carefully.

"Near as I can tell, about thirty gees."

"That's a lot of gees." And a lot of zeroes. He slid the incriminating letter back inside his jacket.

"Yeah, it is." Jay Copperfield lunged at Anthony Mulish. His hand dove into the other man's jacket and probed. His fingers bounced off something hard, a flask. "And, now that Frank's dead, I may never see a dime."

"Stop that!" Anthony hollered and swatted ineffectively at his hand.

"Can anybody join this pummeling party?" chortled Sharon Crumbie, hitching up her skirt from across the lobby.

"Because if they can," put in Dorothy Hall, making a fist of her right hand and swinging her capacious purse in her left, "I'd like a go at him."

Copperfield tugged at Anthony Mulish's jacket. Anthony Mulish stomped on his shoe. Jay Copperfield swore, gripping his foot and hopping around the room.

Both men breathed heavily, sweat dripping from their flush faces. "You haven't heard the last of me, Mulish!"

Crumbie and Hall raced to Jay Copperfield's side. "Are you all right, Jay? Has this bad man hurt you?"

"Him?" snorted Copperfield, rearranging his clothing. His T-shirt was torn. An inexplicable ink stain had appeared on it along with some sort of fruit streak. "This weenie couldn't hurt a mouse. Or solve one's murder. Even if it was found in a cat's mouth with its pink dead butt sticking out and fresh blood dripping off the cat's front paws."

The two women laughed with delight.

"No, the dummy here is playing detective. Can you believe that? He thinks he is Hercule Poirot trying to solve Frank's murder."

"That is a hoot," snorted Sharon Crumbie.

"That's nothing. You should have seen him earlier," interjected Dorothy Hall gleefully. "He tried to get Sheriff Winslow to believe he had actually discovered a second dead body in the walk-in refrigerator!"

The two women cackled merrily.

"Hercule who?" Anthony couldn't stop himself from asking the question.

Dorothy Hall stopped mid-laugh and gaped. "Hercule freaking Poirot!" she belted out.

"Never heard of him."

"Figures." Copperfield glared at him.

"Only one of the greatest fictional detectives of all time," replied Sharon Crumbie.

"Created by Dame Agatha Christie," furthered Dorothy Hall. "The novels are classics."

"Classics? I prefer Dostoyevsky, Dos Passos or even Camus, despite his absurdist notions. Those are classics."

"And he thinks he is going to solve a murder," Jay said to his pals Dorothy Hall and Sharon Crumbie.

"I am going to solve Frank's murder," assured Anthony Mulish.

"Oh, yeah?" Copperfield butted his chest against Anthony Mulish. "Care to make a wager on that?"

"A wager?"

"Yeah. I'll bet you that not only can you not solve Frank's murder but that I or even these lovely, brilliant ladies," he waved at the women and they smiled wickedly, "can solve it first."

Sharon Crumbie clutched Dorothy's wrist. "This is just like in the movies, Snookums."

"Yes. What fun!" agreed Dorothy.

"What are the stakes?" Sharon Crumbie rubbed her hands together.

"Stakes?" Copperfield blinked. "Let me think." A smile burst through his whiskers. "I know. If any of us win, you, TR Ipé, must write a blurb—"

"A glowing blurb," insisted Sharon Crumbie.

"A glowing blurb," Jay inserted, "for each of our next mystery novels."

"I love it!" Dorothy bounced up and down on the balls of her feet.

Anthony Mulish gnawed at the inside of his cheek. Be forced to write words of praise for these hacks? He would rather die first. Well, almost.

Then again, what were the odds that any one or all

three of these losers together could solve the mystery of Frank Ackerman's murder?

Slim to none.

"And when I win, you," Anthony Mulish waved his hand at each in turn, "will each write glowing blurbs for my next novel."

The three authors exchanged troubled glances. Finally, Jay Copperfield shrugged and answered for all of them. "We're good with that."

Dorothy groaned.

"Don't worry, Snookums," insisted Sharon Crumbie. "Trust me, *Tripe* here is incapable of finding his feet to put on his shoes without the assistance of a geriatric aide, let alone nabbing a killer."

"Even Kinkichu and Gary the gargoyle couldn't help you find a killer," snapped Anthony Mulish.

"That's Kikiyu and Garçon," hissed Dorothy Hall, shooting him daggers.

Anthony Mulish paid her no mind. "And as for that silly cat of yours, Copperpot, I'm surprised it can find its kibble in the morning, let alone sniff out a killer."

"You leave my Cuddles out of this," warned Copperfield. Cuddles, the ghostly sidekick in his latest series, was based on his own very real cat Cuddles. "I don't take poop from anybody when it comes to Cuddles. She is worth any ten of you and a dozen of your lousy hermit crabs."

"And the name is Copperfield!" raged Copperfield, spittle flying from his mouth, landing on Anthony Mulish's feet.

Anthony Mulish cringed as he looked at his shoes.

"Do we have a bet or not?"

"That's rich." Anthony Mulish polished his shoes, one

after the other, across the back of his slacks. He would remove and burn his pants later. "Any one of you, all three of you could be Frank's murderer."

"Do we have a bet or not?" repeated Copperfield.

"If you think one of us is the murderer, then prove it!" shot Dorothy Hall.

Three sets of eyes taunted him.

Anthony Mulish pulled in a long, slow breath. "I shall." He reluctantly shook Copperfield's outstretched hand.

The deal was done.

38

Ameena teetered a dozen steps out of The First and Last Chance Saloon.

"Hello, Meeny," bubbled Giselle, running to meet her.

Ameena bristled. *Meeny?*

"Have you seen Anthony?" asked the agent. Not that she actually cared. Asking was merely a diversionary tactic. One meant to deflect the slut from whatever she was going to ask of her. Like asking her to read one of her no doubt amateurish, over-sexed and clichéd manuscripts.

"Last I saw him, he was speaking with some of the other authors, Meeny."

"My name is—"

Giselle reached towards the agent's head with absolutely no respect for the other's personal space and flicked her hair from her ears. "Ooh. I love your earrings. They're darling."

Ameena caught the overpowering scent of patchouli on the young woman's slender wrist. "Thank you."

"I know these are diamonds," she pointed. "But what are those black stones in the center?" Giselle leaned in for a closer look.

"These?" Ameena pushed back her hair to better expose the diamond drop earrings that adorned her ear lobes. "Black opals."

"Black opals?" Giselle gasped. "I've never seen such a thing. Absolutely beautiful."

"They were an anniversary present from my husband," Ameena said with a smile of pride.

"You are so lucky. Your husband must love you very much."

"Yes. Thank you." Ameena let her hair fall. "If you don't mind my asking, have you ever been married, Ms. Mimieux?"

"Call me Giselle, remember, Meeny? No, never married. But I hope to be soon." A luxuriant dark eyelash fluttered as she winked.

"Oh? Who is the lucky fellow?"

"TR, of course, silly."

Ameena's jaw dropped to her heels. "*My* TR?"

"He's not *your* TR now, is he, Meeny? After all, you *are* happily married."

"Of course, but—"

"TR isn't gay or anything is he?"

"No, but he's…"

"He's what?"

What could she say? He was TR. He was Anthony Mulish. He was not marriage material. He was barely human material.

As far as she knew, he had never had a serious girlfriend.

The agent shook herself mentally. "I really must talk to TR. Where did you say you saw him last?"

"Downstairs." Giselle pointed downward, as if Ameena didn't know Up from Down.

"Thank you."

"Is everything okay, Meeny?"

Ameena stifled the urge to slap the young creature

across the face with her handbag. The bag cost over six hundred dollars. It would not do to have the leather defaced by Giselle's cheap makeup or its eighteen carat gold buckle dented by the cartilage of her pert little nose. "I've learned something about Frank's murder. I think TR should know."

"You can tell me. I'll tell him."

Ameena hesitated then said, "No, I'd better tell him myself." She didn't trust this Mimieux creature. She was mentally unstable at the very least. Plus, she wasn't ruling out the possibility that the young vixen was also a murderer. Alibi or not.

"Okay, see 'ya."

"Wait. Before you go, Giselle."

"Yes?"

Nate Saget leaned in the door leading to the hospitality suite, one curious eye on them, while making a show of skimming through his program booklet.

"Sheriff Winslow mentioned, that is, he said that Matt is your brother."

"That's right. Same dad, different moms."

Matt had seemed so normal. Had the two been born on different planets too?

Ameena massaged the steel ropes that had once been her neck muscles. "But Matt told TR that you and he, that is, Matt, had..."

"Had what?"

"Had a thing," Ameena said awkwardly.

"A thing?"

"You know." The agent felt her chest heating up. "A sexual thing." She meshed the fingers of her two hands together.

Giselle giggled. "My brother is a real jokester. Always

kidding around." Her face went serious. "He's crossed the line this time."

Giselle patted her pouty lips with a fingertip. "I hope TR didn't get the wrong impression. If he did, I am going to kill Matt."

The young woman smiled, exposing two rows of teeth so flawless and white that only nature could have bestowed them upon her. Ameena's Fifth Avenue dentist could not have duplicated their perfection.

"Have you seen him, by the way?" inquired Giselle.

"Matt? No, not today," answered Ameena, suddenly wondering whether that was relevant. Matt and Giselle were an odd pair and were going to need watching.

Ameena went one way and Giselle the other.

39

Anthony Mulish turned around and discovered that Giselle was gone. So much for his secret weapon.

"Anthony!"

Ameena hurried down the stairs, arms waving. She tripped on the bottom step and fell into his arms.

"Ameena? What's wrong? Are you all right?"

She burped, blushed and put the back of her hand to her lips. "Sorry."

"Are you drunk?"

"Of course not." Maybe a little but that was nobody's business but her own.

Ameena pulled herself together. "I just had the most interesting conversation with Nate Saget." And with Giselle but that could wait for another time. It was important now to focus, which was hard enough because for some reason she could not get the childish phrase eeny, *meeny*, miny, moe out of her head.

She could absolutely kill Giselle.

"Who?"

"Nate Saget. The cozy author."

Anthony Mulish looked at her, his face blank.

Ameena gave a general description. "He writes as Lee Walters. He said he met you this morning at some coffee shop on the other side of the creek."

"That's right. I remember now. Can you believe the

nerve of the man? He asked me to provide a quote for his next novel."

"I know. He told me. So do it already."

"What if I don't like it?"

Which, face it, thought Ameena, was definitely going to be the case. Anthony Mulish liked nothing unless he had written it himself. "Give him a quote anyway. You're a big celebrity now. Think of it this way. A blurb with your name attached will go on the front cover of every book jacket of his. Free publicity for you," she added, knowing it would seal the deal for poor doomed Nate.

"I'll consider it," allowed Anthony Mulish, swayed by the lure of free publicity.

"Fine. It's a minor point anyway. Nate told me something far more important."

"It will have to wait," Anthony Mulish replied. "I have a murder to solve." Dorothy Hall, Sharon Crumbie and Jay Copperfield had left in a proverbial cloud of dust, probably running around sniffing for clues already. He couldn't let them get ahead of him.

The stakes were high. His reputation was at stake. This was far better than any infantile scavenger hunt his childhood friends used to drag him into.

"This is about Frank's murder. Maybe more."

"What do you mean?"

"Nate thinks Frank's ex-wife could be involved."

"Beulah? Why her?" Winning this bet looked suddenly to be very easy and quick work.

"According to Nate, Beulah threatened to kill Frank."

"Yes, yes," Anthony Mulish said, disappointed that her news was of no use to him at all. "He told me that. That means nothing. Plenty of people threaten to commit murders. Few carry out their threats."

"He also told me that Beulah carries life insurance policies on all her authors."

"What does that have to do with anything?"

"Maybe she carried a life insurance policy on Frank. A hefty one."

Anthony Mulish paced the alcove. "Beulah is Jay Copperfield's alibi."

"He's also one of her clients."

"You think he might be next?"

"I have no idea." A headache pounded around inside Ameena's alcohol-soaked brain looking for somewhere to go. Had Anthony sounded hopeful there?

"Beulah and Jay are involved in this somehow. I can feel it in my bones. Interesting."

"What's interesting?"

Anthony Mulish explained about the bet with his cohorts. He could never consider them his peers. "The loser has to blurb the winner's book."

"I see," she replied, carefully remaining neutral in her tone.

What she was really thinking was that authors were as bad as children. Worse even. Childish in every way. Fifteen percent was far too little to be charging in commission for putting up with the lot of them. It ought to be double that amount, easy.

"Wouldn't you love to know whether or not Beulah held a life insurance policy on Frank?"

"I don't know about this life insurance being important. They were divorced," replied Anthony Mulish.

"That doesn't mean a thing. Maybe they had taken out policies on each other while they were still married. Couples do that, you know," countered Ameena. "And never cancelled them."

Ravi had a two million dollar policy on her. She had a four million dollar policy on him. He was the big bread-winner of the family so it only seemed fair.

"I'll ask the sheriff. He might know."

"Why don't I handle that?" suggested the agent. "It will leave you free to concentrate on more important things." And give Sheriff Winslow one less opportunity to strangle, stab, mutilate or plug six full-metal-jacketed bullets into the upper torso of her best-selling client.

"Good idea," concurred Anthony Mulish. "Did you stop to consider that Saget could have been lying?"

"No," Ameena told him. "I didn't." Could the nascent author have been lying to her? "Why would he lie? What could he have to gain?"

Anthony Mulish shrugged. "I have no idea. Why would he lie?" He locked his hands behind his back as he began pacing once more. "To hide the truth. To misdirect you and, therefore, me. And the authorities. As to what he has to gain, that would depend on what he has or has not done."

"You are suggesting he might have murdered Frank?" said Ameena.

"I am suggesting that if Saget lied to you, he has his reasons. I believe I'll see what else I can learn about our Mister Saget."

"You do that," replied Ameena. She rued ever getting mixed up in any of this. She rued becoming Anthony Mulish's agent. "I'm beginning to think that mysteries are best when they are fiction and kept on the page."

"You cannot give up now, Ameena. I need your help."

"What do you expect me to do?"

"Keep your eyes and ears open. You have a way with

people. Talk to them. Listen, learn."

"You left out possibly get murdered by one of them," she said sourly.

"Chin up," urged Anthony Mulish. "I've got your back."

That was no consolation. In fact, it had the opposite effect on her nerves. "What if this is all for nothing, Anthony?"

"What do you mean?"

"I mean, what if Giselle really did stab Frank?"

"That's impossible. She has an alibi, remember? There were witnesses stating that she could not possibly have committed the murder."

"But what if she did? She confessed. What if it was all an act? A maniacal, genius plot to hide the fact that she really is the killer?"

Ameena scrubbed her hands over her face. "What if the witnesses are mistaken? Or maybe the murder happened earlier or later, or she has an evil twin sister, or... I don't know what."

"Do you really think the witnesses could be wrong? I'll tell you what, I'll find out who reported seeing Giselle and go over their stories with them. Will that make you feel better?"

"Yes. It would."

"Good. There is one other flaw in your theory, however."

"What's that?" she was afraid to ask.

"If you believe for even a minute that Giselle is guilty, that she planned this elaborate charade to hide the fact that she brazenly stabbed Frank to death—"

"Yes?"

"Then you are crediting her with a great deal of cunning and cleverness. Ameena, do you really believe Giselle has the capacity to brutally stab a man to death, proclaim herself guilty, knowing she would be proven to be a liar at worst or insane at best?"

"But—"

Anthony Mulish refused to yield the floor. "And then pull the wool over everyone's eyes, the eyes of the sheriff too?"

Ameena glared daggers at the author. Sometimes she absolutely, positively hated Anthony Mulish *and* TR Ipé.

"No. You're right," she was forced to admit. "It's not possible. Although she certainly has pulled the wool over your eyes."

Ameena threw her hand over her mouth. She hadn't meant for that tidbit to slip out. She was angry. Not thinking straight.

"What is that supposed to mean?"

"Nothing. I'm tired. And, you're right, maybe a little tipsy." She performed a little wobble for his benefit.

There was no point warning him about the vixen's intentions. Giselle was doomed to fail anyway. If she didn't know better, she might think that he was enamored of the woman-child. But Anthony Mulish was not the marrying type. He refused to even keep a dog, a cat or a pet goldfish. The nearest thing he had to a pet was Hermie the hermit crab. And he was a figment of the man's imagination, existing only on paper. "I'll go telephone Sheriff Winslow."

"Good idea. I am going to have a word with Jenny."

"Why Jenny?"

"She worked for Frank. She may have more information than she has been sharing."

"Such as?"

"Did I tell you Copperfield is suing Ackerman Publishing over royalties?"

"No. It's news to me." But she wasn't surprised. Authors were rarely a happy bunch. Especially when it came to their royalty money. "Are you sure?"

"Yes. I found a letter to Frank written by Copperfield amongst his personal effects. I confronted Copperfield about the matter and he confirmed it. This is not something I should be concerned about, is it?"

"No. I review each royalty statement carefully when it comes in. I'm sure everything is aboveboard." Damn. The first thing she was going to do when she got back to Long Island was to reopen those statements and study them line by line. She had them in a drawer somewhere.

"Good. There's a lot of money at stake."

Ameena agreed. "I'll make that call to the sheriff now." Not that she held up much hope that he would tell her whether or not Beulah had a life insurance policy on her ex, if he even knew or had a way of getting that information.

"Do you know where I might find Jenny?" Jenny Garrett wasn't the bookkeeper, but she might also have some insight into this whole royalties issue. Anthony Mulish could not get the nagging worry out of his mind that Ackerman Publishing might be cheating him out of his fair share of his royalties the same way they had reportedly cheated Copperfield. He was determined to track the young woman down.

"If she's not in one of the panels, try outside. The woman smokes more than a chimney."

"One thing before you go, Ameena." Anthony Mulish held up a finger. An unsettling thought had occurred to him.

"Yes?"

"Do you have a life insurance policy on me?"

"No." Not yet, anyway. In fact, could she have two policies? One for Anthony Mulish and one for his alter ego, TR Ipé? It was an intriguing idea. She'd run it by the lawyers. "I'm not even sure that would be ethical."

Ethical or not, it could be very profitable. Ravi would call it good business sense.

40

Ameena stepped outdoors but only momentarily. Frigid wind gusted twenty miles per hour. Snow swirled around her, biting her exposed cheeks and hands. There had to be a foot of snow on the ground already.

With no end in sight.

This was what she imagined the surface of Pluto to be like.

Reluctantly, she dialed the sheriff's office. A woman answered and she was put through to Sheriff Winslow at his home.

"Why are you calling me, Ms. Chowdary?" Sheriff Winslow said angrily. "I'm off duty." Technically, he was never off duty. That was one of the major drawbacks to his job. But she didn't need to know that.

"TR and I were wondering if Beulah Ackerman held a life insurance policy on her ex-husband, Frank."

There was a long silence. She heard the sounds of a ballgame in the background with much accompanying moaning, groaning and shouting.

"I have no idea. Why?"

"One of the authors here at the conference, a Nate Saget, maybe you met him?" Her question answered with silence, she continued. "Anyway, he mentioned that she often carried insurance policies on her clients. I thought perhaps—"

"That she took out a million dollar policy on the victim and then snuffed him? Don't you think that's a little obvious? You are reading too many mystery novels. You are becoming a victim of your own habits."

Ameena's temper flared. "It so happens that Nate Saget also told me, and TR, that Beulah had made threatening comments toward Frank."

"Gee," Sheriff Winslow said against a background of sudden, drunken cheering. "What do you know? A divorced couple hurl threats at one another. If I arrested every man and woman for that, I'd have practically everybody in the county behind bars."

"I'm only trying to help, Sheriff."

Sheriff Winslow sighed into the phone. "I know. Look, I'll telephone Ackerman Publishing on Monday. I'll see if they can tell me the name of his insurance company and whether he has a policy naming his ex as beneficiary."

"The policy could be in Beulah's name."

"I'll check on her too," snapped the sheriff. "Anything else?"

"How is the case coming?"

"Like I told you, we have one dead man and one stolen vehicle. Our killer, whoever he or she is, is long gone."

"There's been no trace of the stolen car?"

"Have you looked out a window lately? It's snowing to beat all. Hard to send out searchers in weather like this. Our killer is probably holed up somewhere sitting out the storm."

"What about the melon?"

"The what?" Sheriff Winslow swore. "What the—" More invectives followed. "What kind of moron—"

"Is everything all right?" Ameena asked.

"Huh? Yeah, sorry. Watching the game. What were you saying?"

"I was asking if you found anything on that cantaloupe. Any evidence?"

"You're kidding me, right?"

The agent took that for a no. His cutting the connection clinched it.

41

Matt corralled Anthony Mulish in the booksellers' room where he'd gone in search of Jenny Garrett. "Excuse me, Mister Ipé, sir?"

"Hello, Matt. How's the head?" Anthony Mulish asked, remembering how he had clubbed the young man in the ear the night before with a film canister.

Had it really been only one night? It seemed ages ago.

Then again, it was a dead body ago, very possibly, two dead bodies ago.

"Fine, sir." Matt rubbed said ear. The truth was it still stung. He had discovered several drops of blood on his pillow that morning.

A bookseller interrupted them and shyly asked Anthony Mulish to sign a stack of his novels for her.

"Of course," agreed Anthony. The bookseller shoved some books aside, set a dozen copies of Death Gets Cozy in front of him on the table. She handed him a fancy ballpoint pen.

Anthony Mulish settled into a chair and began autographing. He had gotten halfway through writing Anthony in the first copy when he realized he was signing Death Gets Cozy. He hurriedly scribbled out Anthony and, with a flourish, signed as TR Ipé.

Would the bookseller complain? Would she make him pay for the damaged stock?

Rather than find out, the author set that book at the bottom of the pile. By the time the bookseller discovered his mistake, he would be long gone. Glancing up to see if the bookseller had been watching, he realized Matt was hovering. "Is there something you wanted, Matt?"

"Actually." Matt shuffled his feet. "I wanted to apologize."

Anthony Mulish placed his hand down on the title page of the open book he was about to sign. "Apologize? For what?"

"Well, you see..."

Anthony Mulish narrowed his gaze. "It wasn't you that hit me in the supply closet last night, was it? Getting your revenge for me boxing your ear, were you?"

"No, sir. Not at all!" Matt waved his hands furiously through the air. "It's nothing like that. I would never do such a thing!"

"What is it, then?"

Matt took a big breath. "I lied to you, that is, I may have given you the wrong impression about me and Giselle."

"Ms. Mimieux?"

"That's right." Matt blushed with discomfort.

"I don't understand." The author realized he had been doodling inside the book with the pen. Large blue circles and squiggles marred the title page. He hastily scribbled his signature and added that book to the bottom of the stack too.

"She's my sister."

"Who is your sister?" Matt was the most exasperating young person he had ever met.

"Giselle, sir." Matt stared at the carpet.

"Giselle is your sister?" blubbered Anthony. "But you said—"

"I know what I said, sir. And I apologize." Giselle had come down on him like a swarm of bees. She had made Matt promise to apologize for his little joke ASAP. He didn't see what the big deal was but fear of his big sister clobbering him had spurred him on. And quickly. "I was joking."

Anthony Mulish stared at the college student in jeans and a rumpled gray sweatshirt. "A joke? Jokes are meant to be humorous. Your comment about you and your sister, that was in poor taste, young man. Very poor taste."

"Yes, sir," Matt said softly. "I guess I wasn't thinking." Anxious to change the subject, he asked, "How is your head, Mister Ipé, sir?"

"Fine, fine," dismissed the author.

"I sort of feel like it is my fault that you got hurt. If I hadn't told you about the supply closet, you never would have been attacked. Did you find what you were looking for?"

"I found the microphone. Before I could examine it more closely, someone knocked me unconscious." A bit of an exaggeration but he was a writer, after all. "When I woke, it was gone."

"Bummer. On the bright side, you could have been killed."

The possibility had crossed the author's mind. "I prefer not to dwell on the thought," said Anthony Mulish.

Ignoring the author's wishes, Matt said, "Why would somebody want to keep you from taking a look at some crummy microphone? Do you think it could have been important, like a murder weapon?"

"Frank was stabbed to death. Not bludgeoned, Matt."

"I didn't mean Frank, sir. I guess I should have said *potential* murder weapon."

"Potential?"

"Forgive my saying this, but maybe somebody was trying to murder you. With that microphone. The killer might have tampered with it."

"That was what I was attempting to learn. And now it is missing and we will never know if it was a case of mere negligence or attempted murder."

"In either case, it wasn't me, I swear. If I had noticed anything dangerous about any of the equipment, I never would have set it up. Not that somebody couldn't have switched it afterward. Not me, of course," Matt was quick to insist. "But the room was set up hours before your talk."

"Of course."

"But somebody."

"Your sister perhaps?"

"Giselle? Nah, she's harmless."

Anthony Mulish wasn't sure he agreed with that assessment but there were more pressing issues at hand. "Who had access to the microphones?"

"Practically everybody here. The school doesn't exactly keep them under lock and key." Matt's gaze shifted around the room then landed once again on the author. "It could be someone in this very room."

Anthony Mulish cleared his throat to dispel the choking sensation that had crept in. Matt Mimieux had an unsettling way with words.

Once again he was struck with the thought that finding and exposing a killer was one thing. Being the potential target of a killer was quite another. He had many more novels to complete. His *oeuvre* was incomplete. And he had wasted valuable months writing cozy mysteries.

Anthony Mulish wished to live a long and productive life yet, as had Herman Hesse, for instance. The writer had won a Nobel Prize for literature and lived to the ripe old age of eighty five.

In a perfect world, he would achieve the same and more.

Glancing at the open title page on the table, he was surprised to see that he had inadvertently doodled a rather poor rendition of Hermie the hermit crab.

With a frown, the author set down the pen before he could do any more book damage. He was not the world's greatest multitasker and he knew it. "Did you tell anyone else about the supply closet, Matt? More precisely, did you tell anyone that you had told me about it and that I was going there?"

"No, sir!" swore Matt. "Who could I tell? It was late. I didn't see anybody."

"Pity. I am helping the police with their investigation, you see," Anthony Mulish told him, stretching the truth a tad. Sheriff Winslow might have used the word *hindering* instead. "Do you have any idea who might have murdered Frank?"

"Actually..."

"Yes?" Anthony Mulish leaned closer.

"I hate to say anything," said Matt. "He's with the conference. The guy did hire me to help out and I can use the extra money."

"Really, Matt." The author squeezed his eyes shut a moment. "If you know anything at all, you must tell me. Who are you talking about?"

"Mister Dooley," the young man admitted.

"Stan Dooley?"

"That's right." Matt opened up now like a dam breaking. "I saw him and Mister Ackerman last night before the murder. They were arguing."

"About what?"

"I wish I knew. I was too far away to hear anything but hollering. But Stan, boy, was he mad. He actually socked Mister Ackerman in the jaw!"

"Did he now?" Anthony said thoughtfully.

"Then what happened?"

"Mister Ackerman called Mister Dooley some nasty names and tromped off."

"Where was this?"

"Outside Mister Ackerman's room."

"What were you doing there?"

"While the film was playing, I ran up to my room. I was hungry and wanted to grab a snack. My room's on the same floor as Mister Ackerman's. I was only gone a matter of minutes. I didn't kill him, if that's what you are thinking."

"Not at all, Matt. Not at all. Did they see you?"

"No. I don't think so. I stayed out of sight. In the alcove where the stairs come out."

A timid fan approached the men and held out a permanent marker and a copy of Death Gets Cozy that she had just purchased. "Autograph, Mister Ipé?"

"Did you purchase the book here?"

"Yes." The young lady shot Matt a puzzled look. "Is there a problem?"

Anthony Mulish wiggled his fingers in come hither fashion. "Give it to me." She handed him the book. He rested it on his knee and signed with a flourish: TR Ipé.

"Thank you," she gushed and dropped it in her tote bag. She handed her phone to Matt. "Mind taking our picture?"

"Sure," agreed Matt.

"Put that away," snapped the author. "This is not the monkey house and I am not on display." He indicated for Matt to give her back her cellphone. "Off with you now." His once wiggling fingers transformed into the strands of a broom as he shooed the red-faced young woman away.

"Tell me, Matt," said the author, ignoring the stunned look on the younger man's face, "why did your sister confess to murdering Frank Ackerman?"

"Like she told the police. She was hoping the publicity would help her get a book deal. She's really desperate to get published."

"That's a very strange way to go about it." Based on what he had seen of Matt and Giselle, the entire Mimieux clan might be unstable. Was Giselle so desperate that she would kill to get published? Not that Frank Ackerman would be alive to publish her, but she might find a publisher willing to take her work once she was behind bars. Sadly, even murderers could become celebrity novelists these days.

"Hard work and dedication. That's what it takes."

"Yes, sir. I'll tell Giselle you said that. By the way, it's nice of you to take her under your wing."

"Under my wing?"

"Yeah. My sister said she is really grateful to have you as her mentor."

"Interesting." Anthony Mulish recalled the sight of her manuscript flying out the window to a wet and muddy grave. Her writing was atrocious. Full of sex and nonstop action scenes. Her prose was so bad he hadn't been able to erase it from his mind. "Do you know where I might find Stan Dooley?"

"You mean now?"

"Yes, Matt, now." The more time the author spent with Giselle's brother, the more exasperating he was finding the boy.

Matt grinned. "Follow the footprints."

"Excuse me?"

"If I'm not mistaken, you'll find Mister Dooley at the chancellor's house."

"I was under the impression that the chancellor was away."

"When the cat's away, the mice will play," came Matt's enigmatic answer.

"Must you always talk in riddles?"

"Take my advice, Mister Ipé. Follow the footprints. If I'm right, they start at the front east exit, near the restrooms."

"I'll do that." Anthony Mulish grabbed a fresh copy of Death Gets Cozy and signed quickly.

"One thing," said Matt before walking away.

"Yes?"

"When you get to the chancellor's house, you might want to knock first."

"Why? Is someone going to come out of the shadows and strike me on the back of the head again?" joked the author.

"No, but what you see through the windows might have the same effect."

Matt moved from the room like an enigma, leaving the author with more questions than answers.

42

Anthony Mulish tramped intrepidly through the deepening snow. He was on the hunt for a killer. He felt like a character in one of his own novels.

Was this how Sherlock Holmes felt when he was tightening the figurative noose around a culprit's neck?

There might be something to this mystery-solving thing. Catching a killer was mentally challenging and invigorating of body and spirit.

When this was all over with and he got back to New York City, he would make a trip to the library and check-out some of Conan Doyle's Sherlock Holmes stories and see for himself. Anthony Mulish had only read *Sir Nigel* and *The White Company*, two of Conan Doyle's historical novels. He had heard that Conan Doyle himself held those novels in a much higher regard than he did his more popular Sherlock Holmes tales.

A feeling that Anthony Mulish understood only too well.

The snow was getting deeper. The temperature was dropping. This morning there had been a mere dusting, now the snow was ten inches deep, more in spots. He took this as a metaphor for the mysteries confronting him—the stabbing of Frank Ackerman, and the case of the missing body.

He was getting deeper into that case too. The two

things had to be connected. He did not know how but he had no doubt that a connection existed.

All he had to do was find that connection, that missing link between Frank Ackerman and the unknown second victim. That would lead him to the killer.

How hard could it be?

He puffed. The air was icy cold. He pictured rime forming along the inside walls of his lungs. His nose dripped without end. He pulled a handkerchief from his rear pocket and wiped again.

This bloody conference seemed determined to kill him one way or the other. Natural or unnatural. In the end, dead was dead.

He stomped his frozen feet on the frozen ground, sending needles of pain up to his knees.

The chancellor's house stood dark and the puce curtains in front had been pulled tightly shut. Footprints filling with snow, two pairs, he noted, swung in a tight arc to the left. He followed them.

The footprints hugged the large colonial house, skirted a thick hedge and rounded to the rear of the home. A gazebo, caked with snow, served as the centerpiece of the barren and colorless garden.

Anthony Mulish paused, catching his breath, letting the spinning top that seemed to occupy his cranial cavity come slowly to a stop. Irregular clouds of moist air dancing past his eyes reminded him that he was breathing.

He heard only his tortured breathing. It was otherwise quiet. Eerily quiet. The looming woods, the bare trees, the mounding snow, the dark and dangerous looking clouds, all settled over him like an encroaching enemy.

Give him the city any day.

He glanced up at the chimney for evidence of activity inside. Nothing. He crept to a stone-framed window near the back. A two-foot gap existed in the pale yellow curtains. Soft light emanated from within. The snow crunched maddeningly underfoot. Who knew snow could be so loud?

The cold wet snow worked its way inside his shoes and clung to his socks, soaking him through. The ends of his toes felt like some sadist was stabbing them with sharpened icicles. He would be lucky to survive this little adventure without frostbite. Matt would be to blame for any subsequent amputation.

Lamenting his lack of gloves, Anthony's numb fingers settled on the cold stone window ledge. His foot slipped on a buried rock as he jostled closer. His nose bounced off the rough stone.

His eyes teared up. For a moment, he was blinded. Wiping his eyes frantically, he gingerly touched his nose. His fingers came back with a trace of blood. He dabbed at his nose with a handkerchief.

Stuffing the bloodied and soiled cloth back in his pocket, he carefully pulled himself up to the window once again. Two pairs of legs, visible from the bare calves to the bare feet, dangled off the edge of a black velvet sofa.

Anthony blinked, cupped his hand over his brow, and peered more intently. Definitely two pairs of legs. Definitely naked. Definitely one male, toes splayed and aiming downward, and the other decidedly female with narrow elegant feet and red toenails pointing towards the ceiling.

Light spilled from an antique brass lamp on the end

table.

A sneeze erupted from Anthony Mulish's nose. Blood and snot splashed against the window. The glass pane resembled the site of a small bird impact. A man's head, tousled hair and glistening eyes shot up from behind the sofa. A moment later, a woman, equally tousled and red-faced, joined him.

Anthony Mulish turned and ran.

He hadn't made it eight paces when he tripped on an unseen stone garden bed edging hidden under the snow. Landing face first, he hissed as the freezing snow hit his exposed flesh.

He slipped and slithered. Dress shoes were not made for trudging through ice and snow. Nor were they meant for running.

Before he knew what was happening, rough hands shot under his armpits and yanked him up from behind. He was spun around.

"Mister Ipé!"

Anthony Mulish struggled. "Do you mind?"

"Sorry." Stan released his hold on the special guest of honor. "Are you all right?" The organizer's cheeks glowed red while the skin around was pasty and white.

"Yes, yes." Anthony Mulish brushed the caked snow from his trousers, shirt and jacket. Snow had managed to insinuate itself under his shirt. He squirmed. "At least, I believe so."

"What are you doing out here?" Stan looked buffoonish in a woman's fluffy baby blue robe falling to his knobby knees and a pair of sturdy black rubber winter boots. Tufts of matted hair peeked from the V of his robe. He was clearly naked underneath.

"Looking for you. What were you doing in there?"

"With the storm coming, I wanted to make sure everything in the house was in order."

Anthony Mulish smiled wickedly. "By taking off all your clothing and climbing atop Eve Landry?"

"You saw that?"

"Indeed I did."

Stan tugged at the lapels of the robe. "Why don't we go inside?"

"Yes, I think that would be a good idea." He waved for the organizer to lead the way.

Inside, they found Eve buttoning her shirt. Her hair was unkempt and her lip gloss smeared. Her shoes stood near the fireplace next to a pair of men's hiking boots. Stan's, no doubt. Four socks, two white and two argyle completed the scene.

"Hello, Mister Ipé." Eve scooped a maroon throw pillow off the floor and returned it to the sofa.

"Ms. Landry."

"Won't you sit down?"

She indicated the sofa. Recalling what the two of them had been so recently up to, and so naked at that, on that very sofa, Anthony Mulish opted for a comfortable high-back velvet chair facing it from across an Oriental rug.

Stan took a seat inches from Eve. Both smiled sheepishly. The organizer struggled to remain decent, shoving the end of the robe between his thighs. "Mister Ipé, I'd like to explain."

"Please," replied the author. "I would rather not hear about your sexual practices. Although, I do seem to remember hearing that you are married, Mister Dooley."

Stan lowered his eyes. "Separated, actually."

"Of course." Anthony Mulish stared glumly at the

empty and lifeless fireplace. A roaring fire was what he needed to exorcise the cold that clung to him like the arms of Death itself. "Let us put that aside."

Eve rose. "Would anybody care for something to drink?"

"I'd kill for a cup of hot tea," said the author.

"I'll see what I can find. Stan?"

He shook his head no. She scrambled to the rug in front of the fireplace, picked up her shoes and socks and departed for the kitchen.

"Listen, TR," Stan said, one eye on the doorway through which the security officer had retreated, "I hope you will keep this between us."

"I do not see why not."

"Thanks," said Stan with a sigh. "Because if my wife found out, she would—"

"Just so long as you are completely honest with me. And tell me what I want to know."

Stan appeared confused. "I'm afraid I don't understand. I'll help you if I can. What exactly is it that you want to know?"

The author leaned back in his seat, confident that he had the upper hand. "It is easy. I want to know what you and Frank were arguing about mere minutes before his death. I want to know why you hit him."

Stan's shoulders sagged. "Do you mind if I get dressed while we talk?" He tugged at the cloth of his robe. "I feel sort of silly in this."

"Please do," the author said with a lazy wave of his hand. Stan didn't look silly. The man looked preposterous.

The organizer picked his trousers, underwear, T-shirt and sweater off the floor. Moving behind a tall wing-backed chair in the corner near the floor-to-ceiling bookcases, he let the robe fall to the ground and dressed quickly. "I saw Frank get up and leave the movie. I knew most everybody would be busy watching Strangers on a Train and that would be my chance."

"To kill him?"

"No! I only meant to talk to him," Stan said, zipping up his trousers. "I mean, we are grownups. Two reasonable men."

"What is it that you wanted him to be reasonable about?"

Stan stuffed his arms into the sleeves of his sweater. "Eve's novel."

"Eve's novel?"

"Yes. She's a writer. A good one, too."

"Go on."

Stan picked up his shoes and socks and carried them to the sofa. He sat. "Ackerman verbally slammed her manuscript. Absolutely tore it apart. Eve was devastated. She spent years writing that novel."

"You should have seen her. Crying her eyes out. Broke my heart." Stan wiggled his feet into his argyle socks. "I thought Ackerman was being totally unreasonable. It was my idea to send him an invitation to the conference, too."

"So Eve was terribly upset. You must have been quite angry."

"Like I said, I did not murder him. I went looking for him hoping that he would give her manuscript a second chance."

"What did Frank say?"

A frown fastened itself to Stan's face. "Ackerman told me that publishing was his business and that I should stick to mine."

"Which is?"

"Tax preparation."

Eve Landry reappeared with a black enamel tray between her hands. On it sat a china teapot, three cups, spoons, cream and sugar. She handed the first cup to Anthony Mulish. He sweetened his tea and stirred slowly.

"I was explaining to TR what happened the other night," Stan said, taking a delicate cup from the tray, to which he added a healthy dose of both cream and sugar.

Eve set the tray carefully on the ottoman in front of the sofa. "What about the other night?"

"The night of Frank's murder," Anthony Mulish explained. "You were not exactly honest with me, Ms. Landry. Your involvement with Frank goes far deeper than merely an opportunity to impress the sheriff with your detective skills."

"You," the author said, pressing his elbows into his knees, "had a very strong motive for wanting the man dead."

"I didn't. I swear. I didn't want Mister Ackerman dead at all." She turned to Stan for support. "I only wanted him to reconsider my novel." The security officer blushed. "I am sorry I was not wholly honest with you, Mister Ipé. I didn't think any of it was relevant."

Anthony Mulish asked, "Where is this manuscript of yours now, Ms. Landry? I did not notice it in Frank's quarters."

"It's at my house. I took it. I was afraid somebody—"

"The authorities?"

She nodded. "Yes, I thought the sheriff might get the wrong idea."

"Afraid he might consider you a suspect." Anthony Mulish sighed and finished his tea. He swiped at his nose with his handkerchief, happy to see that the bleeding had stopped.

"I did not murder Mister Ackerman either, if that's what you are thinking." She squeezed her lover's hand.

"I don't know what to think." The chiming of an antique clock in the far corner near the stairway made him jump. He was alone in an otherwise empty house with two liars, cheaters and possible murderers. That was what he was thinking. Not that he was going to tell them that.

They might attack him. He wouldn't stand a chance. He pictured his dead body stuffed up the cold chimney. An ugly and undignified end to his life and career.

"My money is on Jenny Garrett," announced Stan.

"Frank's editor?"

"Former editor, remember?" Stan replied. "Frank demoted her to copy editor or something."

"Yes. I believe I heard something to that effect." Anthony Mulish tugged at his tie. "You think she would murder him over such a thing?"

That would make he himself somewhat responsible for Frank's death. Then again, Frank was a grown man. Just because he had urged Frank to give him a new editor didn't make him personally responsible for Jenny Garrett's unhappiness and potentially lethal response. Did it?

"Frank was furious when Jenny Garrett showed up here," said Stan, interrupting the author's thoughts. "I got an earful from him at the bar."

Anthony Mulish nodded. Frank had said as much to him.

And she had been the one to "find" him after he had been struck down in the supply closet. Coincidence? Or cunning?

He didn't know but he was determined to find out.

"I wonder where Jenny was at the time of Frank's murder," Anthony Mulish pondered aloud.

"That's easy," replied Eve. "She was in the elevator with me and several other attendees."

"Was she now?" Anthony Mulish stroked his chin.

"You're right," agreed Stan. "I think I saw the lot of you go up in the same elevator after the film."

"The problem is," Anthony Mulish said, "Frank was still alive at that time. Jenny surely didn't stab him in an elevator full of witnesses." He turned to the security guard. "Did Jenny and Frank get off the elevator together?"

"No, I mean, I don't know. I got off on the second floor. I don't know where either of them went after that."

"Is it possible that Frank was murdered someplace other than the elevator?" theorized Stan. "And then the killer dragged him to the elevator?"

"That would take some strength," answered Anthony Mulish. "Frank was by no measure small."

"Besides," added Eve, "why would the killer move his body to the elevator? Wouldn't that be risky?"

"Maybe the killer was going to move the body. Get rid of it. Out in the woods, perhaps." Anthony gazed out the window at the blanket of snow. "The forest could be riddled with dead bodies for all we know."

"That's a cheerful thought." Eve frowned and hugged herself. "We'd better be getting back to the conference, Stan."

Stan agreed. "It will soon be time for the banquet and live auction. People are going to wonder where I've disappeared to."

"Speaking of disappearing," said Anthony Mulish. "Can you think of anyone else, attendee or volunteer, who might be missing?"

"Missing?" echoed Stan. "How do you mean?"

"Is there anyone unaccounted for?"

"Not that I can think of," Stan replied after giving the question some thought. "We capped attendance at three hundred and everybody's here. And I don't believe any of our volunteer staff have disappeared. Why?"

"It means our killer could very likely still be among us." It might also mean the dead body he'd stumbled on in the walk-in fridge was not an attendee or staffer.

"I suppose," answered Eve. "But Frank's killer could have been a college employee, a townie or a random stranger."

"Maybe even somebody who knew Frank was going to be at the conference and followed him here," Stan suggested.

"All very good points," replied Anthony Mulish, realizing this mystery-solving business was a lot more complicated than it seemed on the face of it. "But my intuition tells me there is a murderer among us."

"Does your intuition tell you whether or not he or she is likely to strike again?" Eve asked, zipping up her parka.

"Not if I have anything to say about it," assured Anthony Mulish. "I'll have this mystery solved in no time."

Stan pulled on his gloves and marched to the side door from which they had entered. "By no time you'd better mean about thirty-six more hours." He opened the door, bracing himself against the cold wind and blowing snow. "Because the conference will be over at the end of tomorrow and everybody will be off in all directions. Good luck to anybody finding Frank's killer then."

Anthony Mulish followed them outside. Eve grabbed a key from her ring and locked up behind them. "No luck necessary," he said, plodding through the foot-deep snow. "A good detective uses his wits, his cunning, his—oof!"

Anthony Mulish slipped on a buried patch of ice and went sailing sideways. He slammed into the trunk of a snow-laden pine tree and bounced off.

Stan and Eve caught him and escorted him back to the conference.

43

Anthony Mulish donned his vintage Arthur Miller tuxedo and plastered on his falsest smile. Solving Frank's murder was going to have to wait. This was the big night. Murder Under Cover's banquet dinner, the presenting of the Poe Awards, and—the only thing that really mattered—the bestowing on him of the first ever Murder Under Cover Special Guest of Honor Award.

To be followed by some inconsequential live auction, a dreary event that he'd planned to skip but Ameena had insisted he remain for. He'd seen all the bric-a-brac that would be up for grabs earlier in the auction room. Mostly flea market-worthy tidbits at best. Although that exquisite bottle of Louis Roederer Cristal that Ameena had placed in his basket would have been worth carting home.

Unfortunately, Ameena had scolded him for even thinking of pilfering it from the gift basket prior to the auction. She warned him that keeping the bottle of champagne, which her husband had donated even though he didn't realize it yet, might harm his reputation among his fans.

Such a pity. That Cristal was created at the behest of Tsar Alexander II of Russia. Because of the tsar's worry of assassination attempts on his life, Roederer had gone so far as to bottle the champagne in flat-bottomed, clear crystal bottles in an effort to thwart potential bombers and poisoners.

Of course, Alexander II met a bomb with his name on it along the banks of the Yekaterininsky Canal in Saint Petersburg. Though he had died of his wounds, Louis Roederer Cristal had endured. So something good had come out of the tsar's fears.

"Ready, Giselle?" he called through the closed bathroom door. Coming back to his room late that afternoon, he had been surprised to discover Giselle had made herself at home. Both her person and all her luggage—two purses, her swag bag and a pink Hello Kitty spinner suitcase overflowing with skimpy clothes and shoes—now shared his room.

He hadn't had the heart to throw her out.

"Ready, TR," she cried breathily, applying a delicate line of strawberry lip gloss to her lower lip.

The bathroom door shot open and Giselle exited in a cloud of perfume, decked out in a scoop-neck, blood red minidress. Sparkly gold shoes with three-inch heels adorned her feet. If she'd gone with anything higher, she would have towered over Anthony Mulish and her intuition warned her against doing so.

"You look *sooo* handsome." Smiling, she pressed up on her toes and planted a tender kiss on Anthony Mulish's nose then wiped the smear of lip gloss she'd left behind using the side of her thumb. "You are my knight in shining tuxedo armor."

Anthony Mulish found himself blushing with pride. It was an odd turn of phrase. But, he had to hand it to the young woman, insane and/or homicidal she may be, but she did have a unique way with words. That counted for a lot in his world.

He patted the inside pocket of his tuxedo jacket where he had tucked his acceptance speech. It would be a tragedy to forget it. He had spent hours at his typewriter honing and polishing, polishing and honing each precious word.

Who knew? This little award could be a prelude, a dress rehearsal for the main event, his acceptance speech in Stockholm before the esteemed committee who would be bestowing the Nobel Prize in Literature upon him some day.

Feeling the reassuring presence of the pages of his speech in his pocket, he extended his hand and asked, "Shall we?"

"Yes." Giselle laced her arm possessively through his. "You are going to knock 'em dead, TR."

Anthony Mulish halted in his tracks. That was a poor choice of words under the circumstances and somewhat disconcerting.

The truth was that he was going to figuratively knock the entire audience dead with his speech and do the same, more precisely, to Dorothy Hall, Sharon Crombie and that lout Jay Copperfield when he solved Frank's murder before this weekend from hell was over.

They rode down in the elevator arm in arm, surrounded by gushing attendees intent on pummeling TR Ipé with questions and requests for autographs. Giselle, never leaving his side, ran interference for him.

And she did it like a real pro—friendly but firm.

Keeping the riffraff at bay.

All he had to do was smile and nod. She handled the rest.

Ameena could learn a thing or two from this woman, thought Anthony Mulish.

Reaching the banquet room entrance, Peggy Wethering, having spent hours in front of the mirror and wearing a brand new, ankle-length green dress, practically dripped rattlesnake venom as she greeted TR Ipé with that phony French slut on his arm and shamelessly showing her wares for all the world to see.

Nonetheless, she managed to swallow her bile and say, "Good evening, TR. Welcome. You'll be seated at table number one. That's just down in front of the stage." She waved vaguely in the general direction. The stage and table were half-blocked by the milling crowd.

"Look!" Giselle squeezed TR's hand. "There's Meeny!"

"Who?"

"Meeny. Your agent, silly."

"Oh. Yes, I see." The author spotted Ameena across the room. "In all the years I've known the woman, I did not realize she had a nickname."

Ameena balanced a drink in one hand and chatted with that fan of his. What was his name again? Olaf or something?

"Look," said Giselle. "She's waving us over."

"Must we? The only conversation I'm in the mood for at the moment is a brief one with the bartender."

A thick, thirsty crowd swarmed the bars set up at each side of the banquet room. "The drinks are free, aren't they? I was told the drinks would be free."

"Don't worry, baby. I'll go get our drinks. You go see what Meeny wants."

"If you say so," Anthony Mulish agreed, although his feet seemed glued to the floor. "This weekend can't be over soon enough for my taste. Nothing but drudgery and tedium. Not to mention, I've barely managed to write a single word."

To make matters worse, if a copy of A Cozy Ending didn't show up at his apartment or the offices of Ackerman Publishing, he might be forced to rewrite the entire novel from scratch. That would take valuable time away from his latest literary effort and he was anxious to complete his novel, Philosophy of Paris, and see it on the road to publication.

"Don't you worry, TR. It will all be over soon. Why, we'll be back in New York in no time and you'll be banging away on your novel. And if anybody tries to bother you there, I'll just say 'I'm sorry but the great author is busy working on his magnificent, great American', no..." She stopped and shook her head side to side. "Make that 'his next great *world*' novel."

Anthony Mulish smiled so big, his mouth practically engulfed his eyeballs.

Reeling from the magnitude of her words, Giselle gave him a kiss and sent him on his way.

Ameena exhaled a small sigh of relief on seeing Anthony Mulish's approach. She never thought she'd live long enough to see the day that she actually looked forward to him appearing. But this Ulaf Ulafsson, who kept nattering away at her, was dreary as soggy toast. This guy could drive the Buddha to acts of rage. The young man actually thought Anthony Mulish's novels were works of art.

Works of art? Really? If anything, Mulish's slumber-inducing novels were the works of a brain dead sow.

To top it off, Ulaf was drunker than a proverbial skunk as evidenced by his unsteady feet, slurred speech and watery red eyes.

Her best defense, thus far, had been to pour as many drinks down her throat as humanly possible. Now, all she had to do was wait for Anthony to do what he did best—insult or bore this rube until he went away.

"Glad to see you finally made it," quipped Ameena. "I thought maybe you got lost." The truth was, she was afraid Anthony Mulish had decided to blow the event off. Then again, she should have known better. Nothing was going to prevent the great TR Ipé from receiving this special award tonight. Even if it was for something he looked down his nose at.

"Good evening, Mister Ipé."

Good grief, groaned Ameena, the kid was practically bowing as if in the presence of royalty and Anthony Mulish was thinking nothing of it.

"Yes, hello," said Anthony Mulish. "Olaf, wasn't it?" He ignored the young man's offered hand.

"It's Ulaf, sir."

"Of course. Now, if you wouldn't mind, I would like a word with my agent. Business. You know how it is." He waved Ulaf away.

"Of course, sir." Ulaf turned and blended into the crowd.

"That was rude," Ameena said.

"Was it?"

"Yes. Thanks. I owe you." Anthony Mulish had performed his magic quicker than even she could have expected or hoped. She raised herself up on tiptoes to see if she could spot a waiter or waitress working the room. Why was everybody so damn tall?

"For what?"

"Never mind. It's not important." She could see no good coming of making him aware of his solitary super power, which was to make other people disappear as fast as their feet could carry them. "You aren't drinking?"

"Giselle is fetching me something from the bar."

"She's fetching all right…"

"What's that?"

"Nothing." It wasn't her job to save the great TR from the minx's clutches.

"Why is everyone standing around? Shouldn't we be seated?"

"Anxious to get this over with?"

"Yes." And anxious to get the award which was the only reason he'd driven hundreds of miles from home in the first place.

"Relax. It won't be much longer. At events like this, they like to get everybody liquored up before the awards and auction. It loosens lips and wallets."

"Ameena, TR." Jenny Garrett swept towards them, a bottle of beer in one hand. She wore dark slacks and a matching sweater, reminding Anthony Mulish of a cat burglar. Her hair was thrust upward in a loose bun.

He caught a whiff of beer and cigarettes on her breath.

She gave them each a hug. "Tonight's the big night." She rapped her knuckles against the author's shoulder bone. "I foresee big things for you, TR." She winked conspiratorially. "And I hope that I can play some part in your brilliant career."

Ameena winced. Jenny was laying it on thick, which was mighty big of her considering Anthony had had her demoted.

"Say, did you hear," said Jenny. "The offices of Ackerman Publishing were broken into the day before Frank left for the conference."

"Was anyone hurt?" asked Ameena.

"No, it was after hours."

"Was anything taken?"

"Just the manuscript. Weird, huh?" She hiccoughed rudely.

"What manuscript?" Ameena asked.

"Huh?" Jenny saw Anthony Mulish wildly waving his head side to side behind Ameena. "Oh, just something Frank was considering making an offer on." Her eyes lit up. "There's Dorothy Hall. I've been dying to say hello. You'll excuse me, won't you?"

Without waiting for an answer, she waved goodbye and headed in the direction of Dorothy Hall standing shoulder to shoulder across the room with Sharon Crumbie. Both wore frilly purple dresses, reminding Anthony Mulish of a pair of fuzzy purple dinosaurs, like that one on TV that had fallen out of favor some years ago. Good riddance. The only good dinosaur was a dead dinosaur, as far as Anthony Mulish was concerned.

Ameena had been hoping to have a chat with Dorothy Hall and Sharon Crumbie too. You never knew when an author might be looking for a new agent. The last time she and Sharon Crumbie had chatted briefly, the author had hinted that she might be in the market. "Maybe I should go say hello, too." She made to move.

"One minute." Anthony Mulish blocked her path to freedom.

Great, first she had been stuck with Ulaf and now she was stuck with Anthony Mulish. She just couldn't catch a break.

"Fine." Ameena snatched a fresh glass of white wine off the tray of a passing server. She'd been drinking red and knew it wasn't good to mix. But these were desperate times. She ignored the server's request for a drink ticket. "So what is this business you wanted to talk about?"

The server muttered a curse and moved on.

"I'm looking for Beulah. Have you seen her?"

"Not yet. But with the booze flowing, I'd bet my Beemer that she's around here someplace."

Anthony Mulish searched the noisy crowd to no avail.

"How's the murder investigation coming?"

"I'm getting closer by the minute," bragged Anthony Mulish. "In fact, I've got a couple of new suspects."

"Oh?"

He explained how he'd caught Stan and Eve having sex in the chancellor's house.

"And you think that makes them killers? If it does, lock me up."

"Eve Landry is a wannabe mystery author."

"That doesn't necessarily make her a murderer."

"It may when Frank has harshly critiqued and summarily rejected your manuscript."

"Editors and publishers reject lots of manuscripts," replied Ameena. "Trust me."

"Yes, well, this rejected author has a set of master keys to this entire college. And that includes Frank's room here. Those facts make her and Stan Dooley prime suspects."

"Because he's screwing her?" Ameena wasn't convinced. "On the other hand, I was talking to Dorothy Hall and Sharon Crumbie. They seem convinced it was Matt."

"They think Matt murdered Frank?" Anthony Mulish chuckled. "What possible reason would he have?"

Ameena shrugged. "They rationalize that if it wasn't

Giselle, then it must be him. Maybe working under her orders."

"Don't be ridiculous. Those two are harmless."

"If you say so."

"I also put Beulah up there at the top of the suspect list. Now there is a woman who is dangerous."

"You could be right." Beulah struck her as one very determined woman. "Listen, TR, don't you think it might be best to focus on being TR Ipé the rest of the weekend? Meet your fans? Make some new ones?" Pretend to be human.

"What are you trying to say?"

"I'm saying why not leave the real crime solving to the real crime solver? The sheriff."

Anthony Mulish pulled himself up to his full height and then some. "I solved a murder in my book, if you will remember. And brilliantly, I might add. How hard can it be?"

"This is real life. This is different."

"Please, how different can it be? Interview a few suspects, sift through a few clues, sort out a red herring or two and, voila, I reveal the murderer." He snapped his fingers.

Oh, brother. "I only thought I'd make the suggestion."

"Heard but not heeded. This case is mine and I intend to solve it."

"Good luck with that, TR," Ameena said, meaning exactly the opposite and wishing she'd kept her mouth shut.

44

A murmur erupted from the crowd surrounding Anthony Mulish and Ameena. People shifted uneasily to allow Giselle to pass among them. Attendees were nervous that she just might be a knife-wielding murderer, despite the sheriff's assurance that she was, as he had explained it, crazy but no killer.

"Here you go, TR." Giselle, oblivious to the looks she was getting, handed the author a tall glass.

"What is it?" He peered at the unusual red liquid.

"It's called a Jack Rose," Giselle. "The bartender, his name is Mike, he made is especially for you."

"I have never heard of it. Bring me a martini instead." Anthony Mulish tried to hand the glass back to Giselle. She pouted and refused.

"Won't you at least try it?

He sighed and took a sniff of the drink. "What's in it?" he asked rather dubiously.

"Mike said it's got apple brandy, grenadine and a squeeze of lemon."

"Try it already," urged Ameena. "I mean, it's not like it's going to kill you now, is it?" Unless the vixen was out to poison him. In fact, hadn't she already tried on more than one occasion to do away with him?

"I thought you'd be happy." Giselle thrust out her lower lip even as her eyelids fluttered up at him.

"No, I know what I like." He tried once more to return the drink to her.

This time she accepted it and hung her head. "Mike says this was John Steinbeck's favorite cocktail." She swirled the drink desultorily in her hand.

"Did he, now?" Anthony's brow rose. Plucking the glass from her, he hoisted the drink to his lips and sipped. He let the liquid slide down his throat, savoring the complex flavors whilst imagining Steinbeck at his desk turning out *Of Mice and Men*. "It's wonderful. Thank you."

Giselle grinned and planted a kiss on his nose. "You're welcome, baby."

The crazed, half-his-age vixen was calling him baby again!

Then again, Anthony Mulish was pretty much a baby when Ameena came to think on it. A big overgrown baby, but a baby nonetheless. A baby who seemed to have suddenly found his mother and lover, all wrapped up in a big ball of curves and boobs.

She shook herself at that ugly thought and downed her chenin blanc.

"So tell me, Ms. Mimieux," began the agent. "How long have you been in the States?"

Giselle cocked her head the way a collie does when confronted with a complex puzzle. "All my life. Why do you ask?"

"You know, the accent?" Ameena pushed her brows together, uniting them above her nose.

"What accent?" Giselle blinked in confusion.

"Excuse me?" Ameena was about to let loose a comment along the lines of 'that fake French one you wear like a cheap, knockoff mink stole.'

"There's Beulah," interrupted TR Ipé. "Excuse me, ladies. I must speak with her."

Without a further word, he surged through the crowd, careful to keep his Jack Rose lofted high to prevent spillage.

He interrupted Beulah, who was conversing with the self-proclaimed Poison Queen, Queenie Arthur, to ask, "Why did you murder your husband?"

"I'll take this as my cue to leave," said the hoary-voiced Poison Queen. "Good seeing you again, Beulah." She marched off, stomping TR Ipé's foot with her icepick heels as she did so.

Beulah Ackerman laughed wickedly. "Why did I murder dear Frank? You are precious Anthony, I mean, TR. The question you should be asking is 'Why *didn't* I murder Frank?'

"I was married to the jerk for fifteen too-long years. That he's dead now is no skin off my nose. Of course, it does mean I have one less editor to pitch my clients' manuscripts to."

She laid her fingers on Anthony Mulish's shoulder. "Say, you wouldn't be looking for a new agent, would you, darling?"

Anthony Mulish looked at her hand digging its way into his tuxedo jacket like a ravenous alien creature. Her purple-polished nails looked ready to siphon his blood. Ameena had stood by him all these years, through thick and thin.

Still, now that he was finally successful, should he maybe find himself a nice, new A-lister? One of those high-powered New York agencies with dozens of equally high-powered agents to take care of his every need and heed his every whim?

The downside, of course, would be that those agents may suck even more of his money from his pocket. Not a good thing. Not a good thing at all.

The situation required some serious thought. Perhaps he would ask Giselle, get her thoughts on the matter. That woman had a good head on her shoulders.

The rest of her wasn't exactly Swiss cheese either.

"I'll give it my consideration," lied the author.

"You do that. And to sweeten the deal, I'll even give that little piece of eye candy of yours a contract with my agency." She nodded in Giselle's direction.

Anthony Mulish's brow twitched. Clearly, Beulah had not read Giselle's work. If she had, she had no literary taste whatsoever. He decided to change the course of the conversation. "Did Frank have any enemies?"

Beulah snorted. "Are you joking? How about any author or agent whose manuscript he rejected? And that's only for starters," she said, swilling her drink.

"That is a very big list."

"Frank," said Beulah in an icy tone, "was a big ass."

"He was good to me."

Beulah merely shrugged. "Look, if you really want to know who I think did the world a favor by removing Frank from it, take a look at dear, sweet Jenny."

"Jenny Garrett?"

"That's the one." She grabbed the author's lapels and pulled him closer. "She was threatening Frank. Physically threatening him."

"Threatening him physically?" Anthony Mulish echoed uneasily. Was Jenny Garrett violent? If so, his own life could be in serious danger. Why, he'd had the woman demoted, practically fired.

"Did you know that she beat her husband?"

Anthony Mulish shook his head no.

"Yep. Of course, Jenny's not married anymore. Her husband finally escaped with what was left of his manhood. He's living in the Midwest somewhere, so I heard. Recovering from his bruises. And then there was the big to-do at the office. Jenny took a considerable pay cut. Word on the street is that you're responsible for that."

She prodded her thumb into his chest. "I wouldn't want to be in your shoes, TR." She paused, then said, "Say, do you carry life insurance?"

"Pardon me." He gulped down his Jack Rose in one swift move and fled in search of Giselle. He needed some spot of calm in this sea of madness and evil.

He never dreamed that the world of cozy mysteries could be so dangerous!

45

Instead of finding solace in the arms of Giselle, he bumped into the backside of Jenny, who bumped into Dorothy Hall, who herself shot sharp daggers at him. "Look what the cat dragged in," scoffed the author, casting an ugly eye up and down his body. "The great author himself, Tripe."

Dorothy Hall was drunk and burped loudly twice in quick succession. Blushing, she said, "I need some fresh air." She peered around the room, spotting her partner in crime. "Yoo-hoo, Sharon!"

"Good riddance," muttered Anthony Mulish, still wondering where Giselle had gotten to. Ameena stood surrounded by an unruly mob of wannabe-published authors. She looked like a mule that had just been hit between its big, dull eyes with a sledgehammer.

"Are you okay, TR?" demanded Jenny. She reached out a hand to steady him.

"Yes, quite well." He extricated himself from her clutches and shot his cuffs. What he could really use was another of those exquisite Jack Roses. Where the devil was Giselle? "Have you seen Ms. Mimieux about?"

"Umm." Jenny scratched her chin. "The last I saw of her she was talking to Matt and Sheriff Winslow."

"The sheriff is here?"

"Sure. He is a conference guest speaker, after all. No

surprise to see him at the banquet."

"I see. I hope there's no trouble," he said, worriedly. He also wondered if the sheriff had found any clues on that cantaloupe.

"You and me both. I'm sorry I almost let the cat out of the bag earlier."

"What? A cat?" He was too busy looking for Giselle to pay much attention to Jenny at the moment.

"About your manuscript."

"Ah, yes." At some point, Anthony Mulish feared that, the way things were going, he would possibly be forced to mention to Ameena that not only was there a new manuscript, but that the manuscript was now missing.

"Did I mention that all the office copies are missing? I'm talking the paper copy and the digital files. That is so weird."

"More than weird. It is totally unacceptable. You must find it, Jenny." The only thing worse than writing A Cozy Ending would be having to rewrite it.

"I'll do my best."

"Thank you. What will happen to my book with Frank dead?"

"I'm not exactly sure but I'm guessing somebody, maybe another publishing house, will take over the business. And your contract."

Anthony Mulish mulled over Jenny's words.

She took his silence for concern. "Don't you worry, TR, I've got your back."

What he was afraid of was that she might just stick a knife in his back. "Jenny, I hope you don't hold any grudge over what happened at Ackerman."

"You mean about you complaining to Frank about me and almost costing me my job and me now working for half the salary with a woman for my boss with half my experience?"

"Umm..."

Jenny grinned. "Like I said, don't you worry. I'm not the kind to hold grudges. Life's too short. Know what I mean?"

Anthony Mulish gulped, feeling his shirt and tie press tightly against his Adam's apple. Unfortunately, he feared he knew precisely what she meant.

"What about this lawsuit between Jay Copperfield and Ackerman Publishing?"

"Lawsuit?" Jenny's eyes danced. "That was nothing. Trust me. Jay Copperfield is all bluster. Although..."

"Yes?"

"Now that you mention it, Jay came storming into the offices a few weeks ago."

"He did?" Not that it surprised Anthony Mulish one bit. The man was a brute. A Neanderthal, at best.

"Yep. In fact, he vowed to get his money back and said that, if he didn't, he'd take it out in blood."

"Frank's blood?"

Jenny shrugged.

Stan Dooley rapped his knuckles on the lectern, leaned into the microphone and called for everyone's attention. The microphone squealed like a startled micro pig. Matt jumped to the podium and made some adjustments.

"It looks like it's time for dinner," said Jenny. "We'll chat more later."

As Jenny wandered away to find her table, identifiable by the numbers placed on stands in the center of each table, Anthony Mulish couldn't help wondering if those parting words of hers had carried a hidden threat of some sort.

Ameena was making a beeline for their table assignment when Jenny Garrett accosted her.

"I think I know who killed Frank," Jenny told Ameena.

That stopped the agent dead in her tracks. "Who?"

"You'll never believe it."

"Try me."

"Your star author."

Ameena's brow furrowed intensely. "You don't mean..."

"Yep. Dear old Anthony Mulish, aka TR Ipé."

"You think Anthony murdered Frank?" As low as Ameena's opinion was of her author, she didn't really think he would stoop that low. Or would he? "But he was with me. We found Frank's body together."

"I'm just saying. Maybe he snuck out during the movie?"

"Hm-m." She had dozed off once or twice. That was a possibility "Why would Anthony want to murder Frank?"

"Let's just say he might not have wanted certain things to come out."

"What's that supposed to mean?" Jenny Garrett was talking in riddles. And Ameena's patience was running thin.

Stan Dooley repeated his request for everyone to be seated.

"Ask TR," Jenny Garrett said with a mischievous grin before suddenly retreating. Stirring up trouble was sheer delight.

46

Anthony Mulish's thoughts scattered like dusty, dry oak leaves as his eyes fell on Giselle. His heart unexpectedly warmed. She was seated at their table beside Ameena. Catching his eye, Giselle smiled brightly.

"Yoo-hoo!" She waved her arms overhead, exposing a dangerous amount of bosoms.

Ameena felt suddenly smaller. "Put your arms down, already. He sees you." She grabbed Giselle's right arm and pushed it to the table. "The whole world sees you."

"Sorry, Meeny. I just worry about my baby *sooo* much."

"And I worry about your mental health," Ameena mumbled under her breath. "Both of yours."

There were two bottles of unopened wine standing unclaimed in the center of the round table. She leaned forward and snatched the nearest. It was California merlot and it was free. She fisted the provided corkscrew, popped said cork and filled her own glass before offering the bottle around to her tablemates.

Giselle filled a glass for herself and an even more generous glassful for Anthony as he plopped down in his chair with an audible groan.

Barely acknowledging his companions, he turned to Ameena. "Meeny, you should have warned me that I was getting involved with kooks and killers when I agreed to come here to this godforsaken place."

"If you hadn't written Death Gets Cozy, we wouldn't be here. And, as I keep reminding you, writing Death Gets Cozy was your idea," she shot back. This entire weekend was getting to her, Anthony Mulish most of all. He was getting under her skin even more than the thought of a cold-blooded murderer being possibly on the loose amongst them. "And do not call me Meeny."

"Death Gets Cozy is a wonderful book, Meeny. You of all people know that," Giselle said, coming to his defense. "And A Cozy Ending is even better!"

Anthony Mulish whipped his head around in horror. "Giselle! You know about...it?"

"Of course."

"What cozy ending?" demanded Ameena.

"Not what cozy ending, A Cozy Ending," Giselle explained.

"Say, is that your next release, TR?" asked Stan. Everyone at the table had now stopped their own conversations to listen. "Everybody's been buzzing and conjecturing about what your encore might be."

"Quiet," insisted Anthony Mulish, shutting everybody down with a wave of the hand. "Giselle, explain yourself."

"Well," Giselle began, her voice a mere whisper, eyes aimed at her crotch, sensing she was in trouble, had made him angry. "I-I saw it in your room. On your computer."

"I'm going to ask again, what is A Cozy Ending?" Ameena said in a steely tone.

"Merely a little idea I was toying with," replied Anthony Mulish, putting her off. "Giselle," he said as calmly as he could muster. "Tell me and don't be afraid to answer. Did you destroy it?"

Her eyes flew to his. "Destroy it! Of course, not, baby! I would never ever do that!" Tears welled up in her eyes. "You know I love your work. Same as I love you." To prove it, she placed her hands on his cheeks and kissed him.

Rather than clobbering them both on top of their heads with the merlot bottle, which was what she desperately wanted to do and had been her first instinct, Ameena picked up her fork and stabbed at her salad. "We'll talk about this later, TR."

Anthony Mulish colored. His evening kept getting worse and worse.

"Did I do something wrong, baby?" pouted Giselle.

Anthony Mulish patted her thigh. "Of course not. Let's eat and forget all about it."

"*I'm* not going to forget about it," promised Ameena, jabbing him between the ribs with her bony elbow while chewing on a rubbery bit of peppery arugula. "I'll show *you* a cozy ending."

Anthony Mulish pretended not to hear her. Sometimes it was better to ignore things. Sometimes those things went away.

Sooner or later.

Servers darted expertly among the diners, delivering banquet dishes with silly names like Dead Duck, Vegetable Ptomaine and Stake Thru The Heart.

Anthony Mulish cringed, almost wishing some errant vampire hunter would thrust a stake through his own heart, thus putting him out of his misery.

Sheriff Winslow, who found himself seated across the very same table as the windbag, TR Ipé, and the nutjob, Giselle Mimieux, due to some sadistic god playing sport with him, goggled as the night wore on and on and on. The nutjob had somehow managed to attach herself to Ipé like a remora to a shark. Sure, she was beautiful. He could see why a guy would want her. But what did she see in him?

All he could see when he looked at TR Ipé from across the table, from any angle at all really, was an ass.

And what was all this about a missing manuscript? Could it possibly be connected to the publisher's murder?

Sheriff Winslow shook his head. When it came to a stop, he downed a full glass of white wine. No, he told himself. Nobody would kill somebody over some cozy mystery. Or would they?

47

Reba Lonnegan solemnly carried a sealed envelope up the steps of the dais and handed this to Dorothy Hall, one of the two co-toastmistresses for the event, the other being her bosom buddy, Sharon Crumbie. The winner of the prestigious Poe Award for best hardcover original mystery novel of the year was about to be announced.

Dorothy Hall repeated what the audience already knew. "This award is voted on by this year's attendees of this, the inaugural Murder Under Cover. And, might I add, that Sharon and I are having a wonderful time and hope to come back next year. Thank you, organizers and thank you, attendees."

"Absolutely, Snookums." Sharon gave her friend a big hug.

Being one of the most popular and celebrated authors present, Dorothy Hall expected she herself, or possibly Sharon, would be the recipient of this award. What a boon this would be to her career. What a feather in her already multi-feathered cozy mystery writer's cap!

"And the winner is—" said Dorothy Hall, slowing slitting open the envelope with her thumbnail and extracting the card inside.

Dorothy Hall and Sharon blanched like a couple stalks of white asparagus dragged upstairs from somebody's windowless basement.

"Who is it?" an anonymous voice called out from the tables.

"TR Ipé," Dorothy Hall's voice came out in a strangled whimper and she slumped to one side. Sharon Crumbie propped her up.

Wasn't it enough that the damn fool upstart was Special Guest of Honor? Now the fans had proclaimed him a Poe winner?!

"Boo!" came a catcall from the audience. "I demand a recount!"

Anthony Mulish twisted in his seat to witness Jay Copperfield, hands cupped on each side of his mouth, anger distorting his ugly mug.

"Life isn't fair," Dorothy Hall gasped to her dearest friend. "In fact, life is patently cruel."

"Totally," groaned Sharon Crumbie, about to collapse under the weight of her companion.

Ameena felt a stroke coming on. TR Ipé? That was the last name on the planet that she had expected to hear from Dorothy Hall's mouth. How could he have won? Even she hadn't voted for the pompous twit.

TR Ipé mounted the podium for the second time that night. He pontificated ad nauseam before being gently guided back to his seat by Reba Lonnegan who feared that they were running overtime and that folks would wander off to their rooms before the auction had even had a chance to begin.

Sheriff Winslow sat up straighter as Dorothy Hall and Sharon Crombie, the night's co-toastmistresses, began the auction with a gift basket donated by Nate Saget. The bidding started at twenty-five dollars and stuck there.

Feeling sorry for the young man, Ameena, tipsy and bored to tears, offered thirty-five and found herself the lucky winner of a cheese log sprinkled with bits of stale walnut, a dried salami and an autographed, trade paperback copy of Nate Saget's mystery novel. "Oh, the joy," she mumbled, tucking the sad little basket under the table.

"When are they going to auction off my basket?" Anthony Mulish whispered in her ear.

"You mean the basket that I paid for and put together in your name?" Ameena sniped. "They're saving it for last." Everybody would be good and plastered by then. Drinks were now half-price and the booze was flowing like water over Niagara Falls.

Deputy Rogers chose that moment to come racing into the banquet hall, disturbing all the seated guests, who began buzzing like bees being agitated by a kid poking a sharp stick into their beloved beehive.

Wet snow clung to his rubber boots. "Sheriff, sorry to disturb you, sir."

"What is it, Rogers?" demanded Sheriff Winslow. "You're supposed to be on duty out front."

"I let Sgt. Pepper off her leash to take a pee and—"

"And you interrupted my evening to tell me about it?" Sure the steak had been rubbery, but it was steak and it was free.

And yes, TR Ipé's speech had dragged on for an infinity and bored everyone in the audience—except for Giselle Mimieux and Peggy Wethering, both of whom he noted had hung on the author's every word like they'd come down from Mount Olympus—but he had stuck around for the auction. There was a pair of handcuffs up for grabs once worn by Farrah Fawcett in an old episode of TV's Charlie's Angels.

Sheriff Winslow wanted those handcuffs. He wanted them bad. And he had nearly four hundred bucks cash burning a hole in his pocket just for the occasion. He'd siphoned the money off the meager allowance his wife doled out to him for beer money for just such a special occasion.

"No, sir." Deputy Rogers ran the back of his hand across his red forehead. He leaned closer to the sheriff's ear. "She found a body. A dead body, sir."

48

"A dead body?" The sheriff jumped to his feet. The table shook and silverware flew. He slid back down and apologized to his dinner companions. "Explain yourself, Rogers," he said with forced composure.

"Yes, sir. She was pawing in the snow when I caught up to her and there he was. Male, early thirties is my guess."

"And where is this body now?"

"Lying half-buried in the snow a couple hundred yards away. I left Sgt. Pepper standing guard."

Sgt. Pepper was a sturdy, well-disciplined German shepherd. Probably more reliable a guard over a corpse than Deputy Rogers.

Stan squeezed his head between his hands and groaned. "Could this weekend get any worse?"

"Don't worry." Sheriff Winslow threw his napkin down on the table. "I'll check out this so-called dead body. Probably nothing more than a college prank with one of those store dummies. It wouldn't be the first time." He glared meaningfully across the table at TR Ipé. "Like a cantaloupe with a knife sticking out of it."

"That cantaloupe might contain a clue," shot back Anthony Mulish.

Ameena shuddered. What was happening to her?

While on the face of it Anthony Mulish's pronouncement sounded nonsensical, she knew exactly what he meant. Hell had indeed arrived and instead of coming in a handbasket, it had arrived in a cozy mystery gift basket with a dollar store ribbon adorning its handle. Maybe once she got home, she'd change her focus. Concentrate on sci-fi or romance novels. Forget all this mystery crap.

Sheriff Winslow stood, thrusting his hand in his trouser pocket. "Here." He extracted a bundle of mixed bills and dropped the wad onto Stan's soiled bread plate. "If I'm not back in time, when the Farrah Fawcett handcuffs hit the auction block, bid for me."

"How much?" blinked the defeated and weary organizer. He sensed this would be the first and very last Murder Under Cover conference.

"All of it." Sheriff Winslow hurried from the banquet room with Deputy Rogers at his heels.

Bidding now opened on Cherie Maraschino's improbable fully-furnished and landscaped matchstick dollhouse.

"I hope that thing comes complete with its own miniature fire extinguisher," Anthony Mulish said to no one in particular.

He closed his eyes with pleasure as Giselle massaged the back of his neck with her right hand while with her left she stroked the bronze medallion hanging by a gold braid around his neck. A gift of the organizing committee, along with a plaque commemorating his achievements.

"You look just like one of those war heroes," Giselle gushed.

"Sometimes I feel like one," Anthony Mulish confessed. "Writing is akin to going to battle every day. And the publishing business, that is much like a largescale war unto itself."

Ameena waved for their server. What was taking him so long bringing that new bottle of champagne she had asked for?

While she'd ostensibly ordered it to celebrate the occasion, for her personally it was meant more to blot the evening out. If she was lucky, she'd wake up tomorrow morning and remember none of this.

The server finally found his way to their table, popped the cork on the bottle and splashed fresh bubbly into their glasses.

"A toast," Giselle said rather breathily, raising her crystal flute. "To the one and only TR Ipé."

"I'll drink to that," the agent said, hoisting her glass and thanking her lucky stars that there was only the one TR Ipé and his demented alter ego Anthony Mulish.

As the unexpectedly heated bidding on Cherie Maraschino's donation rose to the incredible one thousand dollar mark, Ameena yanked Anthony Mulish's bowtie and pulled him close enough that their noses bounced off one the other. He could smell her fetid, alcohol-infused breath.

"What are you doing?" he hissed, goggle-eyed. "And why are so many people willing to pay so much for that pile of kindling?"

"It's the herd mentality. Auctions count on it. But never mind that. I know who murdered Frank," Ameena whispered victoriously. She had one-upped every mystery author and wannabe mystery author in the crowd.

"Of course, you do." Anthony Mulish said haughtily.

"Don't you patronize me." She had just figured it out. Put it all together. The who, at least. And everybody knew the what, at least roughly—some sharp, pointy object.

The why she wasn't so sure about. But Sheriff Winslow could figure that part out for himself. She'd done the hard part. Let him do the rest.

"It was Ulaf," Ameena whispered in his ear.

"What was Ulaf?"

"The killer. Aren't you listening? Focus, dammit!"

"Who was Ulaf again?"

"Ulaf Ulafsson. That big phony over there." She nodded her chin in the direction of a table a couple rows back.

"That fellow intent on overbidding on matchstick manor?"

"Yes, your superfan, remember?"

Anthony Mulish stiffened. "My fans are not murderers, Ameena."

"This one is."

"Impossible." Anthony Mulish narrowed his eyes and studied the young fellow in a tan two-piece suit and yellow tie as he raised his hand again, bringing the bid on the dollhouse up to the eleven hundred dollar mark.

A fan in a clearly homemade I'm-Cheering-for-Cherie-Maraschino bedazzled sweatshirt slumped in her chair.

"He really wants that dollhouse, doesn't he? My, my. Just think what he might bid for my basket."

"Focus on the dollhouse, would you?" agreed Ameena. "Think about it, TR, why would he pay so much for that piece of crap? Why would anybody?"

Cherie Maraschino, seated within earshot the next table over, shot her rheumy eyes at the agent and huffed.

"I'll bet there's some kind of clue inside. Some sort of evidence tying our killer to the murder," suggested the agent.

"A clue? Evidence?" Anthony Mulish snorted. "Hidden inside the dollhouse?" he asked incredulously. "Don't be absurd."

He'd seen his agent drunk before. Many times. And the results were never good. Alcohol induced a tendency to babble incoherently. But this was over the top lunacy.

"Wouldn't that make Maraschino the killer?" Anthony Mulish said. "Not that the old thing looks capable of raising a butter knife in her frail, elderly condition, let alone thrusting something bigger and more deadly into Frank's bony chest."

"No. I overheard Ms. Maraschino saying that she'd had to make repairs to the dollhouse because it had been damaged overnight. She was very upset and said it was a good thing she travels with hundreds of extra matchsticks for just that exigency."

Dorothy Hall called for last bids. There were none. Sharon Crumbie banged the gavel and invited Ulaf Ulafsson up to the podium to claim his prize.

Said Ameena, "You know, Anthony, Ulaf told me earlier that he is a big fan of your work."

"So? The young man has taste."

"Listen to me. He said he was a big fan of *your* work, you." She poked him in the chest. "Anthony Mulish. He's read every one of your novels." That alone could have been enough to send him over the edge and turn him into a psychopathic murderer.

"I still don't see your point," said Anthony Mulish, feeling she'd insulted him somehow but not quite understanding how she'd done it.

"Think about it. How did he know it was you and not TR Ipé? How does he know so much about you before this weekend?"

"He didn't murder *me*, Ameena. He murdered Frank. That is, if he murdered anybody at all." He patted Giselle's hand. The young woman was hanging on their every word. "What sort of evidence could possibly be in that pile of matchsticks?" he scoffed.

Ameena fumed as Ulaf carried his newly-won dollhouse from the podium and started toward the exit.

Anthony Mulish was quite certain that Ameena had gone off the deep end. His fingers tapped out a tune on his empty champagne flute.

Yet, the more Anthony Mulish thought about it, the more he became convinced. The murder weapon could be hidden inside that ridiculous dollhouse...making Olaf, or whatever his name was, the killer!

Anthony Mulish knew he had to act and act quickly. If he didn't do something, and fast, a killer could escape. Worse, Ameena might steal his thunder and claim all the credit for herself.

Anthony Mulish leapt to his feet, bringing the auctioneering to a halt with a cry of "Stop that man! He's a murderer!"

49

Clutching his prized matchstick house by its base, Ulaf twirled around.

Every eye in the audience locked on him. For one awful moment, he froze. Then his feet came unstuck and he started running to the nearest exit, one of the doors leading to the lobby.

Anthony Mulish, much to his own surprise, found himself chasing after the young man. Giselle hurried along behind him.

Even Ameena jumped into the fray, lifting her skirt and plowing through the crowd toward Ulaf.

Ulaf darted past Jay Copperfield. The disgruntled author couldn't have cared less about Ulaf. He stuck out his foot, tripping Anthony Mulish. "Oops, sorry about that, TR."

"Hey!" shouted Giselle, yanking her beau to his feet. "That wasn't nice." She drew her arm back and socked Copperfield squarely in the jaw. He went down like a bag of bones, leisure suit and all.

Ameena was forced to climb over the fallen author, lying on the carpet like a beached whale, in her pursuit of Anthony and Ulaf.

Approaching the exit, Hall and Crumbie, faster on their feet than Anthony Mulish would have suspected, mowed him down. He hit the floor with an oomph! All the air flew from his lungs.

Giselle, running short of breath, hauled him up once again and propelled him forward. Ulaf struggled with the handle of the door, trying desperately to push it open without dropping his precious cargo. Handfuls of matchsticks littered his wake.

Dorothy Hall and Sharon Crumbie pursued them all, feet stomping, tongues lashing, determined to find out what was going on.

"One way or the other," huffed Sharon, unused to such effort, "this is great material for my next murder mystery."

"You mean *my* next murder mystery," charged Dorothy, inching past her best friend with a sudden burst of speed.

Bystanders ran in every direction, chickens fleeing an unseen fox and finding no way out of the henhouse.

Anthony Mulish managed to get a hand on Ulaf's coat collar. At that same moment, Sharon Crumbie paused long enough to remove a purple high-heeled shoe from her foot. She whirled it with surprising accuracy, knocking Anthony Mulish upside the head.

Anthony Mulish clawed at his ear, howling in pain. Giselle, worried that Ulaf might escape, kicked him where no man wants to be kicked. The young man dropped to his knees. Anthony Mulish tripped over him and went down too.

Smashing the dollhouse to matchstick smithereens.

With mutual cries of victory, Dorothy Hall and Sharon Crumbie dog-piled atop them, smirking.

Ameena stopped at a nearby table to plop down in an empty chair and catch her breath, stole a startled attendee's wine glass and downed its contents.

"Get off me, you pig!" insisted Sharon Crumbie.

"You get off me, sow!" Anthony Mulish panted. He stuck out his hand. Giselle took it and gave it a pull.

"Don't ever become a literary agent," Ameena said to the woman next to her. "It's not worth it." She thunked the glass down and went to do her job.

Together, Giselle and Ameena managed to untangle the mess that was Ulaf Ulafsson, Anthony Mulish, Dorothy Hall and Sharon Crumbie.

All looked very much the worse for wear.

But most of all the matchstick dollhouse.

From across the banquet hall, dear old Cherie Maraschino could be heard sobbing over its loss. "All that work," she cried. "All those matchsticks…"

"I hope his check was good," Stan was heard saying to Reba.

"Let me go," insisted Anthony Mulish, pulling free of the women who were only trying to help him. He picked up the shattered remains of the dollhouse. "Nothing."

He turned an angry, ugly eye on his agent. "No clues. No evidence." Sweat dripped from his forehead. He mopped himself with a white silk handkerchief. "Only matchsticks."

Ameena blinked. He wasn't wrong. "Then why was he running away?"

"Probably because he was afraid of this moron," Sharon Crumbie suggested whilst pointing her thumb at Anthony Mulish.

Ulaf pushed up to a seated position, propping his back against the wall, breathing hard, not saying a word.

"Look, baby. What's that?" Giselle tugged Anthony Mulish's sleeve and pointed.

"What?"

She whispered in his ear. "Maybe whatever is so important isn't in the dollhouse."

"Clearly," he replied.

"No. Maybe it's in the base. See?" She kept her voice to a whisper. "There's a crack in the base."

"Hmm."

Cherie Maraschino had erected the dollhouse on a plywood base, eighteen inches on each side and four inches tall.

Anthony Mulish bent, picked up the base and studied it.

Ulaf's eyes grew wide as Giselle handed Anthony Mulish a bread knife, which he used to pry off the rear panel.

Anthony Mulish beamed. Inside was a nasty kitchen knife that seemed to bear blood stains.

And one other item.

"My book!" Anthony Mulish handed Giselle the busted plinth holding the knife and pulled out his heretofore missing manuscript.

"Hey!" Ameena snatched the manuscript from his hands. "A Cozy Ending? Really?" She waved the pages of the manuscript across his face and slapped him in the nose with it. "This isn't a few thoughts, this is a complete manuscript!"

Dorothy Hall nudged Sharon Crumbie in the ribs. "This ought to be good."

"Yeah, this is where the windbag gets his comeuppance," giggled Sharon.

"You've done it, TR! You've solved Frank's murder!" Giselle kissed him and kissed him again. "I am so proud of you, baby."

Ameena glared meaningfully at her author. Waiting for him to set the record straight. After all, she had figured out that Ulaf was the murderer, not him.

"Thank you," Anthony Mulish said instead. "It was simple, really."

"You're simple," Sharon said under her breath while retrieving her shoe and squeezing it on her foot.

"But why did Ulaf murder Frank?" Giselle wanted to know.

"Yes, tell us, won't you, TR," taunted Ameena, folding her arms across her chest and silently wishing him a slow, anguishing death by a thousand painful hermit crab bites.

"Maybe he's a writer and Frank cheated him the same way as he had been cheating me," suggested Jay Copperfield, having joined the throng.

"Maybe Beulah put him up to it," suggested Jenny, always happy to stir up trouble.

"I did no such thing, you tramp!" Beulah threw herself on Jenny, raking her nails across the girl's face.

It took both Jay and Stan to pull the two women apart.

"Maybe Frank rejected Ulaf's book," Giselle speculated.

"Enough!" screeched Ulaf. "Enough." He climbed shakily to his feet. "I can't take any more." He plucked bits of matchstick from his shirt.

"You're not even close, you unsophisticated morons." Ulaf balled his hands into fists of rage. He'd finally had enough of their inane speculations. "It was that book. That lousy stinking book. And Ulaf isn't even my real name!"

"What book?" demanded Ameena. Out of the corner

of her eye, she noticed that Sheriff Winslow had re-appeared with both Deputy Rogers and the dog, Sgt. Pepper, a step behind him.

"Yeah, what book?" Sheriff Winslow asked, stepping into the fray.

"That horrible, awful book, A Cozy Ending," Ulaf told them. "I wish I'd burned it in my room. The only reason I didn't was because I was afraid I'd get caught."

"A cozy ending?" The sheriff tipped his hat up his forehead. He'd gone tromping through the snow to take a look at a dead body and come back to find mayhem.

Giselle explained and turned the knife over to the sheriff.

Ameena fumed.

And vowed revenge. A revenge that would be long and sweet. And expensive.

"Yes, that book!" Ulaf nodded vigorously. "And that horrid awful book before it, Death Gets Cozy. How I hated that book." He turned pleading eyes on Anthony Mulish. "You should be writing great American litera-ture, sir."

"You mean great *world* literature," interrupted Gi-selle.

"Yes! Great world literature," Ulaf was quick to agree. "See? She gets it! That's what you should be writing. That's what you were put on this earth to write, Mister Mulish, sir, not that cozy drivel!"

"Oh, brother." Copperfield rubbed his tender jaw. That Giselle Mimieux had one hell of a punch. "Can't you lock them all up?" he suggested to Sheriff Winslow.

"And throw away the key?" added Dorothy.

Stroking his chin, deep in thought, Anthony Mulish said, "The man does have a point."

"Sure he does, baby." Giselle dabbed his dripping nose with a napkin.

"The man is a vicious killer," reminded Ameena.

"But don't you see?" explained Ulaf. "I had to stop A Cozy Ending's publication. I couldn't let you keep going down this dreadful, ruinous path. Think of your career. Your mark on the world of literature for all posterity." He sobbed. "It's beneath you."

"I'm thinking of his posterior," muttered Copperfield, lifting a foot and planning to strike the bum author in his bum. He took a quick step in retreat when Giselle waved her threatening fist at him.

"You see, sir, I had a girlfriend who works as a temp. She spent a few days typing at Ackerman Publishing and heard whispers about your new cozy. It was already bad enough that you had written the one. I couldn't let another get published. I had to save you from yourself."

"By murdering Frank?" Ameena was more confused than ever.

"Yes. And by destroying the latest manuscript. I urge you, Mister Mulish, please, quit now and promise me you'll only write literary novels from now on."

"Well..." Anthony Mulish was torn. On the one hand, the man was a criminal, a thief and a murderer. On the other hand, the young fellow made some good points.

And Ulaf was a fan of his work, so he couldn't be all bad.

"You said Ulaf wasn't your real name," reminded Anthony Mulish. "Who are you?"

"Good question, TR." Giselle rubbed Anthony's belly.

Ameena could have sworn she heard purring sounds emanating from him.

"Karl Kurkov," he confessed. "I was only pretending

to be Ulaf Ulafsson. It was too late to register when I got here."

"We did have a cap on the number of attendees," admitted Stan.

"Right, so I murdered Ulaf, stole his name and took his place. That was his body you found in the walk-in. After I heard you'd stumbled on it, I moved him out to the woods, figuring I'd either get rid of him later or let the bears and coyotes do it for me."

"Gross!" Giselle's delicate hand flew to her mouth.

"Aha! I knew it!" Anthony Mulish swiveled for all to see, basking in his own greatness. "I told you there was a second body."

"Actually, that would make the real Ulaf's murder the first murder and Frank Ackerman's the second. But, basically, you were right, sir. I didn't mean to murder Frank in the elevator. I'd been hoping for someplace more private. But the elevator door opened and there he was. It was like fate or something, you know?"

"Sick, sick, sick," muttered Ameena.

"What can I say? My girlfriend tells me I can be impulsive." Since nobody was stopping him, he continued. "With the police watching the exits and searching everybody, I hid the murder weapon in that stupid dollhouse. Later, after I deleted your book from your hard drive and stole the paper copy from your room, I hid it there too. I figured nobody would want it and that I'd get it cheap."

Cherie Maraschino appeared out of nowhere and kicked him in the shin with her clunky orthopedic shoe. "I'll show you cheap!"

Nobody moved to stop her as she stomped off more briskly than she had moved all weekend.

Rubbing his shin, Karl Kurkov continued. "Like I said, I am a huge Anthony Mulish fan. I'd do anything to keep you from writing more of this cozy drivel. That's why I had to steal the manuscript and murder your publisher." He turned to the author.

"You understand, don't you, sir?" pleaded Karl Kurkov. "Later, I took the real Ulaf's car and dumped it in the woods. I reported a stolen car afterward hoping the police would think the killer had fled in it."

Sheriff Winslow nodded. "That explains why we never could make sense of that stolen car report."

"And the copy that went missing in New York?" Jenny Garrett asked.

Karl Kurkov frowned. "I paid a guy I met in the Bowery to break into Ackerman Publishing. And your apartment, sir."

"I've heard enough." Sheriff Winslow grabbed the culprit. "And I'm going to want the name of that accomplice."

Karl Kurkov grimaced.

Deputy Rogers cuffed him. "Let's go, Kurkov, if that's even your real name."

"Now I've seen everything," said Ameena.

But she hadn't. Because the next thing she saw was Anthony and Giselle locking body parts and making out like a pair of horny teenagers.

"I think I'm going to throw up." Ameena clutched her stomach. All that booze, all that commotion. Her insides floated on a sea of trouble. She had to do something. And quickly.

To Dorothy Hall's horror, Ameena buried her head in the author's capacious cross-body purse and puked.

50

Ameena clutched the wheel of her beloved BMW. Soon she would be home. Soon she would see Ravi and her children.

And her wine cellar.

Soon.

But right now, she grimaced as she glanced in the rearview mirror and saw Anthony Mulish and Giselle ensconced in the luxury leather backseat, holding hands and grinning like a pair of love birds.

As a small reward for solving the murder of Frank Ackerman, Stan, on behalf of the College of the Alleghenies, had allowed Anthony to take home that desk chair he'd been drooling over in his room. The damn thing was poking out of the trunk, blocking her vision.

She'd been half-tempted to drive straight off the road and straight over the nearest cliff. Almost any fate, any death, was better than having to endure a nine-hour drive with those two.

But she had TR Ipé's A Cozy Ending manuscript locked up securely in her suitcase. The man was not going to get off easy.

She'd put up with him, his shenanigans, his pompous purple prose and snooty personality for far too long to let him steal from her what was rightfully hers.

She'd get her commission and then some.

Reaching the city, Ameena dropped Anthony Mulish and Giselle off outside the entrance to his brownstone apartment. Giselle wiggled her butt out of the backseat. She yanked the desk chair out of the trunk, leaving a small dent and two long and very deep scratches in the hatch, in her wake.

"We'll talk soon," said Anthony Mulish, exiting.

"Count on it," snarled Ameena.

"Buh-bye, Meenie!" Giselle blew her kiss.

Ameena watched in wonder as Anthony Mulish plonked himself down on the desk chair, grinning like a well-fed cat. Giselle rolled him along the sidewalk to the front steps of his building.

It appeared that Anthony Mulish would never be rid of the woman. Not if Giselle had anything to say about the matter anyway. And Ameena had a very strong feeling that the young woman did.

"Good," she said to the blessedly empty space of the BMW. "Why should I be the only one to bear the burden that is Anthony Mulish?"

With that, she shot into traffic, defying death and blaring car horns.

She couldn't wait to get home. The worst was over. The last leg of her journey could be enjoyed in peace. She popped a Bollywood soundtrack in the CD slot. With Anthony Mulish gone, there was no need to put up with that classical crap.

Fighting traffic along Central Park West skirting the Jacqueline Kennedy Onassis Reservoir, she got stuck behind a water delivery truck, weighed down with thousands of five-gallon jugs of purified water, moving at a snail's pace.

Cursing and drumming her fingers, she swiveled her

eyes towards a newspaper kiosk. "No!" she shouted. "Shaitaan ka beta!"

Anthony Mulish grinned at her, his face splashed across the cover of the New York Post. Giselle stood demurely by his side.

Noted Author Solves Murder, read the headline.

With a screech and a howl—from her lips, not the BMW which was now busy leaping the curb—she took aim at the kiosk, pushing the gas pedal to the floor.

AFTERWORD

Hi, thanks for reading! If you enjoyed this book, please support me by sharing your positive review online and on your favorite social media platforms. Every little bit helps. Please check out some of my other books too.*

Thanks again!

J.R. Ripley is the bestselling author of A Bird Lover's Mystery series, the Maggie Miller mysteries, the TV Pet Chef mysteries (writing as Marie Celine), the Todd Jones comic thrillers and other novels; also writing as Glenn Eric Meganck.

*This message brought to you by the fine folks at Midlist Authors Savings & Loan, who remind me often that my bank account is overdrawn and suggest even more often that I might want to get a "real" job. Sheesh, why is it that banks take money so seriously?

www.ingramcontent.com/pod-product-compliance
Lightning Source LLC
Chambersburg PA
CBHW020357260626
47156CB00007B/2152